The Fire of Origins

The Fire of Origins

A novel

Emmanuel Dongala

Lawrence Hill Books

Library of Congress Cataloging-in-Publication Data

Dongala, Emmanuel Boundzéki, 1941–
   [Feu des origins. English]
   The fire of origins : a novel / by Emmanuel Dongala.
    p. cm.
   ISBN 1-55652-420-X
    I. Title.

   PQ3989.2.D6 F4813 2001
   843'.914—dc21   00-031750

Translated by Lillian Corti
Translation edited by Yuval Taylor

Cover and interior design: Lindgren/Fuller Design

Originally published in 1987 by Éditions Albin Michel S.A., France
Originally published in France as *Le feu des origins*
Translation © 2001 by Lawrence Hill Books

Published by Lawrence Hill Books
An imprint of Chicago Review Press, Incorporated
814 North Franklin Street
Chicago, Illinois 60610
ISBN 1-55652-420-X
Printed in the United States of America
5 4 3 2 1

RITUALS

Man,
You'll awake every morning
to catch the birth
of a new day
you'll watch the dawn, the star
and drink the dew, pristine water
of the source of worlds

Thus, perhaps you'll snatch
in the blink of an eye
of a fissure
the primitive brilliance
of the fire of our origins.

Chapter One

I proclaim the night more truthful than the day.

—L. S. SENGHOR

1.

IN THOSE DAYS, WHEN *nganga* MANKUNKU WAS BORN — BEFORE he became *nganga* and even before he was named Mankunku— the world was neither better nor worse than it is today, it was just different. The earth had long ceased to writhe from the enormous geological sufferings out of which had emerged the walls and peaks of mountains, the faults; its primitive face had already been profoundly disfigured by streams, torrents, and immense rivers flowing peacefully through the savanna, cunningly through the depths of the forest to the mephitic swamps, violently against all obstacles on their various paths to the Ocean. Where there was no water, large expanses resigned themselves to the laws of dunes, barrens, plateaus, and especially of the wind, supreme spirit under the ferocious eye of the Sun. Only the sea had not changed, ever violent and passionate, profound and fecund, original mother, source of life and all beings who shared the earth, the sky, and the water.

The world was different: the ancestral founders had already lived and worked out the laws and rites which would make life on Earth coherent and even if, now, they sometimes revealed less knowledge to old people, they still guided them through the difficult evolution of existence; young people already respected their elders less but they still respected them; the earth and the women no longer produced as bountifully as before but they nevertheless produced enough to relieve the hunger of men and their progeny.

Thus he was born one day in the dry season, in a banana plantation where his mother was left alone, the village being deserted as the men were out hunting or pillaging adjacent territories, the women preparing the earth for planting. Having nothing with which to cover the child, she picked a large banana leaf and passed it through a straw fire which she had lit in order to cook his food: after this infusion of warm spirit, the leaf went limp, became softer than a kapok comforter, as generous and protective as his mother's breast, while the smoke coated it with a layer of oil as greasy as palm oil in order to protect the tender body of the newborn.

She wrapped the child up in the large leaf, pressed him against her chest, and lifted her eyes to heaven in order to express her gratitude to the beings who surrounded her in her womanly solitude: to the weaver birds which circled gaily around their nests, acrobatically suspended among the palm leaves, to the solitary hornbill flying back and forth, all the while snapping his large helmet-like beak, strange and dignified among the little drunken sparrows, to the marauding and rebellious monkeys that jumped from vine to vine, whistling and noisily crunching wild fruits, to the butterflies and dragonflies in shimmering multicolored dresses flying aimlessly here and there as if intoxicated by the light that played hide-and-seek with the shadows of the leaves trembling under the caress of the downy wind; she expressed her gratitude to all those beings who had heard the cry announcing the presence of the new little being in the wide circle of life, among those who were still there and those who had already gone away. For a moment the silent mother and child shared body and soul with the beautiful moire flowers of the lantana bordering the edge of the cassava fields; they feasted their eyes on the violet of the jacaranda flowers lost among other, more ordinary trees; they delighted in the pallor of the taro flowers and the deep green of the peanut plants struggling with hungry tufts of couch grass: thus mother and child took possession of their world and allowed themselves to be possessed by it. Joy of nature, consecration of the newborn!

Finally, she left the plantation and returned to the village, leaving along the trail a trace of the blood that continued to ooze, blood which would later be licked up by panthers and hyenas, blood of sorrow and joy which would perhaps soften the hearts of the ancestors. Before leaving, however, she cut down a palm frond and thrust it into the place where the child had been born in order to preserve the memory of the event. Thus, years later, when the boy had become a man—the man named Mankunku, already known as *nganga*, confronting the turncoat king before the reunited villagers—he would appear with a palm frond in his hand as a reminder to all that his destiny, like his birth, was that of a solitary and extraordinary man.

2.

The women often returned to the village before the men. Those who got back first that day refused to believe in the birth of the child. How could they believe in a birth without cries or pain, without witnesses? Where had this child been born, where was the web of flesh that always accompanied the arrival of a being born of woman, where were the mother's blood and water?

Too tired to take them to the birthplace, the mother told them how to get there: they had only to follow the traces of blood to the place marked by the palm frond; they would see the ashes of the straw fire that had warmed the child, the place where she had buried the afterbirth; they would see the witnesses, the banana trees, the weaver birds, the great leaves of the flowering taro, the acrobatic thrushes, they would hear the barking of the dog-faced baboon, the distant murmur of the river…So they followed the traces of blood which were already beginning to be discovered by the driver ants, noticed the single palm leaf lost among the tall banana trees, and were very moved; they cleared the surrounding land, cut down other palm fronds, planted them around the one left by the mother, then returned singing.

Not all the women of the village went to inspect the birthplace, some stayed behind out of laziness, others out of jealousy; they thus refused to concede the natural origin of the child and insisted that he was one of those beings who exist without having been born. Fortunately, the majority of women not only saw the sanctuary of palm trees but also helped to build it; these women always attested to his birth. What would happen when, not being there, they could no longer give witness? The two versions of the story would compete with each other, but if the version doubting the authenticity of his birth should win out, there would no longer be any material trace of his passage on the earth.

The old men of the clan, being very wise, did not bother to give him a name right away. Why name something that would perhaps prove to be ephemeral? In any case, many did not believe that he would survive, seeing the skinny baby sucking avidly with little nervous gasps, in the manner of a puppy, at his mother's enormous breast. So they called him just "the palm child," then "The Palms," Mandala.

In those days, there were only four days in the week, so there were many more weeks in the year and people therefore lived longer on the Earth. The child survived two weeks, three, then four. They waited three entire moons. The child began to babble, to chirp. He became handsome and strong like the men of his mother's line. It was only then that he was considered a real person, an independent creature meriting a name of his own to distinguish him from the rest of Creation. On account of his extraordinary birth, they chose a prestigious name, that of an ancestor whose exalted deeds were lost in the night of his people's history. The entire family got together and old Nimi A Lukeni, the memory of his nation, presented him to the ancestors: "...so, from this day on, you'll be a man called upon to live, you'll have your own name, that of Mankunku, the one who defies the powerful and makes them fall as the leaves fall from the trees. May the spirit of the great ancestor, noting the palm wine I spit into the wind and the *kimbazia* leaves which I chew up and spit out in front of everybody, consent to watch over you. Try to become strong like him and not to fear any man, not even the powerful. Be worthy of your mother's family."

And the wind responded by accepting the wine, it carried the fine droplets in all four directions, rose, kissed the face of heaven, and brushed the Sun before falling back down on the mother and the father, a great blacksmith. And the spirit of the ancestor accepted the child by stopping once and for all the pain that had continually gnawed at the lower abdomen of the mother since the birth of the child.

Thus they called him Mandala Mankunku.

3.

When they discovered that the child Mandala had green eyes, the family went into a frenzy. They had heard of ancestors with eyes gray as sadness, gray as the sky of the dry season, brown as heat, brown as a woman's breast, black as a secret, black as the heart of a sorcerer. But sea-green eyes, palm green, that glowed in the dark, never! Never had they seen in the clan the green eyes of a wild day-blind creature, the eyes of a wicked sorcerer wandering at night with owls!

Since the people of the Earth always fear things which threaten social equilibrium, each member of the clan tried to find meaning in this event in order to avoid the possibility of ill fortune and its inevitable wake of trouble and tribulation. He is not a natural child, some maintained, but the reincarnation of a panther, or rather of a panther-man come to demand a reckoning of the clan, no, said those who had never believed in the birth of the child, these green eyes are the mark of his bizarre arrival on this earth, the mark of his non-birth, no, no, protested others, we can testify to his birth, this boy is neither a strange child nor a stranger, his mean green eyes are rather a curse from his father's side of the family which has never really accepted this marriage, stop spouting such idiocy, protested the members of his father's family, such a defect can only come from the mother's family because it isn't possible that a family of blacksmiths, workers who by dint of sheer will force metals to take any form imaginable, should transmit any imperfection, any genetic weakness whatsoever! *Nzambi-a-Mpungu*, perverse eyes, mean green eyes!

The mother's family, troubled by these malicious insinuations, took the mother out of her husband's house, and the child along with her. The father then demanded reimbursement for the bride price he had given to his wife's family: two goats, some chickens, ten or so of the most beautiful shells from the seashore, two hoes, and a package of salt; he would say nothing about the dozens of gourds full of palm and pineapple wine which he had contributed for the ceremony. The wife's family rejected the husband's demands, refusing to reimburse him for the least part of his claim because, after all, during the time the woman had spent with him, had she not worked for him? Who was the first to rise, day in and day out, to go and cultivate, plant, weed? Who went twice a month to dig up the cassava tubers and let them soak for days in stagnant arms of the river in order to prepare *foufou*, the flour which sustained them all? Who kept the house in order, washed the laundry, took care of the child, who...who...The family never tired of enumerating, of counting and recounting the multiple activities of their daughter, diligent dragonfly, lithe as a swallow, industrious as a bee, sweet and tender as a mother hen. The polemics between the two families became more and more acerbic. It was during this time that the child was given the name Mambou, child of discord.

It was old Nimi A Lukeni—the one who had given Mandala the name Mankunku—who reconciled the two families, persuaded them to bury the dispute forever, and spared Mandala Mankunku from being called Mambou all of his life. Already so old that he was hardly able to see or hear anything anymore, the wise man spent his days stretched out on a chaise longue in the shade of a kapok tree, a fly swatter in his hand. He could be heard from time to time muttering unintelligible words or bursting out in exasperation when a stroke of the fly swatter failed to get rid of a particularly pesky insect. Only in the evening did he seem to come back to life, when, surrounded by the youth of the village, he recounted, browsing in the library-museum that was his memory, the historic and legendary events which his people had preserved for generations. He always began in a dull monotone which, little by little, became more lively and heated, gradually vibrating as he got deeper into his narrative; sometimes, in a trembling voice, he would break into song, the melody of which would immediately be taken up by a chorus before flying away to the land of the ancestors whose praise he sang. Then, tired, he would go to bed, only to resume his post under the kapok tree on the following morning. So, when he found out about the dispute between the two families, it was to that spot under the tree that he summoned them, each bringing several calabashes of wine. In fact, the entire village gathered about, some wishing to help reconcile the two families, others as partisans of one side or the other, and the rest in order to take in the show and also benefit from the abundant refreshment which was offered on such occasions.

...Old Lukeni savagely chases the fly that has been pestering him and bats it into his hands. Everyone becomes silent. Rituals and counsels of the ages, let the elders guide us! He opens his palms in the generous gesture of one who receives and of one who gives: "Woman, your complaint."

She speaks, accuses, cries, presses her beloved child to her breast. Her family and partisans approve and support her affirmations with cries and phrases thrown to the wind.

"Man, what do you have to say about this?"

He speaks, accuses, boasts about his descent from a long line of blacksmiths. The relatives of the bride protest, boasting about their own lineage. Everyone's speaking at once; voices are raised, get heated, petty insults, the voices rise higher, the threat of more serious insults hangs in the air, crippling speeches which will proclaim a definitive rupture in the clan; they are balancing on the edge, one more word, a gesture and...at this moment the old man raises his hand.

The abrupt silence that ensues is broken only by the cackling of hens and roosters chasing each other in the yard, eager to couple. Eyes turn, ears strain; his voice is no longer his voice but another voice charged with the weight of the elders, as priestly as a mask: "Man, and you, woman, I've seen more suns depart for Mpemba and come back again than the two of you together, and all of you here are my children. I am the last direct descendant of those who, a long time ago, left the ancient kingdom and crossed the river when the world was falling completely into chaos. It was my father who chose, next to the great river, the location of this village which he named Lubituku, the rebirth, while others pressed on, fleeing toward the sea..." He pauses for a moment to allow the wind to carry his words into their earlobes, into their hearts. "Do you know what precipitated this chaos? Well, it was because of the clans, the bloodlines, the families, who fought, killed each other in competition for the throne; clans which made and unmade alliances with the whim of the wind, men who went so far as to make pacts with strangers against their own people. My father chose this place so that our clan might start from scratch. Believe me, it pains me to see all this starting again because of a wicked quarrel..." He speaks for a long time, asking questions without answers, giving answers to unasked questions, distributing blame and praise; he goes back to the dawn of History, returns to the present, questions the ancestors, the world, the seasons, the Earth, describes the colors of the rainbow, and finally comes back to the village, to the clan, to the child: "...one of our ancestors, one of the greatest, the one who overthrew the powerful, I've mentioned Mankunku, he had green eyes. Thanks to his glow-in-the-dark eyes, he had vision which penetrated bodies and read hearts and souls; he could study the looks of wild beasts at night, dazzle those of owls, track down day-blind sorcerers. It's an honor for us to have this child with eyes green as palm fronds, because he's really Mankunku who has returned to us."

He stops, drinks some palm wine from a gourd moistened with fresh water, his face calm and serene. Then he asks for the child, the innocent object of discord. The mother tears him from the protection of her sweet breast and hands him over. Lukeni takes his place with the child at the center of a cross, the crossroad of the four points of the life cycle: the rising of the Sun, its apogee at noon, its twilight when it plunges with a splash into the blood of the sea and the world of the ancestors, and finally the new sunrise. His knobby but agile fingers trace lines and points with white clay on the forehead and temples of the child. "It's you, Mankunku, who have come back to us. May Lubituku embrace you with joy and all the clan be reunited." And the balm of his words on the wind calms their hearts, reconciles their souls, penetrates their breasts and their earlobes, smoothing out the edges of all disagreements...

4.

The child of the palms, Mandala Mankunku, grew up in the shade of palm trees, animals, rivers, and adults. As soon as he could run and speak intelligibly, he spent most of his time trying to understand these beings. He conversed with the savage animals, questioned the adults and the rivers, envied the palm trees' nobility. The Sun was his friend, and the night did not frighten him as it did the other children, thanks to the Moon, who loved him. He had complete confidence in these beings up until the day when the great river Nzadi taught him the lesson which scarred him for life and gave him that unquenchable desire to defy the powerful. Some said that this taste for provocation derived from his illustrious ancestor Mankunku who had been called "the one who overturns the powerful and the drums that pay them homage"; according to others, it was due to the strangeness of his solitary birth in a banana plantation. In any case, it was on the shore of the great river that he resolved to do violence to the masters of this world as often as he could.

He loved the great river, he respected it. He spent hours watching its long undulant course, calm with contained power and glistening in the sunlight; he admired the fishermen who threw their nets into it and brought back quantities of fish: like the earth, the river was also a nourisher. On feast days, Mankunku felt the stream trembling with excitement beneath the clamoring and paddling of the canoeists who struggled for first place in the race they ran in its water. Sometimes he was seized with the desire to be a fish so that he could plunge into it, swim up against its current, live in its bosom. Then, that day, he could no longer resist: he wanted to bathe in it, immerse himself in it, swim across it. The river disapproved; wrinkles appeared on its otherwise calm surface, and little, menacing waves lapped the bank. Mankunku paid no attention, insisting on his bet. The river cleverly let him come out to the middle; come, little one, come; then it blew a whirlpool at the boy's feet. Mankunku was sucked down to the bottom, his head disappearing under the waves. Sink, stubborn child, swallow me, my dirty water, may it distend your stomach, may it choke you! Mankunku's head comes up, he gasps a breath of air, pity me, let me go, I won't defy you any more, I'll always respect you, no, you just don't understand, you dirty urchin, this isn't enough of a lesson, his head goes under again, he suffocates, the blood is beating in his temples, an almost superhuman effort brings him back up, a vigorous breast stroke lifts him out of the whirlpool with his last breath, he thinks he's out of it but the river stretches its long arm out, catches him, pulls him back into the center of the maelstrom, yes, you came after me, obstinate child, I hope that from now on you'll know who's the strongest, the most power-ful, I beg you, let me go, I promise not to defy you any more, the head comes up, another mouthful of air and it goes under again, I just can't go on, I'm suffocating, air, air, for pity's sake, he faints, becomes as soft as seaweed, struggles no longer.

Tired of the game, the great river throws the vanquished body onto the shore. The child's head is knocked against the rocks, the forehead opens, blood flows. Finally, still inert, he is stretched out on the sand. The Sun, who is his friend, takes pity on him, caresses him, penetrates his body, massages his heart; he hiccups, he regurgitates the bad river water, and then he breathes. He gets up, exhausted, sits back down on the sand. He sees the blood trickling down and touches his forehead, feels the wound. He gets angry, Mankunku gets angry, he gets up, his legs still trembling, looks fiercely at the river, spits, howls. Trai-tor! You've betrayed the friendship of one who trusted you. You think you're powerful? I will be more powerful than you! See, I spit, I spit again and piss in your water soiled with the blood of a friend. The day will come when I will swim across you! And the wind whistles as if to carry off these provocative words, to submit them for consideration to all who hear. You too, wind, I defy you, I defy you all! I am Mankunku, the one who destroys, I am Mankunku, the one who overturns!...

Mankunku ran back home. His mother saw him running up with his head all bloody and howled like a madwoman. The women of the village came out, surrounded him, consoled him, then led the child over to the healer. When the latter had disappeared into his house with Mankunku, the mother went back to crying noisily. All the women of the village began to say anything to console her; they pitied her, pitied themselves, explained, justified themselves: it's nothing, mother of Mankunku, these are simply scratches, it happens to all children, why yes, adds another, it is I, Nsona, who says so, it's nothing, see, one day my twelfth son returned from the hunt with an enormous tear in his right thigh and less than a month later there was no trace of it, ah easy, cries Kimbanda, you talk forgetting that the great river Nzadi has punished him and that he never pardons, you're right, Kimbanda, I always thought, like you, that that child wasn't born, that child will never die, oh shut up, you nasty tongues, don't talk about the death of my child, but no, mother of Mankunku, don't listen to these lying tongues that fuss uselessly like a dead leaf in the wind, these old lips that chatter, it isn't serious, pick some citronella leaves, boil them and let him drink a healthful infusion of it after dressing his wound with some juice from fresh tobacco leaves, and so the babbling, chattering, complaining, groaning continues...Finally the shaman-healer comes out of his hut with Mankunku, whose head is bound with a white cloth lightly stained with red: the child is all right, he has only a small inconsequential wound, the skull is untouched; don't forget my two gourds of palm wine and a young rooster for the ancestors of the river...

Before he became a full-fledged adult in the community and began to help his father at his work, Mandala Mankunku had only cried twice in his life. The second of these occasions was some time after his adventure with the river, long after his wound had become nothing but a simple, hardly visible scar on his forehead. He was playing with the daughter of Ma Kimbanda, one of those who had never believed in his birth. They got angry, came to blows. Then his antagonist really hurt him by saying that he would never become a respected ancestor but would remain an old man, blind, deaf, and impotent forever. Since he had not been born, he would never die.

"Yes, I will die!"

"No, you're condemned to live forever, like all things that aren't born."

"Liar! You know that that isn't true. I was born. There are palms on the spot where I came into the world and banana trees too and I will die one day!"

"No, you're the one who's a liar, my mother told me that you're like the wind …"

A strong boy for his age, Mankunku threw his adversary to the ground, thrashed her soundly, then ran off crying. Without origin, without end; without birth, without death; am I condemned to wander like the wind?…"Why no," his mother tried to reassure him, "who are you going to believe, your mother who carried you in her womb or those barren, jealous old witches? I assure you that you were born, you came out of my belly." "Besides," his father added, "the whole village saw the palms there where you were born, why do you doubt it? There's no reason why you wouldn't die, why you shouldn't take your place in the long chain of ancestors next to your forefather Mankunku." These arguments did not succeed in stopping the child's tears. It was only when the healer, his uncle Bizenga, confirmed his mortality that he finally calmed down. But this incident left an indelible trace in the child's soul, and often in his adult life, during those moments of great solitude which must be confronted in all great struggles, he would ask himself again and again if, after all, he was not a man without beginning or end, condemned to wander eternally on the earth, outside the time measured by man-made clocks.

5.

"Ah, what a noble art is that of the blacksmith! He takes the iron, twists it, destroys it, restores it; the bellows animates the fire's flame like that of life; then comes water, poured from the hollow of his hand, sprayed on that living, flamboyant soul to kill it at will. Master of fire, of iron, and of water! And you, Mankunku, you say that this craft doesn't interest you!

"We blacksmiths created the knife, the male weapon, pure as a cry at the dawn of the world's creation; then we created the hoe, female tool which opens the womb of the Earth just as the male tool opens that of a woman, to sow seeds in her. And we created the bells which herald the approach of kings, the lance of the warrior, the axe of the cultivator, the light jewelry of women. And you, Mankunku, you say that this craft doesn't interest you!

"All the males of my line, my father, my grandfather, my great-grandfather, and so on back to the dawn of our origins— all were blacksmiths. Copper, iron, lead, and gold had no secrets for them; like them, I know the source of power, and I'm ready to show it to you. And you, Mankunku my son, you say that this job—this privilege—doesn't interest you!..."

Thus, after the great river, his father was the second powerful figure whom he defied. He, the eldest son, who must continue

17

the family tradition, refused in spite of every entreaty to take up his father's trade. He preferred to take his place in the world of trees, animals, bodies of water, and men, rather than be cooped up for days at a time in the forge, firing metals. Little by little, he became attached to his maternal uncle, a great healer and hunter, who gradually introduced him to the mysterious world of the hunt.

First he taught him to listen to and to recognize the breathing of beasts and their various odors. Then he taught him to distinguish between the two great categories of animals, those one might kill and those one should not strike; then, among the first, he learned to distinguish between those one could eat and those forbidden to the members of the clan. Little by little, he learned all of the preparatory rites of the hunt, how to follow an animal's tracks, how to distinguish a male from a female by the pressure of the footsteps on the grass, how to avoid the wind...He also had to avoid the numerous traps which his master set for him. Look, Mankunku, there's a snake hidden behind that warm stone, show me that you're brave and that I can be proud of you: catch it by the tail. No, Uncle, you should never catch a snake by the tail, or it will bite you. You have to grab it right at the neck, just above the vertebrae...There, Mankunku, we've managed to get the mouth of that magnificent crocodile into our lasso, he's no longer dangerous, he can't bite you, bring the canoe over to it and let's carry it back to the village alive. No, Uncle, it's still dangerous. But I tell you that we've gagged it and it can no longer bite off an arm or tear off a leg. Uncle, it isn't the mouth we must fear, for the strength of the crocodile is in his tail...It was only then that Mankunku really began to hunt. He very quickly tired of common, easy game, and set his sights on beasts of prey. His first victim was a magnificent leopard which he had quickly discovered thanks to the nocturnal acuity of his green eyes. "Look, Uncle, wise master who initiated me in the mysteries of the hunt, I offer you the skin of this leopard, the first powerful animal I've killed." His uncle joyfully accepted this first gift of his grateful pupil, hanging the new symbol of his power in an appropriate place in the collection of feline skins arranged in a delicate array of colors behind the ceremonial seat of the healer.

Before long the exploits of the young Mankunku were innumerable. He killed a lion as easily as a hare, an elephant as easily as a mouse; when he went hunting with the boys of his age, he did not necessarily bring back more game than the others, but he was always the one who tracked the most difficult prey. All this, however, didn't satisfy him. For although he was recognized as a great hunter equal to his uncle, and even though lions and panthers ran off when they heard him coming, Mankunku felt that he was missing something still more profound and fundamental. Was it the knowledge and concomitant power inherent in the craft of the smith?

To the great joy of his father, he returned to the forge and set about learning the noble craft of the blacksmith. He succeeded as easily in mastering the ancestral technique of casting from wax models as he had in learning to hunt. How adept he was! One would have thought that all the experience accumulated in this art since the days of his most remote ancestor was flowing into his fingers. He knew how to create jewels of all sorts, light bracelets of copper and gold for women, thin necklaces and earrings for delicate young girls, tinkling anklets for dancers. He fashioned bells for ceremonies, triangles for making music, enormous heavy hammers for making other iron things. He knew how to control the bellows, a bag full of magic wind, with so much skill that he could revive a fire that, on the point of dying, was nothing but an invisible glimmer to those who did not have his acute nocturnal vision. There are two traditional reasons to respect men: their great age or their skill; Mankunku was respected for the latter. Having been accepted by the regional caste of blacksmiths, he found his place and was admired. What more could he hope for, what more could he desire, in a society where an individual's destiny was nothing but a ridiculous point in the grand design whose plan had been definitively drawn up in the days of the founding ancestors? Yet for all that, Mankunku was not happy.

Of course, his contact with the master metallurgists, great masters of fire and water, had given another dimension to his vision of the world: you can well imagine that to melt lead as if it were common wax, to mold iron in every imaginable form as if you were modeling clay, to make the fire as hot or cold as you wish, all entailed a certain power. Then what was the source of this longing for other learning, this anguished sense of having somehow missed out on something? Exhausted from having to contain so many doubts and questions inside, one day he decided to go and open himself up to old Lukeni, the one who had brought peace back to the clan.

He found him under his tree as usual. With him he brought a gourd of palm wine which he had drawn that same morning, and several kola nuts, so as to dramatize his visit and thus call forth the attention of ancestors otherwise occupied in evaluating other wishes. The old man seemed to be sleeping, hands crossed on his belly where the fly swatter was resting. It was the beginning of the afternoon, the hour when, beaten down by the heat, all the world lounges about: crocodiles on banks of sand, hippopotomi in the mud where they bathe, lions in the groves of the savanna, geckos on warm stones, snakes coiled up in holes in the sand, ant lions at the bottom of their funnels, the river in its bed, men lying on mats under awnings or stretched out on chaises longues under the trees while women enjoy a much deserved rest while chatting and grooming each others' hair; then nothing stirs but the swarming ants, intoxicated by the sultry weather, and some chirping crickets, unable to stop gnawing on the innocent leaves softened by the stifling heat. The indolent wind barely shakes the tree branches. Mankunku stopped near the old man's couch. Should I wake him or not? He hesitated.

"I've been waiting for you, my child."

Surprised, he watched old Lukeni, who had grabbed his fly swatter and was trying, by force of habit, to drive away nonexistent insects. "You were waiting for me? You knew that I was coming to see you this afternoon?"

"Perhaps not this afternoon, but I knew that one day or another you'd come to see me. Sit down. I hear in your voice that you're not at peace with yourself."

"I'm at peace with the family, the clan, and the entire nation."

"You cannot really be at peace with the world if you're not at peace with yourself. Sit down, Mandala Mankunku."

Mankunku sat down cross-legged on the ground. Respectfully, he offered the old man the things he had brought with him. "Old Nimi A Lukeni, accept this wine and these few kola nuts that I've brought to you before I begin to speak."

The old man took the gourd, poured several drops out on the earth to quench the thirst of the ancestors and render them homage, then took a long swig. He cut off a piece of kola nut, chewed it up, spit it out to the wind, then finally took another piece of it and began to chew again. "We have accepted your wine and the kola nut, my child. Speak without fear. Open your heart to us."

"All right: would it be too presumptuous to say that, next to my Uncle Bizenga, I'm the best hunter in the clan? That I can melt lead and work iron as well as my father? That I know better than anyone how to endow a statue of wood or bronze with power, to concentrate hatred or joy in a mask, to chisel out of a statue's face the hidden smile of a living being?"

"No, my child, this isn't presumptuous. You are the best of your generation."

"Isn't it true that a person who can do these things has achieved a certain degree of knowledge and power?"

"Absolutely."

"Then why am I not satisfied? What am I missing? Am I too young? Is youth an insurmountable obstacle to the serenity and wisdom which comes with learning?"

"Don't believe what idiots say on the subject of youth, my child. Youth is a door opening out on life, and it is pregnant with all things possible."

"Well, then what is it?"

"How can I tell you? First of all, serenity doesn't always come with learning. Then, do you remember when you were children and you went around in bands trapping wild animals, driving away the chameleons which escaped by camouflaging themselves the colors of the leaves? And sometimes you knocked down those giant anthills that we often find in the forest. What did you see then? There was a queen, some soldiers, some workers, some slaves...Each ant knew his place, his job; thus the colony functioned and each individual felt indispensible because the failure of a single one broke the chain of solidarity. But you, I don't know who you are, and this is the first time that I haven't been able to position somebody correctly in our society."

"I'm the son of a blacksmith."

"And you're a great hunter."

"Just say that I'm a hunter."

"And you're a master sculptor: in wood, in bronze, and in stone."

"It's just that I'd like to know everything, old Lukeni. Why should I limit myself? Why shouldn't I be a weaver, if I want to? Just because my father's a blacksmith?"

"Things aren't done that way in our society."

"And why can't things be done differently? Why not shake things up so that people like me can find their proper place?"

"Watch what you say! Don't get yourself kicked out of the clan by the excesses of speech, which, I know full well, only express the sincerity of your heart. Mankunku, my son, you are a destroyer! I don't pronounce this word as a curse, I'm merely noting the fact. You're a new variety in our field of corn, and I note it with perplexity: will the seeds which you sow transform our field into a garden of abundance or into a plantation of weeds? Go, let me sleep, I can't help you; I don't understand the thirst which floods your soul."

He put his fly swatter down on his belly, crossed his arms on his chest, and went to sleep. Mankunku knew that he must not insist. He got up and went away. Old Lukeni had given him no solution.

He continued to wander here and there. For example, he went and spent a day on the banks of the river watching it intensely as if to remind it of his challenge; but the river remained impassive and did not jump out of its bed in order to strike him, as the young man might have wished; it continued on its tranquil way in its majestic bed. And then Mankunku went walking in the sanctuary which, according to some, including his mother, was his birthplace. He remained there a long time, questioning the trees, trying to discover the bond that might link him to this patch of barely cleared plantation where the *nsanda* tree had been planted. He did not return until nightfall, dragging his feet in the red dust of the paths of the ferrous earth, and also dragging the Moon over the white dust of the Milky Way.

Obviously, during this period, he neglected what was expected of him in a society where each individual has a role to play; in effect, he placed himself outside the limits of the ancestral norms of the clan. He was no longer seen either at his father's forge or out hunting. No one knew what to think of this unprecedented conduct which risked introducing a weak link in the chain of the clan. His parents worried: should they intervene? Find him a woman? In secret, they consulted old Lukeni who, alone under his tree and among the irritating insects which he continually whisked nervously away with his fly swatter, had always defended the child: "Nobody of your generation will understand this child. Leave him alone, above all, don't bother him. One doesn't awaken a sleepwalker. This young man is inhabited by the spirit of his ancestor, Mankunku, the one who shook up the powerful and sometimes overthrew them. Let him go, let him find his own way…"

6.

That morning, while he was working at the forge, Mankunku's father was seized by sudden and violent cramps. He fell on the ground, writhing and howling with pain. They put him on a bamboo litter and carried him to the home of Bizenga, the sorcerer-healer, Mankunku's maternal uncle. Mankunku, surprised in his solitary reverie by the crying and weeping of the women, came running up and, informed of the misfortune that had stricken his father, tore into the house along with all the others. The crowd was told to go away, but Mankunku refused to leave his father. Then Bizenga closed the entrance in order to avoid prying eyes and asked Mankunku to help him. His father was still bent over, clutching his stomach, his face marked with pearls of cold sweat. He moaned continually. The healer examined his stomach, running his fingers over the sick man's belly as if following lines known only to himself, lines which Mankunku's penetrating green gaze could not discern. He groped, applied pressure to particular points, massaged the flesh. Little by little, the sick man stopped bending over and moaning. Then Bizenga gave him a thick puree of papaya. After that, he asked Mankunku, son of the blacksmith and a blacksmith himself, to take up his father's bellows. Mankunku picked up the tool which had been placed beside the mat, and, following his uncle's instructions, breathed purifying air four times over the sick man's face: as the wind blows away smoke, let the magical air chase sickness away from the body! The patient was, by now, completely calmed; they wiped his face. The uncle donned the beautiful leopard skin and put on necklaces made of various bird feathers, the teeth and nails of feline creatures, pouches containing mixtures of hair, powders, shells... Dramatically taking his place in front of the sick man, a buffalo tail in his hand, he asked Mankunku to open the entryway and the windows so that the crowd could admire him in his little kingdom.

Ah, how powerful is Bizenga the sorcerer! Sure of himself and in charge, he speaks, bestirs himself, calls on men and spirits. He dips the tail of the buffalo in a bowl of water, sprinkles the room with it, fills his mouth with palm wine which he spits into the four corners of the place. Go away, evil spirits, sorcerers seeking bodies to eat, if you don't let go of the body of

Mankunku's father, I'll kill you, you know that there are no secrets for me, I see those who are hiding behind this sickness and I say to them solemnly before the entire village that if they haven't let go of this sick man within forty-eight hours, I'll denounce them publicly and demand that the ancestors strike them harshly in turn...Tchk, tchk, tchk, he spits wine out of the open windows, ding, ding, ding jingle his clappers and bells. May my words serve to calm this sick man today, may the power of my words, echoed in the voices of the ancestors, give Mankunku's father back his strength...

Sitting on the ground, across from the magnificent leopard skin he had given his uncle, Mankunku listened in fascination to this rambling harangue and, bewildered, watched his father, the eldest of the blacksmiths, stretched out like a lost child on a mat. His uncle continued to pace back and forth, sermonizing all the while. Little by little, a troubled question invaded Mankunku's soul, dragging him under as he listened to the healer: was the thing he so desperately needed a knowledge of this obscure world, of the forces that ruled people's lives and health? Because, intuitively, he had known since his earliest years that he was swimming in a world where, if each thing was not necessarily the embodiment of a force, each thing at least had a force in itself: the force that issues from the sap of plants, the force of human sexuality, that contained in the great river, that which makes the Moon and the Sun move across the sky, the force which transmutes a bad thought, a bad word, into a physical pain which strikes a man down, or kills him. Sitting cross-legged on the hard floor of beaten earth, his chin resting in the hollow of his hands, which were joined at the wrists but open in the form of a cup, he no longer felt the pain of muscles straining with immobility, such was his concentration. With his green eyes, he tried to trace his uncle's words, but they soon became insignificant, ordinary, then they lost their meaning, became fluttering murmurs before entirely losing their power to vibrate his eardrums. Suddenly he had the feeling he was confronting a great silence, the silence of the universe prior to any human voice, beyond time as it is measured by man-made clocks. He was no longer anything at all, he was everything. He was there, somewhere, watching the river lose itself in the immense ocean, turbulent here, slack there, he was caught up in the whirlpool of galaxies and nebulae, the shimmering stars, the wind. Astounded, he listened and watched. The world was new and beautiful. It seemed to him that he was suddenly exploding from the illumination of his discovery: without a doubt, the knowledge which he most lacked was that which made it possible to seize the force, the power hidden beneath the surface of each thing, to trap it, and, ultimately, to harness it for the good of humankind.

Yes, that was it, the beginning of wisdom, and wasn't it that which constituted the strength of the elders? His body and spirit relaxed then, relieved. Suddenly, his back and his legs hurt him, and in the same moment, the words of his uncle once again pierced his eardrums: "Have him eat lots of ripe papaya, and for two weeks cook his food in palm oil if it's meat, avoid hanging it up to drain, but wrap it up in papaya leaves and allow it to become tender. At the end of two weeks, come back to see me, and I'll give him a purgative which will loosen his intestines. He'll lose a little of his virility, but I'll cure him. For a few months, he must avoid working with molten lead and breathing its fumes." He became quiet, took up the buffalo tail, and once again dipped it in liquid with which he sprinkled the spectators who respected his power. Curiously enough, Mankunku, exhausted in body and spirit like one returning from a voyage, no longer felt the neophyte admiration for his uncle of a few moments earlier; he even found, in his general manner and his way of insisting heavily on what was due him, something of the philistine: "...Since the sick man is a member of my family, I'll ask for nothing, but, given the seriousness of the sickness, you must nevertheless bring me a goat or three chickens and a rooster, in order to get the attention of the ancestors so that they'll help me and all of us in our thankless struggle against the sorcerers who wanted to eat Mankunku's father..." He got up, left the room where his uncle continued to officiate, returned home, went to bed, and fell asleep right away.

Mankunku avidly learned all that his uncle wished to teach him. He had such a hunger for knowledge that he asked many questions, perhaps too many. His uncle sometimes responded clearly, sometimes evasively, sometimes not at all: the master should not disclose everything; the student should remain dependent upon him. Nevertheless, Mankunku sensed that he was approaching the limits of his uncle's knowledge because, since the revelation that he had experienced during his father's episode of lead poisoning, he had developed a facility for discerning when his uncle's words crossed the border between true knowledge and charlatanism. He no longer went hunting or worked at the forge. There were new stirrings in the village, new whisperings. This child will bring bad luck to the clan, said some, he's a destroyer, said others. When consulted by relatives, Old Lukeni told them: "I love this child. If he's a destroyer, so much the better, because in order to build, one must first destroy."

Unknown to his uncle, Mankunku was experimenting with new roots and plants; he tried to determine the effects of different waters by mixing his medicines with morning dew, evening dew, rainwater. He went even further. His uncle had taught him the golden rule of all healing action: invoke the ancestors each time because, ultimately, they were the ones who healed; if you don't do this, not only do you risk the life of the sick person, but the healer himself may rue it. But Mankunku tried out some medicines on sick people without invoking the ancestors. Thus he made a discovery which was to effect him as profoundly as his experience with the river: there were medicines which were capable of curing alone, without the help of the ancestors. He rejoiced secretly; it was his own way of undermining the powerful. Saying nothing to his uncle, he threw himself into his research on substances strong enough to cure sickness by themselves: thus he discovered *kimbiolongo*, the root which restores a man's virility and vitality. He was also the one who discovered the bitter juice of the *kinkeliba* to counteract malaria, the leaves of *mansunsu* for fever and muscular fatigue, *kazu* as a remedy for sleepiness and spiritual fatigue on days of battle and hunting, and many many other things that the people themselves have forgotten. Unlike his uncle, who preserved his knowledge most discreetly, Mankunku began to broadcast and disseminate his discoveries to the people and to teach them how to take care of themselves; thanks to him, old men enjoyed a second lease on life with dynamic young wives, sorcerers were no longer able to afflict people with malaria, no one bothered any more to call upon the healer Bizenga for an ordinary stomach ache.

Mankunku's uncle became frightfully angry one day when he caught his nephew disclosing the ingredients of a remedy to one of his patients. He bawled, shouted, howled, ungrateful child, you want to ruin me, betray me, after all I've done for you,

Uncle, I'm teaching the people to cure themselves, I don't see anything wrong with that, shut up, are you forgetting that I am your master, that I taught you everything, no, I'm not forgetting that, then don't forget either that I am older than you, that I know much more than you, and that I can cause you serious harm, but Uncle, when they come to you, even for a little ailment, nothing at all, they have to bring a chicken, a goat, or a gourd of palm wine, shut up already, you insolent child, you know very well that these aren't gifts for me but offerings for the ancestors, yes, Uncle, I want to believe you, but why is it you who eat these chickens, these goats, you who drink this wine with your wives, stubborn child, stubborn and insolent, you're asking for it, aren't you, well, keep it up then you'll see, if you weren't my sister's son, I'd already have done you harm, I'd have cursed you and chased you from my home! Uncle's eyes are red, his lips are swollen, his face is deformed with anger; Mankunku senses that it would be wise not to poison things altogether, lowers his voice, assumes a sorrowful expression, humbles himself a bit, and addresses his uncle in a repentant tone, pardon me, Uncle, I've acted like a child because I'm not yet very wise, I'm only an apprentice subject to your orders, your age and your knowledge command my respect, I beg your pardon. The master's face relaxes, resumes its familiar composure, his lips are no longer so thick, all right, Uncle, I've come to you in order to learn, and you're right to tell me when I'm in error. Smiling, the uncle pats his nephew on the shoulder; phew, we've come back to the fold, confidence has been reestablished, respect for tradition is observed, the world's no longer threatened, its equilibrium is assured; the goats, the chicken, the wine, and the other gifts will continue to pour in, nothing will change, always the ancestors, the master, the student, and the others.

"It's not so terrible, my son. A young man doesn't have the wisdom of an old man, and a seed of madness can always slip into his head; the important thing is that he should have someone to watch over him, and here I am. Don't forget, before starting on any project, whatever it is, first come and talk to me about it. Young people need to respect their elders, and the day when this rule is broken, the clan will be destroyed, the ancestors will abandon us, and the end of the world will be at hand. I hope that you've understood. Go, get me my pipe and a bit of dry tobacco, then explain to me where to look for the root which restores virility to men and how to prepare the remedy for malaria."

Mankunku obeyed, brought him his ceremonial pipe, then went back home. This discussion which had nearly become a dispute convinced him more than ever that there were things waiting to be discovered beyond the ancestors, beyond the teachings of the elders. "My uncle holds on to the little that he knows in order to enrich himself at the expense of others," he thought. He was encouraged in this opinion when he learned, later, that his uncle had been spreading the rumor that it was he, Bizenga, who had discovered *kimbiolongo, kinkeliba, mansunsu*, etc., but that the ungrateful child Mankunku had stolen the invention in order to build himself up. This accusation was ridiculous, for what was the point of touting oneself in a society where there was no struggle for existence, where every being who is born has its natural place? Mankunku did not want to get involved in useless polemics; he continued to follow his uncle's orders as if nothing were the matter. Furthermore, he followed so well in his footsteps that everyone began to call him *nganga*, that is to say, the one who knows, the savant, the sorcerer, the healer...*Nganga* at his age, he who didn't even have a child yet, this was extraordinary. It seemed as if things were somehow beginning to change in this country.

7.

Two panic-stricken women with disheveled hair, their breasts bared to the wind, come running up to the house where Uncle Bizenga and *nganga* Mankunku are engaged in conversation. "Mankunku, great hunter, quick, arm yourself, we've been attacked by a panther who's prowling around the banana plantations. We had to abandon the harvest and barely escaped with our lives."

Before Mankunku says a word, Bizenga's eyes light up and his lips curl in a grin of satisfaction, as if he has just found a solution to a problem which has been troubling him for some time. He lifts his hand and assumes the role of the great conjurer who knows all. "Women, these are not panthers, but panther-men."

More panicky than ever, the women scatter, shouting as they go: "We've seen panther-men, we've seen panther-men..." Men and children come out of their dwellings. Some run over to Mankunku and his uncle: "Bizenga, Mankunku, there are panther-men prowling about..."

Bizenga interrupts them before they can finish the sentence. "These are not panther-men; they're Jaga spies. They've been preparing to attack us for months. There's only one thing to do—attack them first. Our chief will have to declare war!"

His uncle's words come as something of a surprise to Mankunku. Where does his uncle get this information, and why has he never discussed it with them? And he himself, who is in the habit of taking long solitary hikes in the forest, both by night and by day, why has he never seen any trace of these so-called spies? But he is the only one to think of these questions. People don't dispute the wisdom of a conjuror, a great healer like Bizenga. Instantly believing him, they rush to see the chief.

The latter is surprised, incredulous, and refuses to raise an army on the spot, proposing to send emissaries to the Jagas. Bizenga speaks up, denounces the weakness of the chief, whose hesitations endanger the life of the village, ushers forward the two terrified women who can hardly hold back their tears. The majority follows Bizenga, and they decide to go to war against the enemy. Beat the tom-toms, *ngunga* and horns, sound out! Red *tukula* powder! Let there be two divisions, one commanded by Bizenga and the other by the conjuror's brother. Soon everything is ready, warriors march, women cry out, *ngoma* and *ngunga*. The village is almost empty...

Less than an hour later, Bizenga's army returns in disarray, dragging itself along, conspicuously moaning and complaining; the fighters throw their arms pell-mell into the center of the village. His brother's men arrive a half hour later, ostensibly hiding their faces for shame. Everyone is singing songs of sorrow, soon accompanied by a chorus of women: "Our chief doesn't know how to rule, he has sent our men out to fight unprepared and now we've been defeated. Oh woe! Bizenga, help us!" The chief seems to have understood this maneuver. He walks out alone, abandoned, deserted. He does not speak, does not even defend himself; he listens with his head lowered:

"A king who cannot defend his people doesn't deserve to remain king."

"He has ruined the land by leaving our harvests for our Jaga enemies."

"He no longer respects the elders, he only wants to have his own way with them."

"He's no longer fit to govern."

"Yes. He has led us into defeat."

Men and women call out. He raises his head and looks Bizenga in the eye, then turns and goes away. They seize his royal seat and break it. They tear the leopard skin away from his entryway. The king is dead, long live the new chief...

It was at the end of these unexpected developments that Mankunku attended, for the first time, the election of a chief. Actually, it was rare for a chief to be overthrown by such a stratagem. Though this rather ingenious procedure had been devised by the elders to depose an aging or unpopular chief, this was hardly the case here. It was clear to Mankunku that his uncle had manipulated public opinion. As if by coincidence, it was he, Bizenga, who was appointed.

"What do you think of the choice of Bizenga, old Lukeni?"

"I no longer see, I no longer hear, leave me in peace," the old man responded.

Many understood that he was not very happy with their choice. "And you, young *nganga*, what do you think of it?"

Mankunku, who was indignant about these developments, had stayed on the sidelines during the election. Now that somebody asked his opinion, he remembered one phrase, the phrase which the illustrious ancestor whose name he bore had evidently repeated over and over. This was his answer: "I am Mankunku, the one who overturns. I am the one who knocks down the seats of the powerful and the drums which pay them homage."

He astonished himself with his courage. Everybody looked at him, amazed. Old Lukeni smiled. Somewhat irritated, Bizenga gave the order to begin the festivities.

At that time when the week was only four days long and the lives of those on earth were therefore longer, ceremonies also lasted longer. People danced and drank for two entire weeks. The chief took a new wife and shut himself up with her for three consecutive nights. They tapped seventy palm trees in order to gather the sap for making the palm wine to supply the revellers; they ate forty goats and sheep, two buffalo, an elephant. There were eleven births, while only five people died, including two who choked to death in the middle of a meal; three cases of adultery were reported. Finally, the festival was over.

This election brought new freedom for Mankunku. Since his uncle no longer needed to work full time in order to earn his living—and get rich—there was now only one real healer in the land: Mankunku. He not only took very good care of his patients, he also did it free of charge. Thus he was loved and admired. He fully assumed his responsibilities and no longer encountered barriers between himself and the universe. He adapted his work to his own rhythm. He went out at night, remaining outdoors until dawn to observe the sky, trying to see if any mysterious stars came out to talk with the Earth while people were asleep; thus he discovered new stars which only came out late at night and went away before sunrise; he marked their trajectories so well that he gave a name to each of them. Several times, he got up abruptly in the middle of the night when the trees least expected it, to see if they also did not move around behind men's backs, holding some secret meeting. He passed an entire night at the edge of the great river Nzadi in order to see what became of it during those hours.

Thanks to his unceasing activities, Mankunku made several discoveries which have since fallen into the public domain because his people attribute everything to the revelations of the ancestors. Some of these were of little importance or consequence, others threw the clan into confusion. He discovered that, observed from the Sun or the Moon, the Earth must look like a ball, just as the Sun and the Moon do from the Earth. It was he who solved the problem of the seasons of the year: the tradition, observing the sky, counted thirteen moons in the year, which made tilling the fields quite risky, because the sowing season sometimes arrived at the appointed time but just as often arrived a month too early or a month too late. Many a year's harvest was thus ruined. The elders of Lukeni's time did not succeed in solving the problem, though Uncle Bizenga had succeeded in imposing his explanation: the ancestors were not satisfied with the gifts which had been offered to them and, to punish people, they made the dry season arrive a month too early or stopped the rains a month too late; thus he called for gifts and offerings which he promised to deliver to the offended spirits.

As for himself, Mankunku was troubled by this thirteenth month which disappeared just like that from time to time. Where did it go? At first he thought that there were several moons, each one taking its turn about the Earth at a different rate of motion, thus accounting for the variable length of the seasons. Then he observed a distinctive spot on one of the Moons as its identifying feature, but he found the same spot every month and every year in exactly the same place: there was then only one and the same Moon revolving around the Earth. Since, according to the ancients, the trajectory of time was not rectilinear but circular, that is to say that everything was in a state of perpetual return, it should be possible to find that missing month somewhere. Faced with this impasse, he tried to determine the seasons independently of the capricious Moon. Thus he got to know the stars so well that he succeeded in predicting exactly the arrival of the rainy and dry seasons, basing his calculations on the movement of the Pleiades. But since, for him, knowledge was only valid if it could be used by the people, he tried to tell the people how, thanks to the stars in general and the Pleiades in particular, it was possible to correct the disparity between the thirteen months of the year and the irregularity of the seasons. Nobody really wanted to take the trouble to understand what he was talking about. They complained that it was all too complicated and that it would be necessary to get up in the middle of every night to look at the sky. His word was sufficient for them; they would believe him because he was the *nganga*, the priest, the magician; he had the ear of the ancestors and could penetrate their secrets, they would put their trust in him. Mankunku was troubled by this resignation and became exasperated with his maternal uncle, whom he considered responsible, because, contrary to the practice of the ancestors, his uncle had jealously guarded and shamelessly exploited his knowledge, managing to persuade the people that knowledge was a privilege reserved for a special few. Mankunku swore to destroy this tradition and set out to find a simpler, more accessible solution...and he found it! He was dazzled by his discovery. The solution was so simple that at first he wondered if all the ancestors and all these old men were not charlatans who understood nothing at all (he quickly recoiled from this momentary sacrilege). The solution was simple, but nobody had found it: all you had to do was observe the movement of the Sun! The people would understand that easily enough. The year then only had twelve months, the seasons ceased to be erratic, they became logical and simple. The periods of sowing and harvest could be planned much more efficiently. From this time dates the proverbial observation: "Put your trust in the Sun, the Moon keeps changing."

Not only did the grandeur of the universe fascinate Mankunku, but also the minute world of plants and herbs. Since he had discovered the existence of medicines which acted on their own strength, that is to say without the aid of the ancients, it seemed to him that he had passed by something even more important, and this never stopped tormenting him. He therefore went about rediscovering this world.

Alone in the strange calm of the forest, in a silence composed of breath withheld, he raised his eyes to the giant trees whose tops seemed to brush the sky, for a moment fascinated by the light which the vibrations of leaves in the wind separated into the colors of the spectrum; his gaze slipped along the length of sturdy trunks, got caught in complicated branches, then slid down to stop on the tufted forest floor where phosphorescent ferns reigned in shaded zones. His empathy for these immobile beings was so strong that it seemed to him that his legs also had taken root; he felt their strength and their life rise up in his body, making his sex tumescent, pushing the sap from the soil to the trunk and from the trunk to the tops of the trees, bearing it out to the farthest tips of the leaves. He meditated on the adventurously curving lianas, running down the trees, grasping in their arabesques the aerial roots of the mangroves and streaming straight towards the shaft of another tree, like an umbilical cord linking two lives: if they were any more mobile, he thought, they would be snakes. How varied and unfathomable was life!

He wrenched himself out of his meditation, took a few random steps, as if intoxicated by this sentient universe, breathed deeply to steady his restless muscles, and began to look for the medicinal herbs that seemed most appropriate for his purposes. He gathered them young and full of green blood, with unusual forms, because he believed in the correspondence between form and function; he also gathered rare flowers with subtle tropisms, plants which grew in nearly inaccessible places, as if to protect themselves from banal landscapes; he gathered the strong secretions of carnivous plants; he climbed to the top of the tallest trees to harvest the fruits in permanent contact with rainwater, pure water, and the Sun. With this harvest, he invented a number of drugs, some useful and others harmful. He discovered cough syrups, popularized the use of citronella, encouraged the use of papaya leaves in gastric purges.

Among the harmful drugs, he found a mixture which could kill an elephant in three blinks of an eye. The discovery disturbed him so much that, ever spurred on by the spirit of contradiction, he devoted himself entirely to the discovery of a new mixture which would annul the effects of the first one. "If water kills fire," he told himself, "there must be something to kill the power of this new product." He wandered in the forests for an entire month, collecting leaves, herbs, flowers, fruits, roots, measuring and mixing extracts, then trying them out on animals to which he had administered his destructive product: in this way he killed twenty-five goats and sheep, thirty-six chickens, twenty dogs.

The villagers understood nothing of this sudden epizootic; they found these deaths bizarre and began to panic. They spoke about it to Mankunku, but he didn't listen. At any rate, he had once again cut himself off from the village, as when he had abandoned his father's profession. He was often seen alone, at dawn, coming back from the woods, herbs in hand, shutting himself up at home; he sometimes went out in a hurry to go and gather the sap of a tree, dig up a root, or pull algae out of the fecund swamps stagnating in the underbrush. He no longer took care of anybody. Little by little, people turned away from him, going to consult his maternal uncle, Bizenga. The latter took advantage of the opportunity to denigrate Mankunku, who had deviated from custom by not vowing absolute respect to his master and teacher. "That man is cursed," he said; "he has a troubled soul." Profiting from his age and position, he succeeded in getting all the villagers on his side and took advantage of the situation by demanding higher and higher fees.

One day, among the plant extracts, powders, ashes, and other substances that Mankunku had studied, he succeeded in obtaining the correct mixture which, if consumed a little before or after his destructive concoction, would neutralize the poison! Victory was his at last! For every force, there was a counterforce, for every poison an antidote! Fire and water! Day and night! The Sun and the Moon! All things were dynamically coupled. The right hand corresponded to the left. He was seized by a veritable illumination: "Now I understand the principle which rules the world," he told himself; "even the ancestors didn't understand it: an event takes place because there's no matching image to annul it. The lack of symmetry must be a necessary condition for things to be set in motion, for life to exist."

After he discovered the symmetry of the universe, Mankunku calmed down. As he seemed to have touched on something fundamental, his soul finally reposed in peace. To mark this grand passage, the evening of his discovery he bathed naked in the great river Nzadi, with whom he celebrated a great reconciliation. He swam out to the middle and there threw out the old clothes that he had worn continually during his quest: the water swallowed them up. He got out of the water, dried himself, put on clean clothes, and returned to the village, where he began again to participate in communal activities. Once again he visited sick people, ate his meals with everyone, took part in discussions as if nothing had happened. People hesitated, not knowing what attitude to take with this man whose behavior was as erratic as that of the Moon, especially after all the bad things Bizenga had said about him. In spite of everything, little by little they came back to him and accepted him completely.

Once again, he became their Mandala Mankunku of old, their beloved *nganga*. Besides, the reason for it all had been understood from the moment old Lukeni had said: "He went away, he has returned. One must often leave to better return."

8.

Mankunku spent a good deal of time with Lukeni, engraving in his memory the stories of the past which the old man told him. "The story of a people shouldn't die with those who have lived it, it should be transmitted from mouth to mouth, from memory to memory to the grandchildren of our grandchildren," he repeated. Mankunku agreed, his young soul slaking itself at the fountain of his origins. The names of kings and battlefields paraded past his ears, the itineraries of various migrations, the dates of the best harvests and the worst droughts, all these accounts frequently interrupted by chants which Mankunku tried, for better or worse, to accompany with his *kisansi*, a little instrument he held with both hands, consisting of a resonating drum to which he had affixed some small iron blades which vibrated when he plucked them with his thumbs, their pitch being a function of their length. Occasionally carried away by emotion, the old man trembled and wept, asked Mankunku to walk him through the important places of his life: a tree here, a tomb there, a pile of stones, a bend in the river. He was visibly tired. Mankunku noticed this as he supported this wilted body on enfeebled legs, desperate for a cane to lean on in order to take a step forward.

One morning, Mankunku did not see the familiar silhouette of the old man at the foot of his great tree. He went look-

ing for him and found him lying in his bed, his body burning
with fever; his lips, toughened by the years and even more
dried out by the sickness, could not close over the toothless
mouth in which he saw a tongue jerking in a vain attempt to
moisten them. Mankunku was overwhelmed and, for the first
time, envisaged the death of his old mentor. "No, it's not possible, old Lukeni can't die! He is the memory of our people,
what will become of us? We can't lose all he knows, people
can't live without memory." He immediately began to doubt
his own and panicked. Would he be able to remember all that
he had learned from the old man? Besides, had he learned
everything? "Oh," he said to himself, "if only I could invent
something, a code, some signs to reproduce somehow all that I
know, all that our elders know! To unlock these treasures,
which we'd preserve carefully in some sacred place, you'd only
need to learn the code, the signs." A plaintive cry called his
attention back to the sick man. He was seized by anger. "I will
cure him! No matter what, against all odds, I will cure him!"
He went out running.

After sweating abundantly in the fumes of *mansunsu*
leaves, the old man swallowed various potions made from *kinkeliba*, and this was repeated three times a day. Mankunku then
nourished him with lots of fruit juices and with a wild fruit,
ntundu. After several days, the sick man recovered, little by little; he was once again able to eat his favorite foods and finally
regained his habitual good humor: he was cured!

Mankunku was victorious, although at no point had he
called on the spirit of the ancestors in order to cure old Lukeni.
He was now persuaded that the only important thing was the
medicine administered to the sick man; the ancestors and the
gifts people gave them played a much less important role than
people believed. In this, he was diametrically opposed to his

master, Bizenga, for whom the success of a treatment was proportional to the gifts people gave him and which he promised to offer up to the ancestors. Mankunku watched the patient, who greedily smoked his pipe in a sort of recaptured joie de vivre. He patiently waited for the visitors to depart so that the two of them could be alone.

"Mankunku, my child, thank you for what you've done for me."

"It was my duty…"

"Thank you anyway. Please take this cool wine to the village tombs to also thank the ancestors."

Without protesting, Mankunku took the wine. When he returned, he sat down on the goatskin seat next to the old man chewing his kola nut.

"Father Lukeni, I've taken the wine to the tombs. What would have happened if I hadn't?"

"You know very well, *nganga*, you who have been chosen both by your birth and your green eyes."

"No, I don't know."

"You appealed to them in order to cure me, and I must thank them."

"Do you really believe that we can do nothing without them?"

"Yes, my child, nothing. They are the intermediaries between the All-Powerful and ourselves; they control everything: the rain, the wind, the seasons, the forces of nature. We can do nothing without them. They are not all good. You who are a *nganga*, a wise man, your work is to gather up these forces, this learning, in order that it may be of use to us, men of flesh and bone living on the earth."

"I don't doubt your wisdom, Father Lukeni, but I'm sure that we can do some things without them."

"No, never! Whatever is done without their consent is bad."

"But no, I can cure a person without their help."

"There can't be any curing without them—it's impossible! If you hadn't called upon them, I'd be dead!"

Young Mankunku kept quiet. What could he say? He had not called on them, on purpose, and he had succeeded in curing the old man.

"Don't you believe me?" demanded the old man when confronted with Mankunku's silence.

"Yes, I do," the young man hurriedly replied.

After a moment the old man resumed, "Anyway, we have to believe, if not, what would become of the clan? What common bond would unite us? Without respect for the elders, who'd remember our past, our history? Would you today know that our great-grandparents came from Kongo dia Ntotila? Who'd take care of us old people? Perhaps I might be dying all alone in some badly built hut with the rain pouring in. Everything has its purpose, my child."

"I agree. But there's a vast difference between preserving our common heritage and blindly submitting to long-dead ancestors."

"Watch out, my child, or your lips will utter words which will come back to haunt you."

"I discovered *kimbiolongo* all by myself—what did the ancestors have to do with it?"

"You discovered it thanks to them. They chose to help the people through you."

"But then, what's the use of learning when you hide it from the people the way Uncle Bizenga does?"

"If everybody were a blacksmith, the work of the forge wouldn't be a noble profession."

"All professions would be noble!"

The old man did not answer.

Mankunku could no longer hold his tongue, now he spoke with great ardor. "The ancestors couldn't know everything. I feel cramped, Father Lukeni, I want to move, I need space. I want to shake everything up, to reinvent the world so that I can find a job that can give me joy and peace. Is it wrong to add new wisdom to that which the ancestors have given us? They didn't know the solar rhythm of the seasons which I discovered; we enjoy better harvests—is that wrong? Let them be our inspiration, all right, but the world changes, everything changes!"

"Watch out, don't be presumptuous…"

"We need new knowledge! It's not enough to be just the conduit for the teachings the ancients transmitted, to be just the repository for an eternally fixed body of knowledge. We need to give up this inert aspect of knowledge and seek out its active aspect, which means tracking it down, routing it out of hiding!"

"The search for wisdom doesn't mean breaking with one's heritage, my child, all things follow each other; the Moon catches up with the Moon, the day catches up with the day, and the seasons with the seasons; all things follow each other, everything in good order."

"Yes, but before the day catches up with the day, there's the rupture of night, which lends a new virginity to the one that dawns."

"The day which dawns is a day already dawned, everything always begins again, everything is a perfect circle."

"No, Father Lukeni, the day which dawns is a day which has not yet dawned: it's a new departure, everything is always beginning, a new departure."

"Discussion is no longer possible between us, you reject the conception of the world which the ancestors have bequeathed to us."

"There's nothing new to learn in this world," he cried passionately, "this world is too old, it's at the end of its course! I've had enough of all these symbols, repeated a thousand times, of this palm wine that you spit to the wind on every occasion, of this respect required by an undeserving maternal uncle, of this..."

He became suddenly quiet, as if he sensed that he had gone too far. A shadow of sadness passed over the old man's face. "You're a destroyer, Mankunku."

"No, I'm not a destroyer."

"It's not an accusation, my child, you are what you are. I'll only note that you're unfair to us because you judge our society, our habits and customs, on the basis of what you actually see. Believe me, in the old days, when an uncle took charge of his nephew, he really became his tutor, he guided him through life more carefully than his own father would have done; also, the healers didn't follow their calling in order to get rich but simply played the role expected of them in the grand plan that we've traced out together in the course of centuries, the ancestors and ourselves. Now I have the same impression as you, evil acts are everywhere, uncles are becoming contemptible, healers avaricious, rites and symbols empty. Until now, I lived in a society whose ideal was its own perpetuation. We and our ancestors constructed it so well that we feared anyone who departed from the accepted norms, for the tiniest false movement, the tiniest addition or subtraction, might cause the entire edifice to crumble. Now you, you've done things that a person ought not do, you've run against all the rules, nobody knows who you are, are you a healer, a hunter, a weaver, a blacksmith? You're right, this world is at the end of the line, it can't hold out much longer. What can I do or say? I'm very old, Mandala Mankunku. Perhaps thanks to men like you we'll continue to survive."

"Thank you, Father Lukeni, it's only with you that I can speak so openly, without being punished by the ostracism of the clan."

The two of them became quiet after this long and adamant discussion. The old man had sunk down in his seat, his eyes closed. Feeling overwhelmed by an immense affection, Mankunku reached out his arm and took the old man's hand. He had never felt so close to someone, not even his mother. Lukeni opened his eyes and smiled sadly.

"Last night I had a strange dream, Mandala: I saw living cadavers, their faces white as the Moon, with a strange hairiness only found in the land of shadows, arrive from under the sea in the bellies of great whales. But this is what frightened me: they scattered over our lands like a cloud of crickets, they marched over the tombs of the ancestors, destroyed their offering cups, pillaged our goods. I invoked the ancestors, I called on them to help, they didn't come... All of this is beyond me, I'm too old. I can't wait to die."

Mankunku was shaken. He saw in the eyes of the old man Nimi A Lukeni that faint wavering, he heard in his voice that barely perceptible little trembling that you sometimes notice in very old people who are nearing the end of their lives on this earth. What did it all mean? "It's only a dream, Father Lukeni. In any case, if that happens, we'll find a counterforce, an antidote. Well, good night, take care, get some sleep, don't forget that you're in convalescence."

Old Lukeni died that night.

Chapter Two

There were great winds on all the faces of this world,

Great winds in jubilation throughout the world,

without eyrie or shelter.

Without protection or perspective, and they left us, men of straw.

In the year of straw, on their way...

Ah yes, great winds on all living faces!

— SAINT-JOHN PERSE, *Winds*

9.

PEOPLE SAID: "*They come from the bottom of the waters, from the land of shadows where the dead abide...*" or else: "*They came in great whales breathing smoke, they emerged from the ocean where the spirits live...*"

The first refugees arrived from the regions bordering the Ocean; they were dislocated families, footsore, fleeing forced labor, slavery. These were no longer communities but diverse clans, broken up, mixed together, helping each other, supporting each other, dragging along their meager resources, one a goat, one a mat, the other a stalk of bananas, all fleeing the common enemy, forgetting their mutual rivalries. They weren't going anywhere, they stopped in the vacant territories they found. Hardly had they settled down before the foreign authorities would catch up with them. They would pick themselves up again, their numbers slightly increased, and set out again on their way to the interior, until they encountered other clans which often welcomed, sometimes massacred, them...

People said further: "*It's better not to touch them because their fragile skin will leave dappled flakes on your hands like shale; their faces are like the moon because they're living cadavers, zombies...*"

When people first saw these strange beings disembarking on their shores, they were afraid. While some fled as before a monster, others received them with honors, taking them for messengers sent by the ancestors. When they understood that they were only foreign conquerors, it was too late, their land had been conquered and their power annihilated.

People also said: "*It's better not to fight them because they use extraordinary weapons which spit thunder...*" and others added: "*It's better to welcome them, to ally ourselves with them and their power in order that we, in turn, may conquer neighboring ethnicities...*"

At first, the foreign invaders conducted the conquest themselves, going from village to village, leading their little army. But soon they dominated territories several times larger than their own country. Unable to be everywhere at the same time, they changed their strategy in order to consolidate their power and keep on conquering new territories. Just as a sorcerer will use an owl to travel far afield and carry his curses to a distant home, so the invaders used militias, known as *mbulu-mbulu*. They recruited people from the ethnic groups they had subdued, either by force of arms, or, more often, by corrupting chiefs. They dressed them in khaki uniforms with pants that came down to their knees, put red woolen caps with black pompoms on their heads, and told them a thousand times: "We are the bosses, we are beautiful and intelligent God sent us to civilize you, you are black, the color of the devil, of night, of servants, you are monkey slaves look at your kinky hair your fleshy lips your wide noses while we have straight hair narrow pointed noses thin lips we are the ruling race back off bow your head watch out!" They gave them guns, stripes, taught them to stand at attention before the flag. Then they told them a thousand times: "You men here have been chosen because you're lucky you're a little bit more civilized than the others so make the most of this privilege we're going to send you to subdue those monkeys hiding in the jungle so as to avoid paying taxes and harvesting rubber or ivory for us catch them beat them whip them do whatever you like so long as it pays off or else watch out! Turn around bow your heads a little more faster dirty savage nigger cannibals tip your caps a little farther there that's good now salute the flag take a step back obey your masters or else you're in big trouble order arms at ease! Go into the villages catch all the holdouts and all the lazy bastards who don't want to harvest rubber take them prisoner whip them until the village pays its taxes understand dirty monkeys if not it's you who'll pay for them but if you do your job well you'll be chiefs we'll make you chiefs like us understand is that all understood shoulder arms present arms march one two one two"... They left them, hungry dogs, black blind men, *mbulu-mbulu* of misery, owls, carriers of conquest, killers, thieves, rapists! Where are you going like that, running and pillaging?

...Here they are, coming to a village, suddenly appearing from all sides, guns in hand, crying out raucously in their barbarian language. Panicky women, crying children, men fleeing to hide in the tall grass. They shoot into the air, destroy two or three houses, kill two or three goats with their guns, and finally calm down. Then their boss, the one with the stripes, starts shouting, "Where's the chief of the village?"

He comes out of his hiding place. They pull him, trembling, on legs which can hardly hold him up, they grab him by the throat, throw him down on the ground, hit him with their gun butts, humiliate him in front of his wife, his children, his dependents. Gunshots in the air to remind everybody who's in charge. Then they demand tribute for the victors.

"Are you the chief? Have them bring us ten big fat chickens, two goats, two sheep, three stalks of bananas. Then prepare some nice tender chickens for us to eat right away."

The chief is still trembling, blood running from his nose, his mouth. He barely says, "We don't have any sheep in this village."

"I don't want to hear it!"

They get busy, run, hunt, here chick chick chick, come here little chickens, here's some good corn, come, come on little one, come here, like this, here, here's some more grain, chick chick chick, that's it, come on, there, gotcha, off with your head and those of the other nine, into the boiling water, come on children, come quick, pluck these birds, don't keep these militia of misery waiting, the kids dash over, practically scalding themselves, pull out the feathers...Farther along, baa baa, let's catch the goats, drag them over, tie them to the tree. The militiamen strut about, self-satisfied, proud, indifferent to the the villagers' anxiety, cartridges on their shoulders, feeling invulnerable thanks to their foreign backers. Their black faces contrast violently with their red woolen caps with black pompoms on top. They come from far away, from the North to pillage the villages in the South, from the South to pillage and terrorize the villages in the North in order to establish the new master's law...The women are afraid, this one tries to hide but he sees her, come here woman, no, I don't want to, come here, no; she runs, tries to force her way through the bushes, he starts to run after her, he watches her buttocks bouncing up and down as she runs, his hashish-smoker's eyes glow, he's excited, aroused, he's a real man, he runs faster, faster woman, no, too late, he catches up to her, grabs her, throws his gun aside, clutches her with both hands, she screams, he throws her on the ground, her face is scratched in her fall by the thorny bushes, her eyes fill with tears and her lips cry for mercy, pity, but he doesn't see, he doesn't hear, he tears the cloth from her waist, she screams, bites him, he slaps her, pops his buttons, she rolls on her belly, he pulls her back on her back, she squeezes her thighs together, he punches her with his fist, spreads her legs, his stiffened penis pierces, tears, penetrates, rapes her. Ah! marksmen of misery, killer *mbulu-mbulu*, thieves, rapists!...

The militia have eaten and drunk; they are happy. Their chief, the one with the stripes whom they call *capita*, has eaten the most precious part of the chicken, the gizzard: ten chickens, ten gizzards. He is sated and, hands crossed on his full belly, sleeps in the shade of a veranda, while two women cool his face with fans made of braided straw; a child crouching at his feet digs fat white round chiggers out of his toe with the help of a thorn; sometimes, with a slip of the hand, he digs the end of his instrument a little too deep in the flesh, and the bug bursts, spilling out thousands of white eggs while the face of the guard shudders in an instant of pain and pleasure. The other militiamen keep on drinking, harrassing the women, smoking their big raw hashish cigars...Watch out, the *capita* has finished his siesta. He gets up, sets his weight cautiously on his feet, trying not to irritate the wounds left from the extraction of the chiggers.

He blows his whistle. His subordinates drop everything, the trumpet has sounded, they rush over, assemble in the center of the village under the burning sun: "All right, we've been good to you people. We haven't killed anybody, we're not taking any women with us…" He can't continue. The vapors of the good pepper sauce that the gizzards were in are rising to his throat; he belches with satisfaction and pulls his belly in. Now he resumes: "But watch out! We'll return in five days. Then every man and every woman of this village must give us three kilos of rubber! Three kilos, you understand, or else you're in trouble!" His subordinates understand this last bit. They click their heels together and present arms; in his eagerness, one of them pulls his trigger; the shot blows the red cap off of the *capita*, angering him. He kicks the guilty party in the ass, knocking him face-down on the ground. Trembling, the guard gets up and hands the fallen cap to his boss. "At ease!" he shouts. "Three kilos per person or else we'll take your women captive until you deliver the required amount! Understand? Or else we'll cut off an ear for every kilo short, then a finger, then a hand. Bad news for you dirty monkeys who hide in the forest to avoid paying taxes we are the bosses born to command shoulder arms about face forward march three kilos per person understand or you're in trouble!" He's happy. He puts his cap back on, picks up his gun, and sets out to leave the village. The militiamen shoot into the air, then pick some of the men of the village and force them to carry their booty to the next stop; they turn the corner, they disappear, they're gone…

But some people also said, "*They'll arrive and spread out like driver ants, they'll devour our land, they'll walk on the grounds of our ancestors and desecrate them, they'll take everything from us! We must find a way to fight them, stop them, and send them back across the sea to where they came from.*"

And others went still further: "*We'll have to listen to them, watch them. Thus we'll learn. When we've learned enough, we'll use their own arms to attack them and they'll leave our land more quickly than an arrow in pursuit of an antelope.*"

10.

If entire villages were destroyed or subdued, entire ethnicities dispersed or conquered, if chiefs rallied to join the newcomers, it didn't all happen in the same way or to the same degree. There were those who failed to struggle and abandoned in their flight everything they had, or, taking the foreigners for long-awaited ancestors, kneeled before them; there were those who struggled a little, or rather, pretended to struggle before submitting; there were those who, either due to their naivete or their sense of hospitality, were duped; there were those who struggled heroically and were massacred; and finally, there were those who knew how to resist, taking militiamen as prisoners.

Since the conversation with his old mentor in which Lukeni had described his dream, Mankunku had felt anxious, ill at ease, expecting to see some catastrophe strike the land. The arrival of numerous haggard and famished refugees confirmed his sense of apprehension and plunged him into something of a depression. He no longer played his *kisansi* and reverted to his old habit of wandering around. He only calmed down and regained his focus when some new refugees showed up; he listened to them, questioned them, ascertained a few particulars, then went and closed himself up in his room. There must be a remedy for this affliction, a counterforce, an antidote! The universe could not secrete something whose flow it was impossible to check in some manner or other! He searched and searched. Once interrogated, the refugees were fed and then urged to continue their wanderings outside the lands of the clan. After many conversations with these unhappy people uprooted from their native soil, Mandala Mankunku made several circuits of the village, registering all the paths, the hills, the rivers…

Finally one day he asked Chief Bizenga, who had made everyone call him "king," to call a meeting of all the inhabitants, including the children, in order to discuss a plan in case of an eventual invasion. His father, the most senior blacksmith, spoke, other elders spoke, without arriving at any conclusion satisfactory to Mankunku. They talked of invoking the ancestors, of asking their blessing on the warriors' weapons which were to be left on the ancestral tombs for four nights and four days in order to make them invincible. Mankunku found all this puerile and ineffective, like trying to cure somebody of hunger by describing the delights of a plate of chicken cooked with peanut butter. He awaited his turn calmly, only the incandescent green of his eyes betrayed his impatience. He regretted intensely the absence of old Lukeni, that man who had seen so much and knew so many things. Finally it was his turn; he began to present his ideas: "Look, I think I understand the strategy of these invaders, their militias, and their easy victories. They show up suddenly, taking advantage of our surprise, which brings with it panic just as dogs bring fleas, they quickly subdue unsuspecting populations. Now the only way to combat surprise is with surprise. So this is what we're going to do: we'll place sentinels on every hill around the village and on every passable trail leading into town; when they see those militias of misery they'll ululate like owls, birds of bad omen. All the men, women, children will run out of the village and hide in the bush; we'll only leave ten or so people pretending to go about their daily business. The *mbulu-mbulu* will show up, make a big racket in the village, expecting to cause surprise and panic, but..."

In a flash, they're all surrounded; every man chooses his target, the surprised militiamen have no time to react; one of them feels courageous, tries to load his gun, but the steel tip of an arrow buries itself between his eyes. He falls, head backwards, red woolen cap with black pompom flying through the air as the shot from his gun gets lost in the clouds. Mankunku gives the order to confiscate the guns. Cries of victory. They are hustled, beaten, the red caps fall, the *capita*'s stripes are ripped off, the women spit in their faces, the children join in, some with rocks, others with big stalks of green bamboo. These fierce fellows who believed they were invincible tremble with fear; gray-faced, they beg for mercy, no, the people keep beating them, rapists, thieves, assassins, don't kill them, shouts Mankunku, stop, stop, the women keep on pulling their hair and their ears, kicking them in the belly, the groin, they're frightened, their master isn't there; they've lost, many have swollen and split lips, their blood flows, people are beating them now with rifle butts, stop, stop already, Mankunku keeps shouting, don't kill them, let's not kill them... Finally they listen to him, they stop hitting them, they drag them on the ground, they tie all fifteen of them up and leave them out in the sun in the middle of the village. When the men of the village go off, a female refugee slowly walks up to the chief of the militiamen, dares him to look at her, then spits in his face; she aims at his lower belly and gives him a formidable kick in the testicles. The militiaman howls with pain and, prevented by his bonds from massaging the injured member, rolls on his belly, trying to soothe the pain by rubbing himself on the ground with jerky back and forth movements. The woman smiles and goes back to her refuge in the shade. She has avenged herself.

They take inventory: fifteen new cartridge guns, one hundred and ninety-nine real rounds of ammunition. Victory! No more spears or old flint-lock rifles. It's the dawn of a new age. Who said these people were invincible? The victors share the cigarettes, the hashish cigars, the uniforms; they cut up the red caps, and each one takes a piece to make into a purse in which to keep their fetishes and gris-gris.

King Bizenga, who actually only ruled over a big village, had to concede that his nephew was clever. As for Mankunku's mother, she was so proud of her son that she no longer let people call her anything but "mother of Mankunku." The entire village celebrated the victory: palm and pineapple wine, tom-toms and dances, xylophones and *sansi*, singing. For the first time, the invaders, or at least their agents, had been defeated in battle and that was worth a great deal to a people. But Mankunku had a feeling it was not over; that would have been too easy. He was sure that the foreigners would not let it go at that, they would try to liberate their militiamen by any means, and the advantage would rest with the vigilant. Future struggles could be anticipated, one must prepare accordingly. They made the imprisoned militiamen teach them how to use the guns and Mankunku put together an army of which these arms were the framework.

That army began to wait for the arrival of the invaders.

11.

At the end of the third week, that is, on the twelfth day of the state of alert—there were then four days in a week—Mankunku had to change his army's strategy; far too many of his men were falling victim to the fetishes and magic of the army of the foreign invaders. It had begun the first week. After standing watch three days and four nights, thanks to the effects of the kola nut, three soldiers in Mankunku's army thought they saw dozens of militiamen, wearing red caps, long pants, and boots, sweep through the village in a thunder of gunshot. Without hesitating, they heroically threw themselves into the counterattack, shooting their guns off in all directions, thus wounding several of their comrades; it was impossible to stop them; they shouted, ran, pursued their enemies into the most unlikely places. When they finally calmed down, Mankunku had lost two men and twenty or so cartridges.

In the middle of the second week after that, it was worse yet. A dozen soldiers thought they were being attacked by strange beings with transparent bodies and faces as pale as the Moon; after a moment of panic punctuated by shouts and howls, they grabbed their rifles and fired in all directions. Alas, this seemed to neither kill nor frighten the attackers; when they had used up their cartridges, the faces with the transparent bodies were still there, more menacing than ever. The soldiers took out their knives, lances, and spears in order to chase the enemy away; in the ensuing disorder, some stabbed their own comrades, others ran for several meters before collapsing, exhausted. When things finally calmed down, no enemy bodies were found; on the other hand, several of their own men were wounded and about forty cartridges had been wasted. While the villagers could understand nothing about these incidents, the imprisoned militiamen found some hope, seeing in all this the manifest work of their masters. King Bizenga carried cool wine to the village tombs, pleaded with the ancestors to protect his army; he also hoped for a sign proving that the ancestors had disavowed Mankunku. For a long time, he had hidden this desire, but after his offering, the decision was made: one more incident like this and he would eliminate Mankunku.

For his part, Mankunku was perplexed. What could explain these events? He decided to ban the chewing of kola nuts, but the soldiers, deprived of this stimulant, could no longer stay awake and fell asleep at their posts. It was only on the twelfth day of this that he understood what was happening. It was not the flesh-and-bone invaders who were giving them a hard time, but their irritated spirits, which attacked men kept in a state of constant alert too long thanks to the kola nut juice. The only solution was to ban the kola nut and reduce the length of guard duty.

Therefore, he completely changed his system of defense. He no longer made the entire army stand guard; he sent the soldiers home to sleep at night, even authorized them to sleep with their wives, and only kept a few sentinels on a rotating schedule of duty; in any case, nobody had to stay up all night any more. Thus Mankunku succeeded in outmaneuvering the magic spirits sent by the enemy.

———

While they were expecting a troop of militia guards armed to the teeth, most likely arriving at dawn or even in the middle of the night to attack the village and deliver their imprisoned friends, it so happened that three men showed up one day at the hour when the sun is at its midpoint in the sky; or rather, two armed men and another strange being, his face not pale, white, or transparent like the ones in old Lukeni's dream, but red as a cock's comb, with a white pith helmet on his head. He wore a white long-sleeved shirt buttoned up to the neck with two fat side pockets stuffed with God knows what. Unlike his guards, he wore white pants that came down to his ankles, under which his feet were well protected by sturdy boots. At his belt there hung a small weapon, a handgun. In addition to their guns, the two men who accompanied him carried big packs on their backs; they spoke the language of the region and never stopped shouting, repeating, "We come in friendship, don't shoot, friends, we are friends." The sentinels surrounded them, disarmed the guards, and conducted the three men to the center of the village, all the while ululating the cry of the owl. Everyone came out, excited, curious, to see this strange creature with the reddish face, the long nose, the big red ears, "don't shoot, we've come as friends, don't shoot, friends..." And now the children are crying, pressing up against their mothers, frightened; or else, hidden behind their mothers, they stick out their little heads and ask, mommy mommy, what's that, what's that there, pointing with their fingers at the thing, it's a man my boy, but why is his face red like *tukula* powder, that's the way they are where he comes from, and where does he comes from mommy, I don't know, it must be there where the sun sets after drinking the blood, but why doesn't he stay home, what's he going to do here, shut up you dirty brat, interjects a big male voice, let the grown-ups talk, the child bows his head and presses all the more closely up against the sheltering wall of his mother's body, "friends, don't shoot, we've come as friends..."

Chief Bizenga comes out. On his right, Mankunku his nephew, the most admired man in the village, doctor, scholar, warrior, and poet; behind them, the king's advisers. The king sits down on his sculpted throne, his feet resting on the leopard skin given him by Mankunku; his entourage follows suit. His guard remains standing, not with the old flint-lock rifles of local manufacture but ostentatiously sporting the rifles seized from the invading troops.

"Bring a seat for the stranger."

A goatskin seat is set down in the shade across from Chief Bizenga. The stranger sits down and, a little way off, his guards do likewise. He removes his helmet, wipes the sweat which is rolling down his forehead. Mommy, mommy, why is his hair straight like the beard on an ear of corn, silly, it's the hat that he wears that flattens it, mommy, mommy, can I touch it, no, it'll come off and stick to your fingers like the wings of flying termites, mommy, mommy, shut up, cries the exasperated mother.

"We are friends. We have come in peace."

It is the first time that the stranger has opened his mouth: all eyes plunge into it; although he evidently has a pink tongue and white teeth like everybody else, the sounds he emits are different, incomprehensible, strange. What barbarian speech! While the interpreter, one of the guides, translates, the stranger unbuttons his sleeves and rolls them up to his elbows, unfastens the two buttons at the neck of his shirt, and fans himself. Mommy mommy, look, he has arms as white as cassava flour and his chest is hairy as a chimpanzee, silly boy, that's because he comes from the land were shadows live, a land where there's no sun, mommy mommy, can I touch his skin, no my child, splinters would come off in your hand like the scales of a fish, I'm scared mommy, I'm scared of this guy with a red face and white arms, smack, a slap, I told you to shut up, scolds a big male voice.

Chief Bizenga makes a sign. People bring him palm wine in a gourd. He offers some to his guest; the stranger reaches over, accepts the vessel, hesitates to carry it to his lips. Chief Bizenga takes it back, carries it to his lips, drinks several mouthfuls of it to show the stranger that the drink isn't poisoned. He gives it back to the guest. Clearly embarrassed, the man surreptitiously wipes the place where the king's lips have touched the gourd and, with the edges of his lips, barely tastes the drink.

"We are friends, we have come in peace," he repeats. (The interpreter translates.)

"We've offered you a seat, we've offered you cool wine," responds Bizenga.

The interpreter's translation: "We also welcome you as friends."

"I thank you," Bizenga resumes, "but we don't understand this kind of friendship. You send armed men to us who steal our livestock, pillage our harvests, rape our women, sack and burn our houses, then you come crying peace, peace, we've come as friends. If that's what you call friendship in your distant land, it's not what passes for friendship here."

The interpreter's translation: "You and the men you've sent here are livestock thieves, rapists, plunderers. Maybe that's the way you act in your distant land, but don't come here to talk to us about peace, peace, friends, friends!"

The stranger isn't happy to be treated like a thief and a rapist by these natives; his face gets even redder. Mommy mommy, his face is burning, he'll catch fire, bang, a whack, I already told you to shut up you stubborn brat, shut up or I'll send you back to the house. The face loses a bit of its color, he's civilized and diplomatic, and he's alone in a horde of hostile faces, he must control himself: "Believe me, O great chief, you're mistaken about our intentions. We've really come here as friends. It's true that some militiamen got out of control and went sacking and pillaging; I've been informed about that, but that's a vile minority who haven't followed our orders. Besides, I know that you've taken some of them prisoners here, I'm glad of that; deliver them to us and we'll punish them in accordance with our laws. As for ourselves, our hearts are as white as snow, and my presence here should make that perfectly clear."

The interpreter's translation: "We haven't sent those militiamen here, they didn't act on our orders. Give them back to us, we'll shoot them as our law requires. As for us, believe me, our hearts are white as... as..."—the interpreter hesitates, searches, finds—"our hearts are as white as the white hair of wisdom."

"I'm happy to learn that the heart of the stranger is as white as white hair, the sign of wisdom. I'm also glad to learn that those *mbulu-mbulu* of misery didn't come here by your orders. They are surely rebels with stolen arms. I propose to the stranger that instead of shooting them as his law requires, we will punish them better ourselves, we'll bury them alive and plant a great *nsanda* tree on the spot to commemorate and seal our friendship."

At this mention of friendship, Mankunku interrupts without asking permission to speak: "Uncle Bizenga, don't listen to this man, his speech is as sticky as gumbo, we can't depend on it. He's surely lying. It was he and his brothers who sent those militiamen. I've questioned them, I've talked with them; it really was these foreigners who gave them guns and unleashed them on our villages and our land like hungry vultures. This man is lying; don't fall into his trap!"

Bizenga listens to his nephew's speech with irritation. This young man born of the latest rainfall is really getting to be impossible. Will it be necessary to put him in his place once and for all to show everyone who's the chief in this village, or would it be better to disregard his interruption and continue as if nothing had happened? He hesitates for a moment and, cleverly, allows his silence, mirror of his uncertainty, to be taken for the silence of kings, pregnant with wisdom. As for the stranger, while not understanding the language of this land, he believes he can guess the words of this tall man with the hard, scowling face. He turns around and really looks at Mankunku for the first time, he wonders how he failed to notice him sooner. Startled by the color of his eyes and also fascinated, as if seized by vertigo in confronting their depth, he plunges his gaze into them; he sinks into the thick depths of the great Nzadi River, he splashes about, he goes under, he takes fright, he emerges at last to find himself in the immense equatorial forest, green and inaccessible to his soul; he hears cries and whispers and, unable to

understand, he invents horrors and phantoms which only add
to his increasing anxiety; his spirit sinks a little deeper into this
heart of darkness and goes crazy, not knowing how to escape
from the trap of this mysterious and fantasmagoric world. His
body, which has also taken fright, heats up, and beads of sweat
glisten on his skin. By dint of a superhuman effort, his gaze
finally bursts out into the burning noonday sun. Whew! He is
saved, he tears himself away from Mankunku's green eyes, he
fans himself, taking the time to pull himself together.

Mandala Mankunku has also plunged his gaze into the
depths of the foreigner's blue eyes, ultramarine eyes: in them is
an immeasurable procession of forges manufacturing at an
astonishing speed an incalculable number of rifles and maybe
even repeating rifles; he doesn't understand, he is terrified, he
searches behind these factories and these munitions for the
tombs of their ancestors, the secret of their power; he can't find
it, his spirit can't grasp the logic of this world and the man
before him becomes all the more formidable; he wants to
escape, to withdraw his gaze, but it drags itself further through
the blue sea of the stranger's eyes; there he discovers great boats
plowing the oceans, men in chains, dragged over the face of
the earth and sea, endless teams of dockworkers. His anguish
becomes more oppressive, he breathes badly, he is afraid.
Abruptly, his gaze escapes, comes back up to the brilliant and
reassuring tropical sun, to the immense green expanse, calm and
reassuring, of the great equatorial forest. His chest is no longer
constricted; he breathes more easily, but the impression of
uneasiness remains. He gets up suddenly and leaves the assembly without a word: this world into which the stranger wants to
pull them is a world with which he wants no compromises. All
eyes follow him until he is nothing but a barely visible shadow
on the edge of the forest.

The king has made no attempt to detain him, on the contrary, he breathes more easily now. As for the stranger with the long nose, the straight hair, and the red ears who frightens little children, he relaxes perceptibly on his goatskin seat. Among the council, glances hesitate, hands and feet fidget, tongues want to speak, to call for Mankunku's return or at least for his presence in these negotiations with the foreigner; but already they no longer dare, the elders remain silent, the chief does what he wants, offers to and demands from the powerful stranger what he alone decides…There has been a sudden rupture between the chief and his counselors.

The stranger, followed by his interpreter, accompanies Chief Bizenga to his dwelling to negotiate behind closed doors. They go in. Before his hosts have even offered him a seat, the stranger opens the great pack which the escorting guards have carried for him: waxed cloth from Holland, pearls from the Indies, bombazine, basins, a large red blanket, glassware. Bizenga is bedazzled. He caresses the bombazine, rolls the pearls over his fingers, laughs, notices the red blanket, touches it, pats it, unfolds it, wraps it around his shoulders, takes it off, admires it at arm's length, laughs, and wraps it around his midriff. Ah! This will be the new symbol of royalty! Yes, the stranger says to him, you look handsome in it, now Bizenga is no longer self-conscious, he paces, sways, struts. All of this is for you, continues the stranger, and there's a lot more; a lot? asks Bizenga, yes, comes the hurried answer, even guns, even guns? yes, even guns.

Ah, he pats, he smooths, he plays again with the pearls, strings the beads around his neck, I'll be rich, I'll become a great king, and I'll rebuild my kingdom, I'll subdue the enemy clans, you'll fight by my side, won't you? Of course, after we've signed the treaty of friendship we'll be at your side no matter what happens. Well, you should have told me that sooner, I'll sign on the spot, right away!

The stranger pulls out his trump card, a strange gourd made out of glass, then a goblet. He pours a little drink in it, drinks it himself. He fills the glass half full again and offers it to the king. The king tastes it, he coughs, stunned. That's strong, it stings, that's a man's drink, stronger than palm wine or even corn liquor. He empties the goblet. He is happy, he asks for more.

"First let's sign the treaty," the stranger says to him.

"Give me another drop, just a little drop."

"No, let's sign the treaty first and I'll give you the entire bottle."

"I'll sign anything you want right away. And after that we'll kill chickens, goats, we'll have a feast, we'll plant a tree, the tree of friendship."

"We have to sign in front of witnesses."

The king calls to one of his guards: "Go get Nkazi, Mbemba, Mahuku"—a wink at the stranger—"they always do what I tell them to." The three men arrive at a leisurely pace, irritated, uncomfortable with the chief's way of handling this affair, his flagrant violation of what until now had been the communal tradition.

They are most of all amazed by the absence of Mandala Mankunku, the most celebrated man in the land. But the stranger has his three witnesses. He pulls a piece of very thin fabric out of his pocket. Intrigued, Bizenga takes it, pats it, caresses it, looks through it, then gives it back to its owner, who explains, "This little piece of paper here, I have to send it back to my country so that the chief who rules in my country will know that you are my friends; then he'll send you even more gifts and, in case of war, we'll always be at your side. We'll protect your country as if it were our own. Of course, in exchange, we'll expect a few little things—true friendship is not a one-way street, it ought to be reciprocal—some ivory from time to time, a little rubber sap or palmetto, and if someday we should need it, you'll give us a hand in building a road, for example, or a bridge. There, that's all, it's no big deal." (The interpreter translates.)

Bizenga listens to the interpreter, then turns to his three counselors as if he were going to consider their advice. They hesitate, then Mahuku speaks: "Chief Bizenga, you're the chief, and it's not for us to remind you of certain things, but you shouldn't forget that on such occasions we're all supposed to be present. We don't know this man, we don't know where he comes from, or what he hides behind his blue eyes. The elders have said: If you're looking for a fiancee, wait for the dry season, it's only then that you can tell if the girl is decent because she'll no longer fear to wash herself on account of the cold. We therefore say to you, Uncle Bizenga, wait a bit. We have no way of knowing if this man is decent. Let him depart and we'll discuss this matter in accordance with custom, in the presence of everyone, especially Mankunku."

The name of Mankunku precipitates Bizenga's anger. Surprised, the counselors listen with their heads bowed. "Mandala Mankunku, Mandala Mankunku, is he the only one in this land? Who raised him, who taught him everything he knows? Who's the chief around here? Don't you understand that things have changed, that the world has changed? Don't you see that our little isolated world is finished? Aren't you smart enough to understand that our health, our future prosperity and power, depend on this man? Mandala Mankunku, Mandala Mankunku, I've had enough! Enough! This man's offering us guns, cloth, peace, friendship; he's ready, he and his brothers, to get himself killed for us in case our neighbors attack us, and what does he ask in exchange? A few pieces of ivory, a little bit of sap from the wild rubber tree which grows by itself. And you'd refuse him that?" (The interpreter translates.)

The foreigner cheerfully observes the three counselors give in. Their rebellious impulse hasn't gone very far. He has the chief, the chief has them. He unfolds two copies of the piece of paper, he goes over to Bizenga and, running his finger over the document, assumes the tone of a good friend: "What you see here is my name. Here, you'll draw an X under your name, which I've written there, along with those of your counselors. Here. Take this pen."

Bizenga clamps his fist over the pen as if he were holding his machete. The stranger corrects the placement of his fingers. The chief traces the sign of the cross, the three others do the same. It is finished, it was finished. A simple sign had just changed the history of the world, of their world. Years later, when their descendants would gather in front of the governor's mansion to protest against their exploitation and victimization, this very piece of paper, now yellowed and dog-eared, would be shown them. Then they would read that their ancestors had ceded sovereignty over their land, that they had agreed, in signing this piece of paper, to exchange a kilo of ivory for every kilo of salt, to work for days on end with no remuneration, to deliver a monthly quota of rubber and so forth, in sum, that they had accepted, either out of ignorance or greed, an unequal exchange which would for a long time remain the mark of their relations with the land of these strangers.

For the moment, they congratulate each other. The stranger carefully arranges the documents in his large pockets, he lowers the flaps, buttons them. He is satisfied, mission accomplished. He takes out some other bottles; he gives two to Chief Bizenga who sets them cautiously in a corner for himself alone, then he opens the others: people drink, rejoice, their tongues are loosened. Even the three advisors have forgotten their reservations, they love the new drink. Everybody goes out, walking to the center of the village, toward the great tree beloved by old Lukeni. Bizenga has his old flint-lock rifle brought out, loads it with powder, shoots into the air, taya ta ta ta resounds the weapon, emitting a cloud of white smoke. The sound runs off, penetrates the forest, ricochets off the walls of the mountains and becomes an echo, the echo climbs back up to the tops of the trees and frightens the birds which fly away squawking. Women yoohoo, men shout, and children clap their hands. Bizenga has a hole dug, buries the gun, has the cartridges brought to him, which he also buries under the same tree. "From this day on, war between us is finished. Peace will reign between our two countries and our two peoples as long as no tree with cartridges for fruit grows out of this gun. May the ancestors approve." (The interpreter translates.)

Finally, the stranger takes out a flag. He plants it next to the buried gun, unfolds it so that the people can see its colors. "This flag is the symbol of my country. All those who touch it are free. You've touched it, you are free, you are under the protection of my great land."

The pact of friendship is sealed. Tom-toms, fires, dances, joy! The imprisoned guards are liberated, pardoned, offered drinks. The stranger looks on, amused; he is no longer frightened. He has come, he has seen, he has conquered. He watches the gyrations of the dancers who come and go, touching each other. All of a sudden, he flinches: whatever happened to the man with the green eyes?

12.

The stranger, tired of the festivities, his ears fatigued by the constant drone of the tom-tom, his musical sensibilities too long offended by unaccustomed rhythmic syncopations, gets up, lifts his Springfield repeater, and goes out to explore his new territory. He goes out of Lubituku, Mankunku's village, and the surrounding forest, taking the path that leads to the river. He feels good; the air under the branches is cool, and the light filtered by the foliage seems to vibrate with the leaves stirring in the wind; occasionally interrupting this ineffable trembling, there appear through openings in the greenery shafts of light as thick as a projector's beam. Innumerable multicolored birds dart here and there, tittering, insects chirp, branches creak. He is overwhelmed by the strangeness of this new world, he slows his pace, suspiciously observing the large variegated petals of indolent tropical flowers.

Finally, he catches sight of the great river, slow, majestic, its great sleeping ophidian skin shimmering with scales composed of a thousand little suns. Enormous sated crocodiles stretch out on the sandy banks, from time to time closing their yawning maws with a dry clatter in order to trap the dozens of imprudent insects who have ventured onto their tongues. Troops of hippopotomi amuse themselves in the muddy water, chase each other with their clumsy paws, caress each other with the softness their powerful mugs permit, spout geysers of water through their nostrils. A herd of wild boar slakes its thirst a little farther along, after having gorged itself in a cassava plantation. Legions of aquatic birds swim, bathe themselves, take flight only to return to skim the surface of the water before lifting off into the air again. The soul of the stranger isn't held back by the magical quality of the scene which unfolds before him: he grabs his repeater, loads it. He aims and pushes the trigger: the noise, amplified by the sonorous chambers integral to the structure of the forest, is so strong that it startles even himself. For the animals, it signals a cataclysm. The birds take flight in scattered flocks, the crocodiles throw themselves into the water, the frightened hippopotomi also dive in. But the stranger has regained his composure. He shoots at everything moving, the flying birds, the crawling reptiles; a big kudu passes in front of him, he shoots it in the foot; the antelope rolls on the ground, tries to get up on his broken foot but, stricken with pain, falls back down in his own spurting blood, bleating woefully; the man has no time to finish him off, he's already shooting at a jabiru, which, wounded, collapses into the water. Finally he stops. He is satisfied, everything belongs to him, he can do what he wants.

He walks away slowly, nonchalantly, like a lord inspecting his domain; he leaves the rustling forest foliage which has once again fallen into a strange and noisy silence. He heads for the banana plantation, traverses gardens giving off the strong scent of pepper plants, climbs the little slope which hides the savanna...and his heart nearly stops: elephants! Not just *one* elephant but a herd of elephants, a horde of elephants with oxpeckers flying overhead, elegant in their white plumage. He rubs his eyes, is it a mirage? He looks again, they're still there! "They're mine!" Ah yes, they're his, no doubt, within shooting range. Seized by a sense of power, he loads his gun, his beautiful Springfield repeater. He aims at a handsome male with enormous tusks and shoots: trumpeting in pain, the animal collapses. The others, surprised, don't understand, don't see where the danger lies. Now there's no stopping him, he loads, shoots, he loads, shoots; he hits a female, who collapses, her calf circles around her body, tries to revive her, he is stricken in his turn and sinks down into his mother's blood. The animals still understand nothing, they circle around, sniff the air, look for a traditional enemy to charge, they find none. The hunter no longer even aims, it's enough to just shoot into the herd, his bullets will find an animal to kill. He loads, he shoots, he loads, he shoots. Tired of circling around, the animals stop searching for the invisible enemy and begin to run to the opposite bank of the river in an infernal clamor, and finally disappear, raising a thick cloud of dust. The man still continues to shoot, load, shoot, never stopping until, as the dust settles, he notices that there are no more animals and that he is shooting into the void. Then he goes down to look at his victims; not all of them are dead, they bleed, moan, suffer, wheeze. He continues to advance towards the mountain of wounded elephants, who flounder in blood, mud, and dung. A thrill of joy runs up his spine. There are thirty or forty elephants. He clambers on the bodies, caressing the beautiful ivory tusks as he goes, reaches the top of the heap, recalls one of his favorite heroes, stands up straight, poses as a conqueror ready to have his monument erected for posterity: "At the head of this corps of centenarian elephants, I gaze out over mysterious and millennial Africa and…"

Suddenly he comes back to himself, feeling a bit ridiculous, because the villagers, attracted by the shots, are all around him. Forty or fifty elephants, piled there, one on top of the other! They can hardly believe it, they who were hardly able to kill one elephant a month, which was, in any case, sufficient to feed them all. The man with the red face, the straight hair, the white arms, who frightens little children, is really much more powerful than they had imagined. But what is to be done with all these tons of meat? For the first time, they are confronted with the problem of overproduction.

The stranger, confident and triumphant, pretends not to notice the natives transfixed with admiration before this new demonstration of power. Nonchalantly, he picks up his gun, his beautiful six-cartridge Springfield, and walks back up to the village.

13.

Then a wave broke over the land: those who came as peacemakers escorted by heavily armed guards, those who brought civilization and set themselves up as administrators, those who came to exploit the land in order to get rich, those who arrived bearing crosses to save the souls of tribes still submerged in barbarism; men of science who came to study the land, the animals, the plants, and the natives, hardy adventurers dreaming of marvelous Timbuktus, geographers searching for undiscovered Monomotapas, gold diggers feverishly hunting for the golden talents of a new Ophir... They swarmed over the land like a cloud of locusts, devoured leaves, knocked over trees and mountains, massacred men and elephants, traversed bodies of water, took possession of lands, bodies, and souls. They defied mosquitoes, tsetse flies, amoebas, and snakes; they tackled buffaloes, warthogs, and giant forest hogs; they held out against sun, rain, and wind; and even went so far as to walk on the graves of the ancestors...

Nothing stopped this triumphal march to the strains of *jours de gloire arrivés* or God save the king. A more powerful, sophisticated, cynical world was taking possession of a world that was less powerful, less sophisticated, and more naive. It was not a clash such as is heard when two clouds crash into each other, head on, in tornado weather, shattering the shell of the sky with thunder and lightning; rather, it was sometimes a simple stroll, that of the hunter breaking trail with gunshot and contempt, crushing the twigs of the path under his boots, sometimes a light, spinning waltz permitting the dancer to elude and wind around the obstacles in his path, a waltz whose steps included corruption, persuasion, bluff, and various other tricks. That which animated these new conquistadors was truly extraordinary! But what was extraordinary wasn't this world burgeoning with all sorts of life, this world of luxuriant plants, of unknown fruits and flowers, of unique animal species such as the giraffe with its long neck, and the amphisbaena with two heads which can move forward in either direction, no, it wasn't this world where a simple tornado could become a marvelous spectacle in which all the forms of the cosmos were unleashed, what was extraordinary was the incredible ease with which they enlarged their new empires; they didn't buy them, they didn't really occupy them, it was really much simpler: they simply declared that these lands belonged to them and they were theirs, along with everything above or beneath.

Those who conquered Mankunku's land were called Belgian or French, but what difference does it make? They might as well have been called Portuguese, English, Germans, Turks, or Maoris for all that it might have changed their behavior, because all people bent on the conquest of other people are alike. They occupied the basin of the great Nzadi River and were only stopped in the West by the Ocean; to the North, nothing stopped them; in the East they ran into the Muslim Arabs, the first traders of Negro slaves in that part of the continent, who continued to depopulate entire regions with their raids, as frequent as they were cruel. These Arabs who, with their archaic blunderbusses, had terrorized populations, broken families, pillaged, kidnapped young girls for their harems, they who had enriched themselves by forcing tens of thousands of men, women, and children to walk from the interior to the East Coast fettered to each other with chains heavy enough to hobble a buffalo, they who had forced columns upon columns of men to march from the interior to the coast in frightful conditions, necks wedged into the forks of tree branches less than a meter in length between any two slaves and held in place by a rivet of iron at the throat, even these Arabs were unable to hold out against these newcomers who proceeded to dispossess them of the sources of their wealth; having finally met their match, they were hewed into pieces and subdued along with those whom they had subdued. And when the invading foreigners had overflowed the basin of the great river, they continued on their way to the great lakes.

They wrote: *"We have a sacred mission, to bring civilization to these primitive tribes, and we will never falter. We will also establish for our country a vast empire on which the sun will never set, an empire which will be the envy of the rest of the world; thus we will affirm our power."*

Others added: *"There are territories for the taking, servants at our pleasure. The rights of man do not apply to Negroes. Besides, the natives have no right to anything, whatever one gives them is a genuine gratuity."*

Still others: *"I won't speak to you of the licentious customs of these folk, the pen of a monk refuses to set such things down on paper. The Gospel says that we are all brothers, that is certainly true, but the African is our little brother."*

But, to be sure, others also wrote: *"...We've seen nothing which justifies the hypothesis of the native inferiority of the Negro, nothing which proves that he is of a different species than the most civilized. The African is a man endowed with all the attributes characteristic of the human race ..."*

They continued to march, to climb over mountains, to traverse forests and rivers, not stopping until they encountered other foreigners from the same lands but who competed with them. Then, having run out of territories to acquire, they devoted themselves to what they called the *development* of these conquered lands.

Chapter Three

And in the savanna without soul

Deserted by the breath of the ancients

The horns howl, ululate without mercy

Over the accursed tom-toms

Black night! Black night!

— Birago Diop

14.

MANKUNKU'S COUNTRY WAS DIVIDED INTO LARGE CONCESSIONS which sometimes divided a village in two or three. The new proprietors seemed to have a single objective: rubber. The way of life, the village, no longer existed; the week had been changed and now consisted of seven days, the last one being reserved for the Lord. Mankunku, like the others, had been obliged to abandon all of his former activities for the sake of the only thing that counted any more: rubber. Every two weeks, the collectors sent by the administration came to carry off the quota required from every inhabitant, bringing as return payment an armful of cotton goods for Chief Bizenga, who distributed them among his wives. Rubber! A matter of life and death! When villages refused to obey or didn't furnish the required quantities, the foreigners sent a squad of locally recruited militias, the *mbulu-mbulu*. They would show up with their noisy boots, shoot their guns in the air, and put the frightened villagers to work. But when, as sometimes happened, these militiamen were unable to exert their authority because they were too close to the region where they grew up, the foreigners dispatched soldiers recruited in other districts, who were called Senegalese riflemen, though not all of them came from Senegal. The anger of these "Senegalese" was frightening. If people didn't do what they asked right away, they didn't hesitate to beat them bloody, rape the women, burn their houses down; if the offenders ran away, they'd run after them, drive them into an impasse, and throw grenades at their feet to watch them jump. In the North, people called them *tourougous* because, for some reason, they took them for Turks. In any case, for Mankunku's people, who had never seen Muslim Arabs, these strangers had bewildering manners. They walked around with canteens slung over their shoulders, using the water sometimes to make tea, sometimes to wash their sexual organs before eating or praying. Their way of praying was also curious: they took off their boots, faced the rising sun, spread out a mat or cover on the ground, bowed down on it, positioning themselves so that their buttocks were more elevated than their heads, then, executing a series of back-and-forth movements, enough to make you seasick, swaying like a trotting camel, they would cry out, Allah, Allah, Allah Akbar, several times, and all this several times a day. After prayers in which they pleaded for God's mercy, they cracked a kola nut, put their boots back on, picked up their guns, and continued on their sanguinary mission.

As for the local *mbulu-mbulu*, they used so much ammunition that their bosses began to require an inventory of every last cartridge. The solution was simple: they cut off the right hand of any individual troublesome enough to oppose them. In any case, not all of their bullets were used for repression: sometimes they were used for hunting game, and sometimes they were simply lost from shots fired by accident. In such cases, in order to avoid the fury of their foreign masters, they still carried back severed hands to justify themselves, either by cutting off the hands of living people or by taking advantage of a natural death to remove a hand from the corpse. The ritual was always the same: the foreign commander counted the number of bullets, counted the number of the hands (which were often smoked so that they would not decompose en route) and, if one count corresponded to the other, simply declared: "*Malamu* (very good). Throw the hands in the river."

Every morning Mankunku and his countrymen would get up a little earlier, even before the cock's crow; they would walk for hours in the forest, carrying machetes and containers, before discovering the rare trees they sought. They bled these accursed plants, which discharged white latex blood that they gathered in their basins. It took them twelve or thirteen workdays to collect the required quantity. When the plants became rare, Mankunku saved the village from punitive exactions by discovering vines whose sap resembled gutta-percha, but this substitution was only good for a while; the harvest of rubber diminished irreversibly and, at the same time, the repression augmented. Rubber, rubber, rubber! The echo of this word still reverberates in the deepest forests of Mankunku's country. The tears and the blood that it made flow have not yet really dried up.

There was no longer time to cultivate cassava, peanuts, or yams because the women were harvesting rubber, there was no longer time to clear the land for new plantations because the men were harvesting rubber. For the first time Mankunku's land knew famine. The weavers had ceased to weave, the blacksmiths to forge, the singers to sing, everybody was out looking for rubber. Even their relationship with the forest had changed: she had become hostile to them because she didn't understand the thirst for destruction that had suddenly swept over them, so she often set fatal traps for them—hidden green mambas emerged suddenly from the leaves, striking with fatal venom; poisonous thorns wounded them; treacherous brambles tore their skin or threw them off balance, pushing them into pits they hadn't seen. On the other hand, she seemed more and more inclined to hide her edible fruit and game from them. For their part, they hated her at the same time as they feared her. All trust was broken between the forest and these men who had always lived in material and spiritual symbiosis with her; they became mutually exclusive, parasites of each other. Oh! rubber, red with the blood of an entire people!

When there was no longer enough natural rubber sap, attention was shifted to the harvest of delicate palm kernel oil. But things became really difficult when there was no longer either enough rubber nor enough palm kernel oil. Since the logic of the foreigners was to always extract something from the occupied land, they found a substitute, a tax to be paid in cash. Thus they instituted a three-franc tax.

Just mention "three francs" in Mandala Mankunku's country! Senegalese riflemen were unleashed on the land, the local militia recruited in the North of the country were unleashed on the South, the ones recruited in the South were unleashed on the North. They had the right to do anything. People fled before their approach and hid in the hostile forests. Woe to the man who died without having paid his three francs! They would spread out the nude body in front of the family and ask one of his relatives to give him twenty-five strokes of a whip in public. Sometimes the foreigner accompanied the militia, and, one time, in a neighboring village, to demonstrate his power and also perhaps to amuse himself, he lined up five rebels in a row and shot through them all with a single bullet!

In this life of forced labor, only the seventh day was welcome. Not the entire day, however, because in the morning it was necessary, no matter what, to participate in the great ceremony celebrated by the foreign missionary: dressed in his chasuble, taking refuge behind his makeshift altar dominated by an immense cross, he came and went, muttered a bizarre gibberish, kneeled, rang little bells, sprinkled people with water...How long it was, this ceremony! But it was worth the wait because afterwards came the actual respite of the seventh day, the day when they could forget rubber, palm kernel oil, and the three francs.

Ah, those Sunday dances! The best drummers were chosen; first they tuned their instruments by warming the skin of the tom-tom on a straw fire in order to give it the right tension, then they positioned themselves lightly inside the circle of dancers, and away they went! The orchestra might or might not, as they pleased, include xylophones, *sansi*, or *massikoulou*; there was sometimes an accompanying chorus, sometimes not— but there was always the tom-tom, source of vibration, of rhythm, source of life. There were all kinds: enormous ones coming all the way up to one's shoulders that were played standing and gave out a somber, almost monotonous sound, thus maintaining the essential vibrations; the smallest, played kneeling, were not only rhythmic instruments but also, when played by a skilled musician, were capable of yielding melodic modulations. Between these two extremes, there was an entire intermediate range of tom-toms. And buttocks jiggled, torsos undulated as if they lacked spinal columns, hands clapped, pieces of cowrie were tossed at the feet of the best dancers.

Quickly they would form two rows, women on one side, men on the other; the latter would keep stamping their feet, shaking their agile behinds, and wriggling their chests in a constant movement up and down and side to side. Then there was the assault, slow, controlled. The women on one side, the men on the other, hop to it, they would imitate the act of copulation by thrusting their sexes forward, men against women, then would back off, stamp, jump, advance, and hop to it!...Stop these obscene gestures, oh my God, sweet Lord Jesus, pardon them, they know not what they do.

One morning, the missionary happened to arrive at the moment when they were performing these dances he had never seen before, and he was overcome with rage, turning even redder than the foreigner who, long ago, was the first to set foot in Lubituku. The tom-toms became quiet; everyone looked at him, intrigued. He fumed, choked, shouted, over here quickly, interpreter, you're all obscene, what license, fornicating under the eyes of God, may the Lord forgive my eyes for looking upon this diabolic scene, stop these dances immediately...They were forbidden to dance on Sunday, the day of the Lord. This was how the people of Lubituku learned that these dances, which went back to the time of their remote ancestors, were an offense against almighty God, and that the deed they had done in order to have children, that deed which best expressed the sense of communion with the world and the continuity of life, was a manifestation of obscenity.

That evening, Mankunku sat down beside his father under the tree where old Lukeni, whom he had loved so much, and who had loved him so much, had been accustomed to take his seat. The tom-toms had been silenced and the dancers dispersed in sadness and restrained anger. Night had fallen. In the distance, they could see Bizenga's house, the only one in the village that was lit with a petroleum lamp. Mankunku thought of old Lukeni: "You were right; your dream said that they would walk on the graves of the ancestors and that the ancestors wouldn't react. Well, that's exactly what's happening. How I'd love to be at your side, old Lukeni!" In spite of himself, his glance wandered over to his Uncle's house; that man and his little family were the only ones who had profited from the arrival of the strangers. He turned to his father, whose back leaned against the tree; he had aged a great deal, work had exhausted him. This man, the eldest of the blacksmiths, had become a commoner with patched garments, running through the forest to gather palm fruits or rubber sap. Mankunku felt a lump in his throat. "Father, how could it have come to this?"

His father hardly budged; his eyes, barely illuminated by the moon and stars, seemed to have turned inside himself. He murmured, "My son, it's always too late by the time we understand. Take a dense forest, cut down one of its trees, nobody will notice a thing; keep on cutting them down and, in a moment, without really understanding why, you'll have the vague feeling that this forest isn't what it used to be; keep it up and the day will come when suddenly you'll realize: well, this forest has really changed. But then it's too late."

Yes, Mankunku admits to himself, it was thus that slowly, insidiously, the order of things changed in their lives, being transformed into a new order that was flimsy, unstable, and, above all for him, irrational. But his father's response didn't satisfy him. He asked the question in a different way: "Why did it happen?"

"Why ask such a question when the evidence is in front of you: open your eyes, my son. Before these foreigners showed up, we lived in a just world, there was understanding in our villages, the forest gave us plenty to eat, and the earth was fertile. They have brought misery with them. I curse them," he concluded, spitting on the ground.

Mankunku stiffened, as if stung by a wasp. "Father, I know that it's not for a son to teach his father to recognize a river, but I believe that what you've said isn't exactly correct. We weren't so just as that! Have you forgotten the quarrels about witchcraft between the clans? Remember, they nearly killed me, and, who knows, perhaps they'd have buried me alive under a *nsanda* tree just because my eyes were green. Our society was also a violent society."

"It wasn't you, Mankunku, that they wished to eliminate; you were different, and they thought that you were a sorcerer, a maleficent spirit, and that's what they wanted to get rid of."

"That's all I've heard, all my life, 'You're different!' Do you think that a society lacking the flexibility to hold onto those who are different is a good society, a just society?"

"We held onto you, my son."

"It's thanks to old Lukeni that I'm alive today."

"There will always be an old Lukeni in our society to save and preserve that which ought to be saved at any given moment."

Mankunku didn't know how to respond to this declaration, which was more an act of faith than an argument. He also didn't want to fly in his father's face, so he changed the subject: "The foreigners have made their contribution to our present misery, perhaps, even for sure, but we also have to look the truth in the eye, Father. Without our cooperation things wouldn't have gone so badly, they wouldn't have had such an easy time of it. Just think how cheaply we allowed ourselves to be bought off: an armful of cotton goods even though our weavers are the best in the region, some glass baubles, some mediocre, badly cut jewels, even though the ones produced by your workshop are a thousand times more beautiful. Where do we get this taste for things that come from elsewhere? Have we neither honor nor self-respect?"

"It's your Uncle Bizenga's fault, he has become a stranger to his people."

"It's you who put him where he is today. We get the leaders we deserve! We'd better do everything we can to see that future generations don't assume that all of this was the fault of the foreigners. We must never forget, father, our own appetites and our own weaknesses."

"I don't understand you, Mankunku."

"You don't want to understand me. You're afraid to recognize that our society had arrived at an impasse. Old Lukeni had sensed it. But who knows, misery's good for something—may the shock provoked by these foreigners help us get through it."

His father looked at him, puzzled; he really did understand why they said that his son was different. He quickly averted his eyes before a bad thought could brush his soul and thus harm his son. The Moon had already risen high in the sky without diminishing the brilliance of the Milky Way. At this season, the Morning Star was visible, just at the tips of the treetops on the horizon; this meant that before long the cock would crow, it was time to go to bed, tomorrow was a workday. In turn, Mankunku looked at his father, who was lost in his own world. He put his arm around his bent shoulders: "Father, we have to get some sleep."

They got up. Once again, he looked at that old face; the eyes of the father then fixed on those of his son. "Good night, my child. We are all responsible, including yourself."

"I know. Good evening and good night to mother."

Thus ended the seventh day of the week.

15.

In order to pay the three-franc tax it was necessary to earn money, and there was no longer any point in looking for the now rare rubber trees, the exploitation of which was more and and more expensive. The youth of entire villages were recruited to build roads and, in compensation for their free labor, they were exempted from paying the tax. This was also the period when work began on the railroad that would connect the great Nzadi River with the Ocean. The pay seemed relatively good, and so, in order to give his exhausted parents a respite, Mankunku signed up, hoping to earn enough to pay their part.

During their first weeks on the job, the men were set the task of breaking up great blocks of stone that the foreign engineers had previously disengaged with dynamite. Once the block was marked, Mankunku would raise the heavy hammer and let it fall on the enormous stone mass; the hammer would rebound at the shock, which would shake his forearm and run all through his body to the very soles of his feet. After several such blows, he would succeed in cracking the rock open, and the small pieces thus torn off from the block would be piled up in a basket which he would carry on his back or on his head to the actual building site; there, the small blocks would be crushed by a pneumatic crusher, until nothing was left of them but a pile of little pebbles more or less uniform in size. There were a hundred or so men doing this work, and the worksite swarmed like a termite colony. In the evening they went back home, bent over, heads buzzing with the sound of hammer blows. The first week, Mankunku's palms were covered with blisters which throbbed painfully; his mother treated the swelling with an ointment made of palm oil, lamenting all the while, "Mankunku,

I keep telling you to get married; at your age you might have had at least five children. Allow me the consolation of seeing my grandchildren before I die."

"But mother," he protested, "stop being so silly, you're not going to die. I'll think about marriage later, now I don't have time, there are too many things to do."

"Oh, accursed life, what have we done to our ancestors that they abandon us like this?"

"Our ancestors are dead, mother, and it's up to us, the living, to find our own way out of this mess. You'd do better to ask your brother what he's done to us."

"Be quiet, Mandala, they'll hear you, don't blaspheme and don't speak of Bizenga like that; he's your uncle and your master."

"You always defend your brother, don't you?"

"Let's not talk about it any more. You can't keep on breaking rocks like that, your hands are nothing but sores."

"That's nothing, if you knew that Lounda crushed two of his fingers with the hammer, you wouldn't feel sorry for me. No, what we're really afraid of at the worksite are the rockslides when they blast those enormous boulders loose with dynamite. There have already been three deaths this week."

"Be careful, Mandala, you're my only child, the ancestors didn't want to give me any more."

"Don't worry, Mother, I'll get by. The important thing is that you'll never have to worry about those damn three francs."

At first, there were a hundred of them at the worksite; now, at the end of the second week, there were only twenty, most of the workers having run away because the work was too painful. The work no longer progressed due to the lack of manpower. The administration launched a conscription, and it began just like the days of rubber and the three-franc tax. Soldiers would surround villages and take all the inhabitants to a bush doctor who would designate future workers according to their weight and the circumference of their chests. In turn, clans and entire villages left the recruitment zones to take refuge in distant territories, even crossing the river in order to escape the local authorities. The recruitment became a veritable manhunt, and the game captured therewith was dragged back like cattle, with ropes around their necks, to the assembly points. Some populations resisted with blows of knives and machetes, but the *mbulu-mbulu* made swift work of crushing such opposition.

After having spent close to a month crushing rocks, Mankunku and his companions were sent to work at the central worksite. Lined up for the length of several miles beneath a sun as hot as the Christian Hell described by the missionaries, they carried heavy railroad ties of burning metal and set them down on the beds of gravel and pebbles they had previously made. Sweat rolled off their brows, burning their eyes. The worksite was so far from Mankunku's village that he could no longer go back home in the evening, so he slept under the open sky in makeshift camps set up by the railroad company. As for the masters, they had movable houses that they transported and set back up each time they moved. But Mankunku slept between two comrades who came from very far away and didn't even speak the same language as he. After a period of total incomprehension, they nevertheless succeeded in explaining themselves in a colorful pidgin wherein gestures were just as important as words and onomatopoetic expressions. Djibril and Djermakoye were their names. Mankunku didn't understand how they could have come from so far away, so he often asked them questions about their land.

"I'm Djibril, I'm a Sara, I come from Chad; there are many of us at this worksite."

"I'm Djermakoye, I'm a Banda, I come from Ubangi."

"How many days did it take you to walk here?" asked Mankunku.

"Oh! The ten fingers of my hands and the ten toes on my feet wouldn't be enough to count them."

"This isn't possible! I knew that the earth was big but not so big! Your country must border that of the foreigners, because I know that they come from even farther off."

"Don't talk to me about that voyage," said Djibril. "After capturing us—because we were scared to look at the sea—they made us walk for ten or fifteen days to get to Bangui."

"Why were you scared to look at the sea?"

"Among my people, we believe that those who look at the sea will catch a fatal sickness, either of the body or of the spirit."

"I haven't yet seen the sea," said Mankunku, "I've never left the banks of the river where I was born; but my father has seen the ocean and he's in very good health."

"What can I tell you? It's what my people say."

"When we got to Bangui,"—Djermakoye took up the tale—"we were crowded onto narrow barges with no roofs, under the sun and the rain; sometimes it was impossible to budge for hours on end. Many died of suffocation, while others, tired of stretching up above the crowd to breathe, let go, slid down, and fell into the river. That's how my father disappeared while we were on our long voyage."

"Why didn't you try to fish out those who fell in?"

"It was impossible to stop the barge to fish out all who fell in; we'd never have arrived at our destination. In any case, they hardly hit the water with a splash before a crocodile's tail would knock them out and an instant later the jaws would clamp down on them."

"My God," gasped Mankunku, finding nothing more to say.

Their conversations often ended abruptly because the sentry would pass by and order them to keep quiet. Then they would stretch out under the open sky and, the next day, wake up with their bodies chilled to the bone by the coolness and dampness of these tropical nights. They only slept under a roof during the rainy season, in a large hangar hastily erected to shelter them. Then Djibril and Djermakoye resumed their transport work, each one carrying a fifty-pound bag of cement on his head. Others exhausted themselves under loads too heavy for them—freight-car chassis, rails, barrels of cement, panels of prefabricated houses—over excessively difficult terrain: they had to climb up and down small hills, watch out for trees, make their way around little ravines; on rainy days, when the ground became a muddy bog, covered with dead and decomposing leaves, they had to pull off a veritable balancing act. This transport work was as deadly as the rest; men broke their necks beneath baskets of rocks, others slipped down hills with the freight cars, only to be found crushed at the bottom of a ravine. One day twenty or so harried workers refused to go on despite the threats of the engineer in charge. The foreman took five men at random, among them Djermakoye, attached a necklace of dynamite around each one's neck, and blew them up. The others immediately went back to work.

Men were running to the left and to the right, breaking rocks, pushing freight cars, picking up rails...all under the attentive eye of the white foreman. And Mankunku was fascinated by this man, by these men: where did they get their power? From their ancestors? Look at that man, alone, unarmed, his face flushed from the heat, in the shadow of his white helmet. It would only take two of us, even one of us alone, myself, for example, to disable or kill him; but no one dares, something's stopping us. There he is, alone, giving orders, imposing his will on tens, hundreds, thousands of us. And on me too, Mandala Mankunku, whose ancestor overthrew the mighty! Moreover, nothing seems able to resist his will. If a rock got in his way, he would make it disappear in a noise of a thousand guns; if a mountain got in his way, he would chop it in two and dig out a tunnel to pass through; if a river got in his way, he would throw a bridge over it and continue right along. Where did it lead, this pursuit of an endlessly receding horizon? Mankunku braced his muscles, picked up the burning railroad tie, set it in place, went back to his companion to get another one. Yes indeed, what would it take to stop them? Of course, the ancestors occasionally took their revenge: some mornings the workers found rails still attached to their ties hanging in the air over the emptiness left in the wake of a landslide that dragged away thousands of cubic meters of earth; well, that didn't discourage the foreigner, he just began again, making them work twice as hard, reinforcing the edges of the embankment, going through it all again. The deaths of dozens of workers was a matter of indifference. Traveler, if one day you ride the train that goes from the great river to the Ocean, listen attentively to the clatter of the wheels on the rails because each of them, every single clickety-clack, denotes a death; then think a little about all those men buried in the mountains through which you will pass and remind yourself that here there's a death for every railroad tie. Perhaps this will help their souls to rest in peace.

That night, upon returning to camp, Mankunku found Djibril stretched out on his pallet. He had lost a lot of weight; his eyes receded into sockets too large for them; the skin was stretched tight over his face, narrowly molding the bones of his forehead and jaws. Moaning, he held onto his belly; his ration of dried salt fish lay untouched by the side of his bed. Mankunku put his hand on his forehead: "What's the matter, Djibril?"

"I told you, it's the sea. I'm going to die because I've seen the sea."

"But we haven't yet reached the Ocean's shore."

"Its spirit is gnawing out my insides. My stools are full of blood, my belly is killing me, my chest is squeezing me."

He was close to delirium. His malady had begun the day Djermakoye died, a death that had affected him strongly; since then he had eaten nothing, he was no longer able to swallow the bad salt fish that they imported from Angola. Poor man, to come more than twelve hundred miles from home, to work on a railway line whose use he didn't understand, then to die alone, abandoned, without friends or family; for Mankunku believed that he would die like thousands of others, ground down by this monstrous railroad. Many a native of Chad and Ubangi, people of the interior unaccustomed to eating salt, succumbed to grave intestinal troubles as a result of eating the salt fish which was the essential item in the workers' diet. When the fish was actually putrid and they refused to eat it, they were neverthess debited for distributed rations in the foreman's book, and the next day, they returned to their hard labor. Famished, emaciated, many of the workers also died from tuberculosis.

Mankunku decided to go and find the person in charge of health services to bring his friend some help. He arrived in front of the prefabricated cabin inside of which the foreign masters took their meals and stopped timidly. A sentry, a Senegalese wearing a red cap and dressed like a Zouave, came over and snarled, "You, get the fuck out of here, what do you think you're doing here?"

"My friend is dying. I would like to ask the doctor to come and see him."

"The doctor doesn't have time, he's eating. Go, get the fuck out of here," he said, raising the butt of his gun menacingly.

A blind rage took hold of Mankunku; he tightened his fist, turned his back, and went off into the night. The zealous servant continued pacing in front of his masters' house, his gun on his shoulder.

Returning to Djibril's side, he saw him twisted with pain and coughing up blood. Mankunku no longer understood anything, he couldn't see how dysentery could provoke bloody vomiting. Other workers gathered around the bed and spoke in a frightened manner that also seemed threatening: "Pick him up, get him out of here..." "We better not let him die in here, it'll bring bad luck to the whole camp..." Two sturdy fellows took tight hold of Djibril, took him out of the camp, picked him up, and threw him to the edge of the forest. Mankunku, who had followed them with a blanket, covered him and sat down next to him. The two of them stayed like that under the light of the stars and the shadow of the forest, Mankunku holding Djibril's hand, so as to transmit, throughout the sad damp night, the warmth of his friendship to this man from a distant land at the other end of the earth. They did not speak, in the midst of the rustling leaves, the swishing wings of nocturnal birds. Suddenly, Djibril clutched at his hand, coughed ever so faintly, and relaxed his grip. He was dead.

Mankunku remained a long time beside the body of his co-worker, his friend, watching the constellations appear and disappear in the sky, thinking of the thousands of dead at rest, scattered all over his land. They had all died of exhaustion and of the sorrow of being so far away from home. And it wasn't only the ones who had come from far away who died, but the indigenous people as well. The only peace that the railroad had left behind it was the peace of cemeteries. Oh! the horror of the days of the machine!

Mankunku buried his friend early in the morning so that the hyenas would not steal the body and then, although completely worn out, went off to the worksite. He who had been defying the powerful all his life, now tried with all his might to understand. These men were strong, powerful, with an almost infinite power, he thought; he wondered—oh heresy—if they were not more powerful than his ancestors. And, while thinking about the events of the previous night, he took note of his own downfall: confronted with the sickness of his friend Djibril, his first thought had not been to make use of his own learning, he who was a *nganga*, but to call on the foreign doctor. What in the world did they possess, and what did he have to do to discover their secret?

He made minute observations of the deeds and gestures of these strange foreigners; he tried to see if they ate as he did, if they had teeth, if their blood was red, if they farted, burped, pissed, if their excrement was real excrement, if they had penises, and if they fucked like he did. After a discreet but methodical examination, he came to the conclusion that they didn't have anything that he, Mankunku, didn't have. Then where did they get their power? Mankunku sweated beneath the sun, suffered, tightened the enormous screws that held the ties to the ballast; his calloused hands had hardened and no longer ached as they had at first; he grabbed the burning steel rails, turned them over, scrutinized them: he who was a blacksmith was intrigued by the steel. By dint of so much thinking, so much reflection, he had become taciturn and introverted; without realizing it, he worked with a certain zeal, thus aggravating his comrades, who accused him of currying favor with the foreign masters. He did not take offense, continuing to look for what it was he had missed during those nights when, alone by the great river, he had pursued wisdom and interrogated the heavens, during those days spent collecting and studying plants. These strangers had solved the problem of the repeating rifle, the problem of signs in which one could hide thoughts, problems which he had been incapable of solving. Had he then, he, Mandala Mankunku, been completely off course?

16.

Three tired militiamen, the famous *mbulu-mbulu,* arrive in Lubituku, Mandala Mankunku's village. Guns slung across their shoulders, the red cap with its black pompom sitting at a proud angle on their heads, they try to maintain a haughty and commanding air. They have just completed a tour of the surrounding villages, either supervising the harvest of palm kernel oil or collecting the three-franc tax. Their only baggage is a little basket on their backs, because they know that they can, for the asking, eat, sleep, have a woman in any village they choose. They head for Bizenga's dwelling; he comes out, welcomes them obsequiously, bids them enter, they sit down. Have you traveled far? Not too tired? What would you like to drink, water, palm wine, corn liquor? Make yourselves at home, stay a while, have something to eat before you go, hey, Nzoumba, wife, kill three chickens for us and cook them up nicely for our guests...They sit on a mat and eat. Bizenga takes care to offer them each a gizzard, the finest and tastiest part of the chicken. They dig into the feast, dipping their fingers into the oily pepper sauce, tearing off the thigh meat with their teeth, breaking the bones to suck out the traces of marrow, drinking, burping, farting to relieve their stomachs and intestines of unpleasant flatulence.

They have eaten, they remove their caps and boots, unbutton their pants and shirts, and stretch out on mats to take a nap. Bizenga orders the playing children to stop making noise, the talking women to be quiet, so as not to disturb his guests...

The siesta is over and the hour of departure nears. One of the militiamen, ready before the others, goes out for a stroll around the village. The others are still getting dressed, putting their things in order. Chief Bizenga notices the baskets the militiamen have been carrying: they're full of dried-out human hands. A gleam of horror passes before his eyes, he feels like vomiting. "But what are you doing with these hands?" he asks timidly.

The guards smile. "If we don't strike those who refuse to deliver rubber or pay taxes, we're very severely punished, and sometimes the white officers of the State even go so far as to shoot us. So, rather than allow ourselves to be killed, we kill the recalcitrant villagers, and the proof of our labor is these hands. Sometimes," he adds with a playful smile, "we cut off their dicks."

"But...but...what do they do with these hands?"

"Well, that depends on the boss. Some count them and then throw them into the river; others have them smoked and use them for pipe-stoppers which they take back to their country...But you, don't you worry, you're a very good chief, nothing of the kind will happen in your village, we guarantee you."

The guard who has gone out walks through a nearly deserted village. All the young people have gone away to put in their day of forced labor; there remain only a few tired old men and women who pass the time getting even older under the great village tree or in the shade of the verandas of their houses. Turning the corner of a hut, he notices a woman, Mankunku's mother. "Woman, come here."

Trembling, she comes forward. Not very young, but she'll do, thinks the militiaman; his eyes, red from smoking hashish, light up. He tries to pull off her cloth wrap, Mandala's mother cries out and pushes him away; he holds onto her, tries to turn her around. At this moment, the men show up at a run. The woman's husband, Mankunku's father, is furious, he faces the militiaman and shouts at him to leave his wife alone. The soldier gets angry: "Who do you think you are? Besides, why aren't you out gathering rubber?"

"You can't do anything to me, my account is paid, my son works and my wife and I, we've paid our three-franc tax. Leave my wife alone."

"You lie, you idiot, trash, monkey, jungle bunny, just watch out, I'll fix your ass! Show me your kilos of rubber or palm kernel oil right now or you'll see what's what!"

"We paid the three francs!" Mankunku's father takes out of his pocket the precious roll of papers which he carries with him at all times.

The guard grabs them, and, since he doesn't know how to read, pretends to scrutinize them. "These papers are worthless!" He tears them up and throws them into the wind.

Mankunku's father is no longer able to restrain himself, he punches the *mbulu-mbulu,* who falls down; humiliated, he gets up, cruelty in his eyes, brandishes his gun, and fires; Mandala's father sinks to the ground, a clean kill. His wife howls, throws herself on her husband's body. The companions of the victim are paralyzed. The gunshot has attracted the two other militiamen, who show up at a run, brandishing their arms. They hold the entire village at gunpoint. The killer cuts off the dead man's right hand and throws it into the basket his friend has just brought over; then they make everybody line up and march them down the path to the village center. Mankunku's mother is left alone with her husband stretched out in the dust under the burning sun, next to the basket full of hands. The animals have sensed the drama, they prowl around, bleating and cackling. The soldiers order the old men and women they've led out to sit down in the sun, then beat them black and blue. They groan, writhe, cry, howl, their shaky old legs won't let them escape. Chief Bizenga comes out, sees what's happening, he's horrified but doesn't dare to intervene and goes back inside.

The three militiamen have finished their work; they leave the groaning and bleeding bodies to thrash around in the dust with the flies. They burn a few houses on their way, kick in a few doors, then go back to pick up their things from Bizenga, who asks no questions and shakes their hands. One of them notices that he forgot his basket of hands, he goes back to Mankunku's father's body, beside which his wife is weeping. He senses something amiss. He spreads out the hands on the ground and counts them: there are only eighteen, one is missing; he figures it out, he grabs Mankunku's mother brutally, tears off her wrap: the hand which she has devotedly hidden in the cloth, close to her body, falls out. The guard takes it and throws it into the basket. The woman seems crazy, she throws herself on the militiaman, grabs the basket and turns it over; she stretches out her arm to grasp her husband's hand, the militiaman kicks her away, she hurls herself at him again with a cry, bites the hand of the soldier, who, exasperated, swings his gun butt, striking a blow which shatters her skull. He gathers the nineteen hands, picks up his basket, rejoins the other two, and they leave the village of Lubituku with the gifts that Bizenga has given them. Mandala's mother, spread out on the ground next to her husband, dies a slow death amidst the bleating of the goats, the cackling of the chickens, and the barking of the dogs.

17.

Having finished his work for the week, Mankunku set off late in the afternoon to spend the seventh day resting in his village, for the week now had seven days. On the way, he had an odd feeling of sad solitude. His body bent over, his morale crushed by the deaths of Djibril and Djermakoye, he wondered if he was going to spend the rest of his life breaking rocks and laying down rails to pay his taxes. Life no longer had any meaning, it ran with no more reason than streams do after a tornado, without knowing where they're going, slipping one way, then the other, finally stagnating before being allowed to dry up in the sun. The invasion of the foreigners had, as it were, broken an equilibrium; it brought such disorder that it was no longer possible to know what caused what. Things had changed so much in the space of a few years that he no longer recognized the village in which he had grown up. He walked along, nostalgic. He didn't realize that he was there until he had climbed the last hill overlooking his village. He heard strange howlings of dogs and felt terribly ill at ease. He pressed forward; the wind soon brought him cries and lamentations: death had stricken the village.

Mankunku could see that some houses had been torn up, others burned down, but his was still standing. He ran to his father's place, from where the cries came: his mother and father were stretched out on a mat; some women sitting around them, hair disheveled, were crying and dragging themselves on the ground, while the men, silent and sorrowful, stood in a circle a little farther away. There was no need to explain to him: the militia killed them, the militia killed them, he repeated along with other tearful words which mingled with the lamentations of the village. He remained immobile near his parents until morning. In the daytime, the bodies were prepared for the burial the following morning. Then began a wake of several days with the entire village present, even Chief Bizenga. Seated apart from the others, Mankunku watched, for a moment, the faces, imprinted with sorrow, weeping for his parents in the pale glow of the flickering flames in the hearth; then he scrutinized, for a long time, the enigmatic face of his maternal uncle, Chief Bizenga. All of a sudden he got up and disappeared into the night.

Mankunku renewed his contact with this earth, with the things he knew so well not long ago, before the arrival of the conquering strangers. Barefoot, he felt beneath his feet the earth still warm from the day's sunlight; an irresistible force pushed him to his birthplace, with the Moon overhead following him as if he were dragging it behind him in the dust of the Milky Way. He finally arrived at the place of the Palms, the place that had witnessed his birth, a birth which, elsewhere, had been contested by so many; he wondered if the link that bound him to this small plantation now overgrown with weeds still had any meaning, now that this land had been thrown into confusion and his parents were gone. He sat down in the middle of the palm fronds and began again to weep for his parents with the wind rustling in the banana and palm trees, with the murmur of the compassionate river. And with him the sky wept tears of stars, for so many stars fell that night that they have not all been replaced, and even today, if you study certain regions of the sky attentively, you'll find enormous black holes where no light escapes; on the other hand, if you notice a new star, a heavenly body that you don't recognize, go to the land of the Kongo, there they'll explain to you that it's the body of Mankunku's mother which, covered with stars, rose up to heaven to yield this new star which they call Kitoko, the Beauty.

Mandala stayed there all night long; he cried so much that his tears broke out in a fine dew which fell over the whole country and produced an early morning fog such as has not been seen since; this fog was transformed into rain and caused the landslide which caved in the biggest tunnel on the railway line then under construction, entombing dozens of workers, foreign overseers, and their white helmets. He remained there another whole day and night. He focused his thoughts, going over, in his memory, his entire life: his controversial birth, only son of a mother who would never bear another child, the river's betrayal of his friendship, his green eyes, his father's sickness, the ancestors, old Lukeni; oh, old Lukeni, the only one who really understood him! The memory of the old man warmed his heart, alleviated his sorrow; he felt that the spirit of the old man was actually there, close at hand; tomorrow, I'll go carry some cool wine to his grave. Then he thought of his maternal uncle, Chief Bizenga: his heart swelled, inflated with anger. He saw again the *mbulu-mbulu*, the rubber, the three francs, his comrades at work on the railroad, Djibril and Djermakoye; these images came and went inside his head, each time giving more pain to his soul and his badly bruised body. It wasn't possible, an entire people couldn't be condemned to such a destiny. Then he, the man who had always defied the powerful, he made his decision.

A palm frond in hand, a strange look in his eyes, Mankunku sets off at a run, bare feet on the cool earth, crushing little dewdrops which complain, crying, no, no, don't run over us, we're only pure water, sacred morning dew, we are tears weeping with you, Mankunku doesn't listen, he runs, he crushes little ants who also cry out, mercy, mercy, don't hurt us, we've always been faithful to this earth and we'd never betray it, Mankunku runs, wings on his feet, he disturbs the birds which, suddenly awoken, chatter, who are you to wake us up, disturb us, oh look, it's Mankunku, our friend, they change their tune when they recognize him, he understands our language but doesn't answer us, something must be terribly wrong, Mankunku continues, a palm frond in his hand, a strange look in his eyes. Oh, Bizenga, damned Bizenga, the words escape from lips pressed shut. The birds hear the cry of malediction, they repeat it from tree to tree, from height to height, carrying it over to the mountains which send it back from echo to echo out over the earth, out over the men and out over the trees, in the pristine light of dawn; these words travel on, by foot, by canoe, on the wings of birds, in the chirping of crickets, the trumpeting of elephants, the hissing of the boa, the movement of the wind. And all that lives on this earth stops, for a moment, doing what it's doing, feeling what it's feeling, so as to keep company with Mankunku in his trek: the great river forgets his bed and flows out over the plain, flooding the fields, capsizing the canoes and huts of the fishermen; trees sway frenetically on their trunks, unable to pull themselves up by their roots to follow Mandala; moles forget their fear of light and come out of their burrows to be present at the great event. Mandala's words continue to ride the wind to the ears of all living things, from the sneaky chameleons to the huge silent mangroves of the swamp, from the immense elephants to the tiniest streams nourished by the morning dew, from the graceful gazelles of the savannas to the robustly flowering guava trees...all the way to the ears of the old hypocritical owl who flees the light. The owl, creature of misfortune, sorcerer's bird, flaps his wings, runs along on his little feet then spreads out his wings and flies, flies, flies to Bizenga's house to warn him. The *popodi* bird sees the owl, stiffens his crest and insults him, hideous owl, bird of misfortune, nocturnal sorcerer, devourer of souls, why are you in such a hurry to fly to Bizenga's house, the other birds take up these insults in the languages of their various tribes, and the parakeet with wings of congo red cries loud enough that Mankunku can hear him, watch out Mankunku, Bizenga's a sorcerer and the owl is his messenger...Ah Bizenga, cursed chief, it's you who have betrayed us, howls Mankunku, it's because of you that my mother and father are dead, I'll kill you, Mankunku runs, the palm of his birthplace in his hand, wings on his feet, faster than the hare of the plains, muscles stronger than the crocodile's tail, more supple than the elephant's trunk, his heart swollen with his mother's spilled blood like the great river in the rainy season, Mankunku runs, *nganga* Mankunku, the one who overthrows the mighty and the drums which pay them homage. He emerges suddenly onto the village square.

Uncle Bizenga, the chief, has already been warned by his various messengers, the owl, the bat, and the crow. He stands outside, an ironic smile on his lips, on the far side of the circle of villagers who, abruptly awakened by the distant sound of Mankunku's footsteps, have hurried out of their dwellings. Mandala Mankunu arrives, hurls his palm frond into the circle, and, without a word, disappears.

Everyone remains there, fascinated by this great green frond with a thousand fingers, long phalanges teetering in the wind. Mankunku has transformed himself into a palm frond as green as his eyes, Mandala has become a palm frond as on the day of his birth, solitary as a palm tree, exalted among trees. Bizenga has a moment of fright, he withdraws a step, chews more nervously on his kola nut, fills his mouth with palm wine, tchk, tchk, tchk, he spits on the leaf, die leaf, dry out and turn gray so that the soul of that damned Mankunku, the accursed sorcerer who only lives at night, may die. You've seen it, haven't you, he calls on the crowd to witness, he stayed in the forest two nights in a row with his little demons sharing the bodies of his parents which he "ate," as did his fellow sorcerers, you're all witnesses, right, he hasn't slept here for two nights, I assure you, I swear to you that this green-eyed man is a sorcerer. The crowd wavers, hesitates, doesn't know which side to take, that of Mankunku the great *nganga* or that of Bizenga the great chief; but Mankunku isn't there whereas the chief is, and he speaks well, he knows the art of persuasion, he has the power of the foreigners on his side . . . yes, they murmur here and there, isn't that Mankunku strange, with all his lonely walks at night, Ma Nsona, I always told you that he wasn't born normally, oh, let me interrupt you, Kimbanda, before this I wasn't sure, but now I think that this man wasn't born at all, he exists without being born, isn't it strange, allow me to take the words right out of your mouths, my friends, from the time I got a look at those green eyes, I knew that he was a curse on our village, I, Lufua, I tell you that a man of his age with no children isn't a normal man and yack yack yack they babble, they chatter, and baa baa baa they bleat, they gossip, they make things up. Bizenga senses that he will win the contest; his confidence doubles, finished, you're finished, Mankunku.

But all of a sudden it becomes very quiet, everyone is still, like the fishes in the river when they see the shadow of the fisherman's canoe: Mandala has suddenly appeared in the middle of the circle. He had gone home, he had drunk his potions, and in his hand he holds the weapon that he had made for himself in his father's workshop. He is standing there, Mankunku, the wise man, the doctor, the blacksmith, Mankunku, in the dirty clothes of a railway worker, his bare feet planted firmly on the ground. Bizenga looks at him and tries to appear haughty and dismissive. He has gained weight since his pact with the foreigners; it is he who collects whatever the village receives in exchange for the rubber and the palm kernel oil, not to mention special gifts the administration gives him; he has become rich, his family doesn't work, he has five wives, he never goes hungry anymore. He is wearing white cloth pants, held up high on his big belly by a belt of crocodile skin, and his fine shoes are imported; his brightly colored flannel shirt is covered by a red blanket thrown over his shoulders like a cape, which, along with the leopard-skin hat on his head, constitutes the new symbol of his royalty.

The two men look at each other, deaf and mute, before this mute crowd whose only sound is its heavy, labored breathing. The two men look searchingly into each other's eyes, and suddenly their gazes shoot from their eye sockets, circle around and avoid each other, waver. Mankunku's gaze sees, in the depths of Bizenga's, a long procession led by the foreigner in the helmet painted with white kaolin, then the chains of men bending and rising to the rhythm of the hoe under a torrid sun, and dockworkers dragged here and there on the face of the earth and the sea, and over the famous caravan route; at the end of this procession, he sees Bizenga himself and other men who look like him, wearing white pith helmets, supervising human caravans, whips of hippopotamus hair in their hands, dressed in the finest cloth from overseas, drinking the strongest imported alcohol, residing in the most beautiful homes... And Bizenga's gaze perceives, in the depths of Mankunku's, an empty region, deserted, where the tombs of the ancestors seem to have disappeared to be replaced by cathedrals of blues and distilled hatreds, by the

train, that immense fuming monster brought here by the foreigners with, as engineers, Mankunku and people like him, he
sees Mankunku at the head of an enormous crowd chasing the
foreigners who, forgetting to grab their white helmets, run
away as fast as they can, climbing into boats and heading for
home, pursued by the shouts and blows of people in revolt, liberated...The two gazes don't understand what they see; not
understanding, they stop staring, while continuing to circle
around and avoid each other, until suddenly they clinch. When
two elephants fight, their trunks twine around each other like a
couple of twisted vines; the two animals push each other back
and forth, each pulling from his own side, until, exhausted,
they disengage their trunks. Finally, each man withdraws his
gaze from the other and trains it onto the crowd to relax it, to
recover strength, to breathe in new energy with a word of
appreciation, an encouraging look, an approving nod, in brief,
with a gesture, nothing more than a sympathetic gesture...But
it is in the nature of crowds that they never know anything
before the denouement of a drama, the people cannot take sides
with one or the other of the great personalities of their town; if
there is to be a confrontation, it must be that the ancestors
wished it to happen, the winner will be the one who was right.

They stare at each other again; Bizenga's face is twisted
with anger as on the day he found his student unveiling his
medical secrets to the people. "Mankunku, you are a sorcerer!"

A hubbub in the crowd: they debate, murmur, get worked
up. This is an extremely serious accusation; you can't simply
deny you're a sorcerer, a "devourer" of men, you have to *prove*
you're not. Yeah, Mankunku, prove you're not a sorcerer, take
up the challenge, the trial by *nkasa*. He gives the signal, they
bring it over, whitish hemlock, genuine poison, more poisonous
than the most fatal of mushrooms. With a smile, Mankunku

takes the gourd, stares intently at Bizenga who keeps blinking since he doesn't know where to look, and empties it in a single draught. He drank the poison, he drank it. He's going to stagger, yes, he's staggering, no, he simply switched feet, don't you think his eyes might be rolling back, no, the sun's blinding him a little, are you sure they aren't getting glassy, no, watch out, Mama, *nganga* Mankunku is going to fall, he's reeling, no, he's moving closer to the palm frond, oh, he's clutching his belly, he's staggering head forward, he's folding, oh ancestors, he's going to fall, he'll be struck dead . . . he's vomiting at the base of the palm frond! The crowd applauds, jubilant, now it can take sides, Mankunku is no sorcerer, he's innocent.

Bizenga's legs seem hardly able to support him, for he can't stand still; he leans first on one foot, then on the other. The innocent are not to be accused with impunity. The crowd is waiting for Mankunku to make Bizenga undergo the trial by poison too. But no, he pulls himself up, his gaze a deep green, even more mysterious than the depth of the great equatorial forests. He looks at Bizenga. Old Lukeni once told him that one day he had seen two buffaloes who, while fighting, had locked horns; they had remained standing, immobile, for an entire month until hunger and thirst overwhelmed them. For his part, Mankunku has imprisoned Bizenga in his gaze. Bizenga is nailed to the spot, only able to shift his weight from one leg to another. The crowd holds its breath; Mankunku doesn't utter a word.

They stayed like that. The sun departed for Mpemba, in a great pool of blood spread out to the west, the moon appeared among her millions of children, a new sun appeared, a great wind blew over the entire land, followed by a rainfall whose length nobody could measure because it hid the moon and the stars, then a new moon appeared. Still, they did not budge.

People waited, waited. Then, the great river, growing tired, went back to its bed, abandoning tons of silt and fish along the way; grains of corn and peanuts that had stopped growing so as not to disturb the dramatic silence weighing heavily on the world by breaking up the ground to get out, resumed their germination; the coconuts, exhausted from waiting suspended on their stems, fell off by the hundreds...

Mankunku continued to stare at Chief Bizenga, who, all of a sudden, had aged. This lasted so long that one by one, the spectators got tired of it and went back to the normal unfolding of their lives. People say that the children of women who went into labor during this epoch had already begun to walk by the time Mankunku finally stopped imprisoning Bizenga in his gaze; as for the hundred-year-old trees for whom time unspools more slowly than for human beings, they say that the confrontation between these two adversaries lasted an entire rainy season. Only the dreadful owl, evil bird that he is, claims that all of this took place in a single morning; you're welcome to believe this bird of misfortune who can only live in the shadows, sorcerer bird allied to his sorcerer master...

Abruptly, Mankunku stops staring at Bizenga. The crowd is thus liberated; tongues are loosened, children cry, the surrounding forest no longer just whispers. Bizenga is also liberated; he moves about, goes from one spot to another, but cannot break the circle he's in. Mankunku holds in his hand the strangely formed knife that he created, that he invented at his father's forge before the arrival of the foreigners. He walks toward Bizenga, who has lost his calm, all his mastery.

"Stop, Mankunku, or I'll curse you."

Mankunku continues to walk toward him.

"I curse you! I call on all of the ancestors to damn you! Ungrateful child, you owe everything to me, I raised you, I taught you everything you know. I am your master, your uncle, understand? Your master! I order you to stop, or else my curse will be irreversible!"

"Traitor!" cries Mankunku. "I, for one, won't accuse *you* of being a sorcerer because that would be too easy and you'd wriggle out of it. But I'll repeat loudly that you're a traitor, you've sold our land, you've insulted our ancestors in order to enrich yourself at the expense of our entire village, plunging us into misery and misfortune."

"That's not true, it's thanks to me that this village has been spared by the *mbulu-mbulu*; take a look at the neighboring villages, all the men have been killed or mutilated and nobody's left but a few sad, lonely old women dying of hunger. I've done what I've done in order to minimize the suffering of the people for whom I'm responsible. As everybody here can attest, thanks to my policy there has never been any commotion in this village."

"If there has never been any commotion here it's because we've always been working, first for rubber, then for palm kernel oil and on the roads, lastly for the railroads and the three francs. Not once have you raised your voice to defend us, all that matters to you are your children, your wives, and your fat belly."

"Listen, my son..."

"I'm not your son, my parents are dead thanks to you."

"Mankunku, I beg you, listen to me, allow some words of wisdom to penetrate your head..."

"It's not from a traitor and a coward that I will learn wisdom; out of greed, you've sold the people for a little salt, a little alcohol, a little fabric. Your words are nothing but hypocrisy and lies. You've accused me of sorcery, I won't forgive you."

Mankunku's face is hard; all of his emotion is concentrated there, accentuating the severity of his knitted brows, the hardness of his clamped jaw, his bulging eyes and palpitating nostrils:

Mankunku's face has been transformed into a mask. The Mask takes up Mankunku's walk, which had been momentarily interrupted by his words. Once again, the crowd is completely silent. Bizenga is terrified. "Halt, You who advance toward me, I am a king, a powerful chief, the foreigners and their *mbulu-mbulu* are behind me, stop or else they'll break you..."

The Mask doesn't stop. Bizenga signals his guard, who brandishes a rifle, aiming at the advancing creature, then firing, practically point blank. But the Mask keeps coming, bullets can't kill it, you idiot, they turn to water, that's not sweat that you see on its body, it's lead, melting like mounds of clay in the rain. With a clean sweep, the Mask grabs the gun and crashes the butt on the head of the gunner, who falls, his skull shattered. By now Bizenga is wild with fear. He tries to ward off his fate, pulls out his gris-gris, a talisman he bought from the Senegalese that is reputed, because of its foreign origin, to be more powerful than the ones made in his own land. He squeezes it, embraces it, rubs it against his body, murmuring abracadabra words...Alas, the power advancing upon him is not destroyed, it continues to come closer; furious, he throws down the charm, grinds it into the dust, invokes the ancestors, calls instructions to the messenger birds, but the threatening Mask is still there. Bizenga howls, he cries, I curse you, where are my foreign masters, my protectors, he talks in jerky, incomprehensible, esoteric phrases. The Mask has had enough of this and raises its strange knife; Bizenga retreats with backward steps, a ray of sunlight glances off the blade, shines in Bizenga's eyes, and blinds him; he doesn't know what to do, where to flee, where to hide; the Mask plunges its knife, with a clean, brutal blow, into Chief Bizenga's heart; it pulls the weapon away before the body hits the ground. Blood spurts out from the heart, forms a little stream which flows to the center of the circle, avoiding the palm frond, and continues on its way to the other side of the circle, into the grass. Then the crowd and the animals begin to react, howl, cackle, plead, weep.

"What have you done?" someone cries.

It's over. The Mask dissolves; the familiar face of Mankunku is seen contemplating his weapon and the corpse at his feet. With his eyes, he follows the stream of blood which, after leaving the village square, flows on toward the river—sorcerer's blood! The grass it touches withers, dogs will not lick it, snakes go out of their way to avoid crawling over it; it turns black like bitterest bile, it continues on its long sinuous path to the river, into which it plunges, boiling, killing innocent little fish. Oh, damned Bizenga!

Mankunku wipes off his knife and goes off towards his house. He is alone. I've killed my maternal uncle, I'm outside the clan. What will I do, what will I do?

18.

Thus Mankunku fell out with the clan. Without losing his head, he tried to think about it. He would have to disappear, go far away and begin a new life; he couldn't remain in the village, not because he considered the murder of his uncle a crime—on the contrary he regarded it as an essential act of justice—but because he feared the reprisals of the militia that enforced the irrational justice imported by the foreigners. It would not take long for them to come and arrest him, torture him, before making him submit to a judgment he couldn't accept. How could they understand all the wrongs Bizenga had done to the village and to the ancestors? Nor could he go to the worksite, that would be the surest way to get himself arrested. There was only one place for him to go now, the great city which had become the capital of the State established by the foreigners. People said that it was an immense city with inhabitants of all races and ethnicities and that you could disappear there as easily as a grain of rice on a sandy beach.

While his wives and children wept for Chief Bizenga, Mandala Mankunku went one last time to his own birthplace. He didn't stay there long. Then he visited the fresh graves of his father and mother, as well as the already ancient grave of old Lukeni. Rest in peace, my ancestors, I ask you to always stay near me and guide me. I've done what I had to do, what my ancestor Mankunku would have done. Now there's nothing more to keep me here, I must leave you; pardon me, and I promise to come back each time I need to revisit my roots.

He went back home, arranged all of his herbs, his discoveries, chemical and otherwise, his blacksmith's creations, his most beautiful hunting trophies, in two small bundles. He slept a little, and at dawn, even before the first cock announced the sun's arrival, he got up, slipped each end of a stick into the knots of his bundles, balanced the stick on his shoulder, went out, and closed up his house.

In this way, for the first time, Mankunku left the village which had seen him come into the world. Only the trees and the wind were there to wish him a good journey, and both still remember it well. Voyager, when you find yourself in an African forest and you hear the wind rustling among the grass and the leaves, make no mistake: it's not only the lives of the hundred-year-old trees and the leaves of one season that it's recounting—it's also transmitting, from generation to generation, just like human beings, the legend of Mandala Mankunku, that friend of the palms who dared to overthrow one of the powerful.

Chapter Four

The day will not save them

and we own

the night.

— AMIRI BARAKA

19.

CITY, GREAT CITY! IT WAS ASTONISHING! NEVER WOULD
Mandala Mankunku have imagined that a place could be so different from a village, even a big village. There were so many different people, ethnicities, races, languages! He was caught,
carried away, snatched up by this maelstrom of sound, movement, color. Here, even the noises were different; whereas those
of the forest had causes and therefore meanings, it seemed to
him that those of the city existed only for the sake of existing,
without purpose, independent of the surrounding world. At
first he found this reassuring because what he wanted, after the
murder of his maternal uncle, was to lose himself in this anthill
without leaving any traces. He experienced a kind of subdued
joy, felt that he was finally free of all constraint and obligation
in this unknown milieu where, a priori, there existed no rules,
no definite duties. His own confidence and calm amazed him:

he had left a world where everything was more or less spelled out in advance in order to plunge himself into another where there was no guardrail, and this caused him not the least apprehension. On the contrary, he thought, in this atmosphere of liberty, he could expand his horizons, more easily learn the secret of the foreigners' power, and—why not?—wind up rich.

He entered the city through the outskirts of town where most of his compatriots lived; his eyes did not register the unsanitary old shacks, the dirty alleys, the canals swollen with stagnant water breeding mosquitoes and flies, the shady dives easily seducing newcomers, the unemployed who peered shiftily at all kinds of rubbishy stuff on display in the markets. On the other hand, he noticed the bicycles, symbol of the newly rich, the beautiful clothes worn by some people, their watches, their shoes. Yes, he really liked the city, to him it was a door opening onto the actual world of today and tomorrow, for he was convinced that the world of his ancestors had ended.

Still carrying his bundles, he kept on walking to the center of town, and there he was struck by something else: the number of foreigners. He had not seen more than five or six of them in his life, from the first one who came into his village to the foremen on the railroad. Here they were everywhere; they wore long pants, shorts, short-sleeved shirts of every color; there were very few colonial helmets, which surprised him because he couldn't dissociate the foreigners from their white helmets and their safari-style white suits. And then he saw their women; so that's what they looked like! He did not dare look them in the eye for fear of being noticed, and hid himself so that he could look them over. He admired, with curiosity, their long hair of varying colors waving in the wind like the beard on an ear of corn, examined their breasts, descended the length of their haunches, their buttocks, their legs, and their well-shod feet;

none of them wore helmets but many carried parasols, strolling nonchalantly along great avenues bordered with mango trees. He found them beautiful, but their beauty left him cold, just as one says a tree is beautiful although it inspires no sensual pleasure whatsoever. His curiosity satisfied, he fixed his attention on the avenue and saw cars, great metallic boxes on wheels, exhaling black smoke as they went. The foreigners were evidently here to stay; they were in charge of everything, they offered jobs, money; you could earn a lot more money now than in the days of harvesting rubber, even more than for working on the railroad. They had changed the country, they had turned it upside down. The native children themselves had adopted the city; they had forgotten all about the "great river," they went to school, learned to read, to imprison things in signs. Would he ever be able to fathom the power of these strangers who, with a handful of men, had succeeded in subduing an entire country?

For several months, Mankunku dragged himself around in the capital, living on his meager savings in a room he rented by the week. He became so accustomed to the city that he felt as if he had lived there all of his life. But one concern became increasingly urgent: the need for money. You had to make money, you could no longer live outside of the new system of value imposed by the foreigners.

One of his friends got him a job as a houseboy with an official in the colonial administration, but he didn't even get through the first day; certainly the world had changed, but still, to let himself be treated like a kid by a woman who lazily dragged her slippers around the house, even if she was the wife of a white boss—it was too much for him, son of a blacksmith, a blacksmith himself, and a great hunter. There was still a dignity in his culture which no foreign civilization, no matter how powerful, could destroy. He found other things, working one day digging ditches, one day sweeping streets, two days moving furniture. But he was getting fed up with these sporadic jobs where he was bounced around from one place to another. And then, by chance, he thought of the railroad connecting the river to the Ocean. The line had been completed, the hundreds of dead buried and forgotten, their tears and cries carried away by the wind and scattered over the Ocean. The line had been completed, inaugurated by the minister of the Colonies in the presence of the governor general; along with dozens of other foreigners, they had drunk a beverage the color of pineapple wine, bubbly as fermenting palm wine, the Saras and the Bandas had been paid and repatriated, and two stations had been named after them, other stations bearing the names of heroes of the foreigners' countries, they had cut with scissors a tricolored ribbon stretched over the rails, but not before several speeches followed by hearty bravos. The line had definitely been completed: nothing remained of all those tears and all that sweat but the click-clack of the cars, full of tropical wood, manganese, and passengers, pulled by big steam-engine locomotives fed with water and coal, later to be replaced by diesel engines fueled with heavy petroleum.

Mandala Mankunku, who had formerly prepared gravel beds, carried ties, laid rails, and dug tunnels, thought with emotion about this railroad, and decided to go and try his luck.

20.

In front of the big building which housed the offices of the railway company, Mandala was seized with panic. He didn't know which door to begin with, he didn't know what language he should speak when confronted by the foreigner he expected to find behind every door; but he was lucky, it was a child of his land whom he found there. Many of them now replaced the foreigners in these offices, for they now knew how to deal with the secret of the signs, to speak the new imposed language, and had adopted the masters' style of dress. Mankunku was all the more reassured because the young man who welcomed him was encouragingly amiable. The two of them sat down across from each other.

"I am Mandala Mankunku, a former railway worker; I left my village a year ago, I have no money to live on here in town, and I'm looking for work."

"What was your job on the railroad? Railwayman? Conductor?"

"I laid rail. I'm one of the ones who built that long metal highway."

"You don't say!" said the astonished young man, and he looked at Mankunku with a certain tenderness; "my father also worked on it; maybe you knew him?"

"There were so many of us..."

"My father came from the coast, he was a man of the ocean."

"I don't think I met him, I'm a man of the river, I laid rail in the river-ocean direction whereas your father was probably going in the other direction."

"I hear that it was very hard."

"Oh yes, I'll never forget it! I saw villages decimated, Saras and Bandas and even Chinese coolies come from thousands of kilometers away to die by the dozen; not to mention the recruitment. In the memory of the people from my region, mention the 'days of the machine' and you'll see their eyes open wide in a horror as great as if you were talking about the days of rubber or of the three francs."

"My father also died for the engine. They never found his body, it was carried off by a landslide."

Mankunku's chest tightened. Oh! those landslides! You had the feeling that the whole earth was slipping away in an infernal noise; this brought him close to the young man, it seemed as though the latter belonged to him a little, that his own heart had adopted him like a little brother.

"Well," concluded the employee, "perhaps misery is good for something, at least we've established an essential basis of communication. What kind of work would you like to do?"

"Anything, as long as I can earn a little money, since that's what counts the most in this world."

"Let's see." He got up, opened a drawer, and began to sort out files. Mandala watched him in admiration. Certainly this young man had a share in the power of the foreigners, a greater share than he, *nganga* Mankunku, could ever have. Henceforth he regarded his own investigations as useless, younger men than he would do them better than he could; he had only one wish and that was to integrate himself completely into the life of the city, do his work, earn money, and forget the rest. The employee came back and sat down. He opened a folder and took out some papers. "There, I'm going to do you a special favor because you're a former employee of the railway. We've just received a Mikado locomotive, and they've asked me to pick somebody to be the first indigenous engineer; I'm going to propose you."

"What does 'engineer' mean?"

"You will learn to drive locomotives."

Mankunku was astonished. "You...you mean that I'll be able to move that heavy machine around, to make it go, cross over mountains, through tunnels, and across bridges?"

The employee laughed at the incredulity of his interlocutor. "But of course you'll be able to do it and do it well. You will be the first, so you'll have to be good, right? You'll make us all proud, and especially me, since I've recommended you. All right?"

Mankunku could already see himself in his locomotive. He was proud, he felt powerful; a wide smile lit up his face. "Yes, of course it's all right. I don't know how I can begin to thank you."

"Oh, don't thank me so quickly, it's not over yet. Give me your papers."

"My papers? What papers?"

"Your identification card, your working papers if you have any."

"I have no papers."

"You weren't given any pay stubs for the salary you received?"

"No. We were never given any paper."

"Ah, that's true, I keep forgetting that it was more like forced labor than a regular job with a set salary. It was really a different era!" He reflected for a minute. "I'm going to prepare a certificate for you, even though I don't really have the right to." He took a sheet of paper and a pencil and began to take down information. "Your name."

"Mandala Mankunku."

"First name?"

Silence.

"Another name in front of that one, a Christian name."

"I don't have one."

"Well, we'll have to pick one." He took out a directory and began to read randomly from it: "Thierry, Rodrigo, Hégésippe, Zachary, Zéphyrin..."

"Those are names?"

"Yes."

"What do they signify?"

"You know, these foreign names don't mean a thing."

"Well, if I need one so that I can work, give me one."

"Wait." He closed his eyes and let his pencil fall on a name: Maximilian. "There, you're now named Maximilian Mandala Mankunku. Will that do?"

"Very well."

"When were you born?"

Mandala was suddenly afraid that the employee would doubt his birth, so he plunged into a long, passionate, and involved explanation. "I was born in the middle of the second month of the dry season, fifteen or sixteen rainy seasons before the arrival of Chief Bizenga, twenty-two or twenty-three seasons before they began recruiting for the railroad. There are palm fronds in the place where I was born, near the river. My village is called Lubituku; you can still find men and women there who can testify to my birth, even though both my mother and my father are dead. I swear to you that, despite the evil tongues of those who make up stories about my birth, I was really born..."

The employee was surprised by Mankunku's desperate concern to prove that he had actually been born, as if a human being could exist on this earth in some way other than from a mother giving birth. "I believe you, I'm sure that your mother gave birth to you, about that there can be no doubt. However, it's difficult to give a date for it. Look. Let's just say that you were born in July and that you're thirty-five years old. No, that's too much, thirty years." He wrote on the paper the name Maximilian Mandala Mankunku, twenty-five years... "Go to a photographer, have him take two photos of you, come back here tomorrow at the same time, and you'll have your papers."

"Thank you so much. What's your name?"

"Poaty. Ambroise Poaty. If I'm not in my office, ask any-body, they all know me, I'm the one in charge of recruiting indigenous personnel."

"Thank you again, and I'll see you tomorrow."

He walked out of the office and stood in front of it for a long time to assure himself that he wasn't dreaming; yes, he had really set foot in there, he had been warmly welcomed, and he was going to come back tomorrow. He smiled to himself and went looking for a photographer.

He soon came across a photographer stretching lazily in front of his studio on which was printed in clumsy letters: "Dékos, certified photographer." As for the studio, it was a lit-tle rectangular wooden hut with a corrugated iron roof. On the wall hung some photos, yellowed and curled by the intense heat and light of the tropical sun, photos of all kinds; the only thing they had in common was the fact that all the people pho-tographed were dressed to the nines. There were some varia-tions: one portrait was set in a circle, a wedding photo in a heart…Mankunku followed the photographer inside. The lat-ter handed a comb and a brush to his client without missing a beat of his sales pitch: "You've done well to come to Dékos, even the Whites come to my studio. Here, comb your hair, you'll see, this'll be the photo of your life. Tell all your buddies to come to Dékos, trained in Europe…" He brushed off Mankunku's clothes, gave him some white powder, "it's to stop the sweat because sweat's bad for a nice photo; but the powder also helps to distribute the light on your face."

The preparations complete, they went outside. The photog-rapher spread a white drape against a wall and had Mankunku sit in front of it on a stool. Then he put his camera on a tripod, with his own back to the sun. A crowd pressed up around the camera and that made the photographer more talkative and sure of himself than ever. "For your photos, come to Master Dékos, whose fame has reached Europe, even the Whites come to him..." A true master of his craft, he counted the number of paces between the camera and Mankunku, came back and did something to the lens, talking all the while. Mankunku, like the crowd, followed this with admiration and respect. Just think! A man who could capture your image, a more-than-faithful image, in a black box and then put it down on a piece of paper for you! He took a rectangular plate, put it in the back of the dark chamber.

"Now, look right into this eye," he said, pointing to the lens. "When I say 'ready!' don't move, not even an eyelash. And you onlookers, don't walk between the camera and the gentleman sitting there, or the mysterious ray that comes out of this box will strike you down. I've adjusted it so that it won't hurt the person being photographed, but the rest of you watch out."

The people respectfully moved back a step from the camera. Then the photographer raised the large drape which fell behind the camera, covered himself with it, and disappeared behind it. "Ready?" he cried.

Mankunku held his neck stiff and stopped blinking his eyelashes. Just at that moment, a cloud passed over the sun and threw him into the shade. The photographer put out his head and cursed at the sun. "Wait until the cloud goes by."

The crowd murmured, disappointed. The photographer pretended to keep busy, giving Mankunku another brushstroke, recalculating the distance, watching the sky. He knew what he was doing, the others didn't, and he knew that they didn't: that was the difference between them. Finally the cloud passed. Once again his head disappeared behind the drape.

"Hold it!"

Mankunku stiffened up again. The photographer's hand removed the cover from the lens, waited for a few seconds, then put it back. It was over. The photographer's head reappeared. People applauded. "Come back this evening," he told Mankunku. The latter was truly impressed; to create with this apparatus an image of absolute fidelity could only be possible if this man had managed to capture a particle of the foreigners' famous power, which Mankunku had stopped tracking down. The crowd scattered, he went on his way.

Mankunku was in Poaty's office early in the morning, and the young man was as affable as ever. When he left, Mankunku had a professional identification card with a fine photograph of himself affixed to it. He was filled with respect for the photo, which was more real than he was: everywhere he went, in all the offices he might visit, as hard as he might try to affirm that it was he himself, Mandala Mankunku, who was there, that it was really he who was speaking, nobody would believe him unless he showed them this card with, above all, this photo. It seemed to him that in this world that was about to hatch open, truth resided in the image and not in the thing itself.

He was Maximilian Mandala Mankunku, soon he would be the engineer-driver of the locomotive from the river to the Ocean: this was how he had landed on his feet in this new civilization being created in front of his eyes, where one spoke a new language made of words taken from diverse ethnicities, including that of the foreigners. He carefully folded his papers, put them in his pocket, and went home to rest. Tomorrow morning, he would present himself at his new job—which he already found more interesting than the craft of the forge—to learn how to master that immense machine which was supposed to move at a speed he imagined to be unimaginable.

21.

Mankunku's apprenticeship did not last long because, with his innate thirst for learning and understanding, he took everything in with remarkable ease. First he learned to recognize the different parts of the steam engine, then how to work them. For him it was a real physical pleasure to activate the sliding distributor valve that set the enormous engine in motion; then he looked out over the cloud of smoke coughed up by the chimneys, he turned the whistles on, he accelerated, and, after a minute, pulled the brake lever, listened to the grinding of the brake shoes as they stopped the wheels. He learned how to suitably lubricate the bogie axles and activate the charge in the tender correctly... However, in spite of this stripping down, this piece-by-piece dismantling of the mechanism that made the engine go, he could never quite convince himself that the engine was nothing more than the sum of its parts. Wasn't there some other more secret power in it, such as the power that makes the buffalo move?

At the end of three months, he became the official engineer of the daily passenger train from the river to the Ocean, from the Ocean to the river. The line was about four hundred miles long and took, on the average, twelve hours, if all went well. In practice, this passenger train almost always came in late; often it remained at a standstill in a station several hours so that another train coming from the opposite direction could pass it, since the line had only one track; sometimes, it was blocked by cave-ins caused by storms or sliding ballast. The voyage was also slowed down by frequent stops for water and coal; travelers dreaded these moments, because, after loading up, the train took off again in an enormous envelope of smoke which slowly settled down on them, getting them all dirty; they gasped, they coughed, they rubbed their eyes, which were irritated by the cinders. Soon enough, these steam engines were replaced by diesel locomotives. This made the train faster and the trip more agreeable.

Regardless of the vicissitudes of the passage, however, Mankunku's train always arrived in the city with great fanfare. One long toot of the whistle, two short, and another long one announced his return. Then children ran and lined up along the track to see the train pass by in a flash, the wind spreading out on both sides, in the midst of voices crying *Mupepe, Mupepe,* the Wind; thus the children named Mankunku the Wind because they were so amazed by the whirlwind of air the long column of cars left behind. As for the adults, they had given him the name Massini, the Machine Man, being as admiring as the children who ran along behind the cars, hoping to catch up with them.

Mankunku kept on signaling his triumphant arrival until the train got into the station, hailed by the bravos and vivas of the spectators. Many came not to meet traveling friends but to enjoy the show, they came to see the train; it was an important moment in their daily lives, just like the dinner hour. They got dressed up as if they themselves were going on a trip and, in their hands, they carried the requisite little white handkerchief, to be waved as a signal of welcome or goodbye. How proud he was, Massini Mupepe, the one and only, the country's first railway driver–mechanic–engineer to master the foreign machine! One long whistle, two short, one long, and he launched his smoke-vomiting engine out across the countryside, crossing forests, river bridges, passing under mountains, accompanied by the incessant clickety-clack of the metal wheels all the way to the other end of the country, near the Ocean. Who didn't know Massini Mupepe?

Thousands of people were arriving now from their villages, attracted by the great metropolis whose marvels were celebrated far and wide. Among them were many young people who, alas, were not all as fortunate as Massini Mupepe; completely out of their element, they would arrive in the great city, drag themselves through the streets looking for work which couldn't be found, and would eventually give themselves over first to petty larceny, then to more serious crimes. In order to avoid such trouble, many of them formed ethnic clubs which became cultural, sport, and mutual aid societies.

The people of Massini's ethnicity formed their own club and had no problem in choosing a leader: they gathered around him and elected him president. Being the most popular man in the country, he did not take long to make his association the most important of them all. Although he had never learned to master the signs which encoded thought and were now being taught in the newly opened schools, he had the concrete power of the machine, that enormous train which he knew how to handle so perfectly; furthermore, the foreign administration pampered him, showing him off and setting him up as an example, and people even said that they were planning to send him overseas to the mother country so that he could learn how to build a train from scratch. In any case, they awarded him a medal and, model employee that he was, he did his best to stand up straight in front of the governor general, just like he'd seen the militias do, in the midst of yoo-yoos, the rhythmic chants of the joyous crowd on the national holiday. Everybody identified a little with Massini Mupepe, the man who would soon be shipped over there to learn to build trains all by himself.

Things had really changed in this country since Mankunku had left his village to become Massini Mupepe. In fact, after the atrocities committed by the concessionary companies, some people and organizations protested in the foreigners' land; the government of the mother country set up various investigative missions which led to the abolition of forced labor. At the same time, a great campaign to eliminate tropical diseases was launched, most notably against malaria and the sleeping sickness which had come into the country along with the emigrant railroad laborers. Massini Mupepe had some trouble understanding how the sanguinary and barbarous colonizers of the days of rubber and the machine, and these devoted physicians who went from village to village in difficult conditions to vaccinate people, operate on them, care for them, sometimes at risk to their own lives and in a hostile environment, could both come from the same country. He did not understand the desire of some of these strangers to teach the children of his country the secret of their signs, a secret which, he believed, made them powerful. Besides, now he was no longer alone, there were other Massinis who knew how to deal with machines, to read and write. Be that as it may, he had to admit that the roads opened up at the cost of so much blood had become indispensible to the country. Really, for the first time, Massini, like the greater part of the population, no longer saw the foreigners as enemies but as people you could live with. It seemed that the transplant had taken root, that the graft had succeeded. Not everything was perfect, but everything was good, they were slowly making their way toward a state of equilibrium which would require nothing more than to be perpetuated as, generally, are all things in the natural order.

22.

The happy period in which tacit acceptance of the foreigners by the people seemed to herald the total success of the project of colonization was over quickly enough, hastened along by events which took place far from Massini's land.

In fact, after the rubber, the three francs, and the railroad, a new campaign of recruitment descended on the country. It was said that over there, on the other side of the ocean, the beautiful land of the foreigners—which was now referred to as the motherland—had been attacked by foreigners even more barbarous and savage than the indigenous people here and that, if they weren't stopped, they would even come to Massini's country to cut the people's throats; it was, according to rumors, the second time this century that these longstanding rivals had acted like this. The recruitment began with enthusiasm; many chiefs of clans and villages made it a point of honor to send off men from their region, many unemployed workers signed up voluntarily, thereby profiting not only from general esteem and admiration, but from the tempting pay they were offered.

Massini had the honor of driving the first train of fighters for the liberty of the motherland. They had been assembled early in the Place de la Gare—since renamed the Place du Départ—in their new uniforms, boots well laced and well polished, the traditional red woolen cap on each head, under the eyes, good-natured for a change, of the ranking Senegalese, tall and very black. They were laughing, singing, joking, surrounded by friends and relations who had come to see them off; one voice had only to lead out with the words of their theme song:

France is our mother

for others to take up the song, at first in voices full of amazed tenderness:

> *It is she who nourishes us*
> *With her potatoes*
> *And her macaroni*

only to finish in a determined and virile tone that allowed no possibility of victory to their prospective, yet unknown, enemy:

> *Marching, marching*
> *We are marching off to war*
> *If the war comes*
> *We will fight like soldiers*

From time to time, their eyes openly shifted to their gear, or they grabbed their guns as if to emphasize some point, set them on their shoulders, smiled, set them back on the ground. Sure of themselves, they had no doubt as to their own importance and the importance of their mission. People envied them a little, these men who would soon discover the wonders of the foreigners' land. Some of them came from Massini's village—most notably De Kélondi, who was nicknamed "Overseas." He wandered here and there, took off his cap, put it back on again. A great seducer of women, De Kélondi was already thinking about the stories he would bring back home to bedazzle his new conquests.

"De Kélondi," cried somebody in the crowd.

"Overseas," he answered, his chest swelling as naturally as a peacock displays his tail.

He walked over to the person who had called him, jabbering a few words in the civilized language of the foreigners to show that, even though he was a harvester of palm wine by profession, he was nevertheless educated. Then there was a man named Moutsompa, said to be the strongest man in the world, and there was...there were so many people that Massini knew! He was sad that he couldn't go with them but also proud, for, as he repeated to all he met, if he hadn't been accepted into the ranks of the riflemen, as the departing soldiers were called, it was because he was too important: he was an engineer, one of the technically sophisticated personnel of prime importance, indispensable to the logistics of the colonial army.

Finally the moment of departure arrived. The territorial governor and a general each made a speech which was translated phrase for phrase by an indigenous interpreter; the soldiers applauded and sang "La Marseillaise" accompanied by bugles and drums, then climbed into the railway cars. They sang "La Marseillaise" some more, waving flags, the crowd clapping the whole time; tears of pride—and perhaps of sorrow—were quickly wiped away but still flowed down cheeks here and there when Massini blew his whistle, one long, two short, one long, and slowly started up the heavy locomotive which little by little built up speed and soon disappeared, carrying off these happy people all known as "Senegalese riflemen." The train rolled off in the direction of the sea where the troops would embark to defend the menaced civilization while the wind kept wafting to the ears of all who could hear the words of their magical song:

> *Marching, marching*
> *We are marching off to war*
> *If the war comes*
> *We will fight like soldiers*

That first departure was the only one where there were real volunteers, because the enthusiasm quickly died down. There were no more voluntary recruits. The administration therefore launched a psychological recruitment campaign. In town, neighborhood leaders were asked to assemble their constituents and read them enthusiastic letters said to have been sent by the soldiers; in the village, such tasks were entrusted to the chief of the clan. The recruitment bonus was doubled, full citizenship—in other words, the same rights as the foreigners—was promised to all who signed up; but all these measures were useless, there were no more volunteers. Then, once again, they let the militias loose on the land. Just as in the days of the machine, they hunted people down, tied the men they caught to each other, and struck them with rifle butts to make them walk in long lines for miles until they reached the assembly point; there, the military doctors would designate, according to their weight and chest measurement, those who would go to defend the beleaguered cause of world liberty. Many mutilated themselves to avoid this conscription, others, trying to fail the minimum weight requirement, fasted too long and died. Exactly 63,344 men were drafted in Massini Mupepe's country, some being taught "La Marseillaise," others the Belgian national anthem, "La Brabançonne," and, among these men, the 63,340th was named Ambroise Poaty, that amiable young man who had made it possible for Massini to become who he was today.

When Massini drove the train loaded with Poaty's group of soldiers into the seaport from where they would embark, the world seemed gloomy to him. For the first time, he left the station without blowing his long and short toots. He pulled out slowly, painfully envisioning the sad men and women whose hearts were still bleeding where a relative or friend had been torn from them. In any case, this was a far cry from the enthusiasm of the first volunteers, the *enfants de la patrie* who had gone off to get themselves killed, their heads buzzing with dreams of the *jours de gloire arrivés*, a gun in their hands and a song in their hearts.

23.

The waves of war only reached Massini Mupepe's land indirectly. To be sure, there were some troop movements and cargo planes stopping off on their way to Chad, but there were no battles; it was also true that the railroad transported fewer and fewer passengers and more and more military supplies of all kinds. If it hadn't been for the great void left in the land by the mass departure of able-bodied men forcefully recruited from even the most distant villages, Massini would never have known that the world was at war. On the other hand, a sense of ill-defined malaise hovered over the land just as the passing shadow of a bird of prey worries the creature on the ground. A certain joie de vivre was missing; was it because the land had been drained of its youth? Was it because of all those women mourning, some for a husband, some for a son? In any case, Massini no longer took any pleasure in driving his locomotive, and often he left or arrived at the station like a thief, that is, without using his famous signals.

More and more, he withdrew into himself, and he who loved the company of others so much now even became a little unapproachable; every day, he dreamed a little more about returning to the village of his birth, which would obviously entail giving up the job that had made him the most celebrated man in the land. After some hesitation, he finally handed in his resignation. His boss was dumbfounded by this development, unable to understand why Massini would quit a job so highly regarded among his indigenous peers on the simple pretext that "the engine no longer brings me joy." As if he could not imagine that a Negro might find pleasure—not to mention happiness—in his work! "No," the boss refused categorically, "out of the question, especially now that we're in all-out war. Besides, you stupid imbecile, if you quit this job, I'll send you to the German front immediately." Massini looked at his boss with the astonished eyes of a villager seeing a locomotive for the first time. A feeling of hatred rose up in him. What right does he have to tell me what I may or may not do? After all, this is my home! He called to mind the first white who had come into his village a good long while ago, he ought to have killed him that day instead of walking out on the ceremony as he had, then he would not be so dependent today on these foreigners to earn his living. He now fully realized that there was a cost for all the things the foreigners had done in his land: the opening of the roads facilitated the transport of palm kernel oil and lumber to the capital, the railroad served to transfer these riches to the ocean, those who knew how to read were necessary for the functioning of their administration, and healthy natives were indispensable for doing heavy labor or supplying the army with fresh recruits. Perhaps the people of his country were a little richer, but rich like his Uncle Bizenga had been, that is, rich with the scraps of the culture these foreigners had brought with them. From that day on, his perception of the foreigners contained something broken; what it was he could not say. Since he had no desire to get himself killed for this particular foreigner, his boss, he chose the lesser evil and decided to remain on the job.

He began to think again about the great river, about his long lonely walks at night in search of the forces that hid behind objects. To have abandoned all of that for the city and the engine—had it been worth taking such a chance?

Life continued like this, in little monotonous steps, until the day the news arrived, at first by rumor, then officially: the war was over! It was in May 1945. This was the first time in his life that Massini remembered a date. A thrill of anticipation seized the country, which awaited, for a few more months, the return of its young men who had gone to war. On that day, women swept their houses, had their hair braided, bought themselves new cloth wraps, to welcome home the men that Massini had the honor of picking up from the ships that brought them here. The crowd filled up the station hours before the train was expected. Joy had returned; young girls, coquettes, and hussies, their beautiful bodies wrapped in cloth printed with tropical flowers, didn't try to hide the little mischievous gleams in their eyes, thus betraying the scenes of pleasure and delight that they already imagined, that they counted on enacting that evening with their returned sweethearts. The war was over. In the Place du Départ, now renamed Veteran's Square, a brass band played, alternating military songs with dance numbers. The militia made themselves amiable; even the foreigners were fraternizing with the natives, their faces, whether pale white or pink, lit up with easygoing smiles. There was nothing but laughter and tears, tears of joy.

One long toot, two short, one long. An ovation from the delirious crowd: Massini Mupepe was entering the station. His train, decorated with flags, came to a slow stop. He gave an extra toot on his whistle. Then the people stormed the cars. The names they called out were all mixed together, they hurled themselves on the necks of the first soldiers they could get their hands on, joy, tears, tears of joy, tussles, turmoil. The militia was ordered to intervene, restore order, and, magically casting off the easygoing air they had affected until then, they reverted to their customary cruelty: in no time at all, everyone was pushed back to the Place de Départ—now Veteran's Square— and made to stand up straight and orderly, waiting, well-behaved, for the soldiers.

Finally the heroes appeared!

They arrived, a stump in place of an arm, a leg or a hand missing! Cripples gleaming with medals planted on their chests which they tried to keep puffed up like the good soldiers they were. The crowd let out a murmur of incredulity and disappointment. If one was looking for a brother, as soon as he was spotted, one checked to see if he was missing a limb. Once again order was disrupted. Friends and relations were embraced; those who were not physically impaired had sad things to say. Alas, many did not return at all, they had disappeared over there, in that land of marvels. Cries and tears of joy were transformed into cries and tears of sorrow; people helped a legless man to move along, lifted gear for one who was missing an arm, held out crutches for a fellow with one leg. Mabiala, from Massini's village, left an eye over there; the seductive De Kélondi was no longer recognizable, he had received a shell-splinter in his left leg and limped slightly. Out of 63,344 who left Massini Mupepe's land, exactly 24,270 did not come back, and one of these was named Ambroise Poaty. Massini searched for him throughout the crowd in vain, he asked all the soldiers he knew for news of his friend.

In the end, those who had gone off to save the motherland and world freedom with a song on their lips came back home with weariness in their hearts. Massini, as leader of the club, invited all the veterans to a reception on Sunday, then found himself like them, his head heavy, his eyes full of tears. He passed by a young woman alone, weeping; her sad face contrasted painfully with her dress bursting with color. He was so moved that he forgot his own grief and went to her side. "Hello, what's your name, sister?"

"Mi...Milete," she succeeding in telling him between hiccups.

"Was it your husband?"

"No, it was my brother, my only brother!"

He didn't know what to say to that. He could only embrace her gently and tell her, before continuing on his way, "Be brave; I also lost a very dear friend, almost a brother."

But this was too much. His eyes, already brimming, burst, spilling hot tears in memory of the friend gone off to defend world liberty. What liberty? Massini wondered. Am I free? Is it liberty to put up with the cruelty of all these militias, whether for rubber, for three francs, or for the draft? He passed near a group gathered around a sergeant-major who had lost two arms and an eye. Without wanting to, despite the buzzing in his head, he felt the words of the hero vibrate on his eardrums, reach his brain, and force their way into his memory; the strident voice of a man embittered by his experience carried beyond the circle of heads surrounding him, nodding in approval at his words: "Yes, what I tell you is true, they called us all Senegalese riflemen. Me, Senegalese? They dragged us from camp to camp, they filled us with alcohol and made us partake in the first battle. When the enemy captured us it was no picnic: they made us dance, dance monkey, you shaker of banana trees, make a face, and your tail, show us your dirty tail, your big black chimpanzee's tail, ooh la la! Isn't it big, mein Führer, dance the bamboula, shake your dirty baboon ass, ja ja ja line them up against the wall and tac...tac...tac...we get sprinkled with bullets."

24.

Curious indeed is the course of historical events: the war that had unfolded thousands of miles away had, more than all the things they'd witnessed up to that point, revolutionized the way Massini's people thought about the world. To begin with, a new kind of foreigner arrived after the end of the hostilities: Lebanese, Greeks, and especially Portuguese. These were small businessmen who ran after pennies with as much alacrity as the indigenous people, in contrast to the first colonizers who led the lives of great masters amid their plantations and their slaves. The newcomers often cohabited with indigenous women, producing swarms of kids which they abandoned from one day to the next without the least sentiment of paternal responsibility when, their business in jeopardy, they decided to move to another region. The country proliferated with children of mixed blood named Gomez, Henriquez, Fernandez, who didn't really know whether they were Africans or Portuguese. The newcomers, gaudy adventurers with no panache, helped a great deal to destroy the myth of the foreigners' superiority. Generally unflattering images of their sexuality and their personal habits were disseminated: they were uncircumcised, they did not know how to satisfy a woman in bed, they only ate kidney beans... Most stupefying of all, the master tongue, the language all men were supposed to speak if they wanted access to civilization or wished to be regarded as "evolved" human beings, was cheerfully massacred by these new colonists; they spoke it with even less skill than the indigenous people who had been to school. So, then, over there, across the sea, in the land the foreigners come from, there were also people who did not know how to read, or write, or speak very well!

But the ones who most efficiently dispelled the aura of mystery and therefore of superiority which surrounded the foreign masters were the veterans, these men who had crossed the venerable Rhine, these soldiers who had passed through European cities as conquering heroes. One had only to see them strut around, medals on their chests, at the reception Massini had convened for them. There they were, the ones who had come home in one piece, those who had lost an arm, an eye, a leg. There was De Kélondi, who indefatigably called out "Overseas" when anyone called his name. Slightly the worse for drink, he would get around with little limping steps, his lameness increasing in proportion to his degree of intoxication. Small, his fine negroid nose trembling like the nostrils of a pure-bred, he had tipsy, red eyes. Since his return, he had abandoned himself to drink. In his left hand he carried a little cane which he said he had taken from a German soldier he had killed. "De Kélondi, De Kélondi," people cried out on all sides. "Overseas," he replied in his drunken voice. His mischievous eyes shone joyfully as if he were enjoying in advance the trick he was about to play. "I'm dying of thirst, like an elephant who hasn't drunk all season long! I'm thirsty," he cried. People laughed. He turned to Massini. "Mr. President, I'm a locomotive which has run out of fuel."

Massini ignored him, being of the opinion that he had drunk enough.

"Massini," he continued, taking the entire crowd as his witness, "if you don't give me more to drink I'll play a magic trick on you with my little black case!"

Suddenly everyone became quiet and looked curiously at the black case. Until then, nobody had paid it any attention. There was a silence, of respect and apprehension, because the veterans were both admired and feared. They had returned with special powers acquired over there, on the other side of the Ocean, and without equivalent here; these powers surpassed in strength all the local fetishes, all the Senegalese amulets; they had brought back talismans that protected them from sorcerers, sickness, poisoning; talismans that enabled them to seduce any woman they wanted! What was De Kélondi going to show them?

Massini hastened to hand him a half liter of wine. De Kélondi grabbed the bottle. "Look, here's the bugler's method." He raised the bottle high over his head, opened his mouth, and a stream of liquid poured into his gullet, his adam's apple going up and down to the rhythm of his swallowing. When he had quenched his thirst, he set the bottle down without having lost a single drop. Applause. He staggered a little more, limped laboriously over to a table, and asked somebody to bring him his case. He assumed an important air, searched his pockets for the key, opened it. The cover of the valise didn't come off completely but pivoted on a hinge and stayed open thanks to a metal bar held in place by a wedge. He took out a wax disc, placed it on a plate in the middle of the case, then took out a handle, slipped it into a hole and began to turn, easily at first, then with more and more force, and stopped when the resistance was too strong. Then he took a needle out of a box, ostensibly examined the sharpness of the point, made a sign of approbation, unfolded a long hollow tube into an S-shape surmounted by a big head, and set the needle into it. Everybody kept on watching him in silence, understanding nothing of these mysterious operations. Then click, the catch was flipped, the disc began to turn, and he delicately set the big head and the needle down on it: at first a crackling, then a voice, yes, nothing less, the voice of a man singing!

The men are startled; panic spreads among the children who hide behind their mothers and fathers; an instant of terror seizes the women: De Kélondi has a box with a little devil who imitates human voices hiding inside it! De Kélondi is proud of the effect he has produced; he stops the record and explains: this is called a phonograph, and this is a record; nobody is hiding inside, you can see for yourself. Massini looks, seizes the contraption, taps it, examines it from every angle, it's true, there's nobody inside. Ah yes, De Kélondi elaborates, it's all in the record. Reassured, the children come over for their turn to touch the machine. De Kélondi moves them aside, puts the record back on, and now the voice of a woman sings! So, they've even made prisoners of voices, Massini says to himself in pleased admiration.

They played and replayed this single record many times even though the songs were in a language they did not understand. De Kélondi changed the needle five times; finally, he stopped the machine while the enthusiastic crowd applauded. He received several invitations—with promises of gifts of two-liter bottles of wine—to play his phonograph in people's homes. He put the machine away and concentrated on drinking. But people wouldn't leave him alone and asked him all kinds of questions. His eyes burned like hot coals and his head registered all the questions they asked him simultaneously, so that he mixed all the answers together.

…they're called bombs, they burst like thunder, the earth flies up, the wind flies at the speed of panic…man without fear that I am, I lay down some nights in the snow…ah, I see that you don't know what snow is, you ignorant fools, savage natives, snow isn't ice and ice isn't snow, snow's white and soft like the kapok that falls gently from the sky when the wind shakes the brances of the ceiba; only this kapok, it's cold, very cold, and as soon as you touch it it melts and turns into water just like ice…you know what they did to us Senegalese riflemen, why are you looking at me like that, no, I didn't say I was Senegalese, you know what they did to us, they gave us aquavit, yeah, my little one, and it was good, then we weren't afraid of anything, we marched out with no fear and no complaint...ah, ah, ah, the first time the Germans saw all those black faces facing them they shouted Gottadammerung and ran away and threw away their guns, ah, ah, ah, that's how we won our first battle...war would be swell if only the enemy always ran away and you could always win without fighting...

"De Kélondi," called out Mabiala, who had just arrived, one-eyed and gleaming with medals.

"Overseas," replied his interlocutor.

"Drunk already?"

"Me, drunk? You've got to be kidding. Remember that time at Marseilles before we shipped out, I drank a bottle of pastis and still managed to satisfy five women in a row? Hey, Mabiala, you remember, in Paris, no, in Berlin, yeah, that's it, while Dresden was burning, with bombs bursting all around, when hundreds of crazy airplanes were dropping fire bombs on the city, underneath the fire, the strafing, the smell of burning flesh, the shouts, the blood, you know what I was doing, the man with no fear and no complaint, I, Corporal De Kélondi from overseas, ah, ah, ah, I fucked a blonde blue-eyed Aryan girl in a cellar that was practically caved in! Better to go up to heaven between the thighs of a blonde than with a bomb up your ass..."

"De Kélondi..."

"Overseas!"

Mabiala wasn't even listening to him; with Massini, he backed off from the guys shooting the breeze. He was carrying a package that Poaty had asked him to deliver: there was a photo of the young man in uniform, an envelope containing some money, and a letter. The young man had asked Massini to accept these few souvenirs, he had considered him almost the sole member of his family, since his mother and father were dead. Massini was very moved. This young boy who came from another region and another ethnic group had adopted him as a parent. After all, did what was called ethnic identity really count in the face of shared suffering? Hadn't all the combatants suffered the same thing in that white, melting snow that De Kélondi talked about? He carefully put the photo away and promised himself to find a member of Poaty's family, even only a distant relative, to give the money to. He thanked Mabiala and both of them turned back to De Kélondi. Mabiala and Massini sat down beside him.

"Hey, De Kélondi," interrupted Massini, "stop telling us about your heroic exploits. Tell us a little about your everyday life over there."

Suddenly, De Kélondi seemed to sober up. His voice lost its drunken animation, the words he uttered became gray and sad like tears shed at a wake. And, as if the dikes of his subconscious had suddenly burst, he began to speak with a broken voice of that part of their life which they had all kept hidden until that moment.

"We were not men over there," he said, "they didn't know our names. I, known to everybody in my own country, I, De Kélondi, they only called me 'Hey, rifleman...'"

"Yes," agreed Mabiala, "we were all 'riflemen.' Over there in the motherland, there were no clans, tribes, or ethnicities. We were all treated the same."

The old fighter takes up the tale more slowly, as if to make sure that his words sink into the ears of the president of the ethnic club. "Back there, when they refused to rent us a room or serve us in a restaurant, it had nothing to do with our tribal origins; no, wherever we came from, we were all brothers there, Negroes. I tell you, Massini, it wasn't worth the trouble to go and lose a leg or an eye defending these foreigners and then come back here and fight among ourselves for stupid ethnic reasons; no, it really makes no sense to defend the foreigners and then kill each other in our own country."

The two soldiers became quiet, then Mabiala resumed: "You've had enough to drink, De Kélondi, let's get out of here."

The old fighter gets the nod from his companion. They empty the bottle of wine and get up. De Kélondi takes his cane, grabs his phonograph, and the two of them hobble off, the one-eyed following the cripple, their medals dangling on their chests, involuntary heroes of a distant war. Massini Mupepe watches these two men, mutilated and old before their time, following with a sad dignity the rails of their lives, but leaving behind them, reverberating in his head like a train whistle, those three words: *our own country.*

25.

The days following the war brought a certain economic prosperity and a certain lifestyle to the country. The Portuguese, Lebanese, Greeks were followed, after a while, by some Hungarians who came to try to rebuild their lives after the invasion of their country, opened numerous boutiques, started small enterprises, hired many workers, and the money really began to circulate. Copper mining accelerated in the south of the country, as did iron and manganese in the north. Massini Mupepe kept on driving his cars full of travelers, merchandise, logs, and minerals. It was a period of renewed joie de vivre, a period when people did all kinds of things, when they cooked up all kinds of schemes, to make money. Thus, Wendo-Sor, a friend of Massini Mupepe's, quit his job as a mechanic in a bicycle shop to take up a career as a musician with a Greek who had started up a phonographic recording label called *Ngoma*, the tom-tom. Besides, the phonograph had become popular, and social progress was evidenced by the fact that fashionable receptions no longer featured the rhythms of the tom-tom, which was, in any case, neglected by the youth, but the sound of the phonograph, which was now plugged in or ran on batteries and played long-playing records. Some people invented a new profession: they set up a place, turned on some music, and made the people who showed up pay money to listen, dance, drink. And one of the first big hits in these dance clubs, bars, or pubs was Wendo's record in which he sang about his miseries and joys with Marie-Louise:

Marie-Louise, solo e ngaï na yo mama …

In all these places, it was only the rhumba, the beguine, the cha-cha-cha, the merengue, it was the rhythms which lubricated women's hips, made them as supple as the body of a boa, made their buttocks bounce up and down in suggestive, lascivious back-and-forth movements; it was music that drugged men's hearts, that allowed their eyes to run languorously over the breasts of women ripe with desire, over buttocks which jiggled and shook…Suspicious activities flourished in and around these places, and the first bordellos opened their doors.

With "Marie-Louise," Wendo not only became more popular than all the other singers but also more popular than Massini Mupepe. To the new generation coming along, the banal, everyday railroad said nothing at all, compared to

Wendo's success...Other names proliferated, sports stars, rich businessmen. It was these city folk who no longer had any organic connection to the villages they came from, these folk who, unlike Massini Mupepe, didn't have a little corner of the forest where their ancestors rested; these folk tried to catch, to grab all the novelties which Europe parachuted into their country. Also, for the first time, the indigenous townspeople began to internalize cultural values imported from overseas. Massini's country was invaded by the songs of Tino Rossi, the tangos of Carlos Gardel, the duets of Patrice and Mario. The radio arrived: Massini was the first to buy one, and he wanted to repeat De Kélondi's trick with his phonograph on those who had never seen one.

He organized a big celebration, invited, in the name of his club, all the people he knew, without, of course, forgetting the war veterans, all ethnicities mixed together. He also invited Wendo and his two rivals, Paul Kamba and Mundanda. Wendo performed "Marie-Louise," as he had to, and Mundanda his new hit, "Poto Poto." Finally, Massini's moment came. In the crowd he recognized Milete, the young woman who had lost her brother in the war, and called her to his side. They took out an enormous box with several buttons and a long wire which extended all the way to the roof. Using a jumper cable, he connected an automobile battery to another wire that came out of the back of the apparatus. He turned the button, and a light came on, pale green at first, then deeper and deeper, which he called a magic eye. He turned another button and music burst out of the box. A smile spread over his face, he puffed up his chest, and waited for acclaim, for the sound of surprise that should greet music without records: but nobody seemed impressed. "There's a phono hidden inside," somebody said. Then Mupepe got angry: "Have you seen a phonograph capture the entire world?" He turned the button, changing stations rapidly; they heard whistling and crackling, "ships on the sea," strange languages, "that's the Americans," other incomprehensible languages, "that's German, that's Russian or Arabic, they sound the same," music, atmospheric interference, "that sounds like airplane noise!" Finally, the crowd seemed convinced; yes, it really was different from the phonograph, "well of course, you fools, it's called a radio, it can pick up news from all over the world…" And the veterans piped up, explaining how, thanks to the radio, they had kept up with all that went on back home in their villages when they were over there at the front in Verdun and the Ardennes, in the burning snow; besides, the radio kept them posted about who was sleeping with their wives while they were gone, who said bad things about them, because the radio was everywhere, told everything, and never lied! Certain guests slipped away discreetly, believing themselves unmasked, while the wives of certain veterans became exceedingly attentive to their husbands, hoping thus to avoid suspicion… At the end of the transmission, Massini wiped the battery terminals carefully, then covered them with a slipcover especially made by Milete to prevent the battery's charge from "escaping."

But as a result of this first success, Massini's house became a meeting place during broadcasting hours which, at that time, only lasted three hours a day. First came the youth, who arrived early, in time for the concert, listening to Wendo, Keita Fodeba, the San Salvadors, humming Adios Pampa Mia, My Canadian Cabin; then came the veterans and other adults interested primarily in following the news from Indochina, where many of their brothers and friends were stationed. In this way they learned that a battle was raging in a place called Dien Bien Phu. The veterans commented on various phases of the battle, explaining to the civilians what a mortar was, a recoilless rifle, a bomber. Initially, the sympathy of the listeners was on the side of the foreign masters because many of them had a brother, a child, a relative, a friend in the foreign army surrounded in that infernal basin. But every passing day seemed to nourish a current of sympathy for these Vietnamese who resisted the power of the masters. Then their sympathy and admiration became wholly one-sided, they hoped for the defeat of the foreign army in which their brothers were fighting. Thus it was in Massini's home that his country-men learned, to their ill-concealed joy, that the masters had lost the battle of Dien Bien Phu. This was in May 1954, the second historic month of May to be impressed on Massini's memory.

From then on, surreptitiously, like a mole making its path, the dogma of the inviolability and invincibility of the masters started to rupture in the collective consciousness of the people. Veterans no longer talked about the news from the mother coun-try, about the burning snow, about Paris-the-most-beautiful-city-in-the-world but insisted instead on their bitter disappointment over there, talked about Whites whom they saw green with fear before going into battle, about the paupers and beggars to whom they had given alms; in brief, the land of the foreigners was no longer the paradise they had spoken of. And then a rumor began to circulate, uncontrolled, on the q.t., since the official radio had not confirmed it and on the contrary minimized it, even denied it (it was at this time that the population first became aware that the radio could lie), and according to this rumor, spread by the sev-eral "educated" natives who read the metropolitan newspapers, non-Whites from all over the entire world had gotten together somewhere in Indonesia, in Bandung, and vowed to liberate the country, the entire continent, all the Blacks in the world. New names began to appear alongside those of the officially sanctioned heroes: Kwame Nkrumah, Sukarno, Nasser, Nehru, Chou En-Lai...1955: a new world and a new hope had just burst forth.

Chapter Five

Do not fear Baas

It's just that I appeared

And our faces met

In this black night that's like me.

— MONGANE WALLY SEROTE

26.

THE LONG TRAIN OF CARS LOADED WITH MANGANESE CLIMBED laboriously up the gentle slope it had just tackled; little by little it slowed down, despite the engineer's signal to accelerate, then it no longer moved at all, its wheels spinning, wearing down the rails even more. Massini came down and, along with some workmen, threw sand on the tracks: the wheels then caught and the locomotive's fierce effort pulled the cars forward, they rolled ahead for a little bit, then the wheels began to spin again: there was nothing to be done, the load was too heavy. Fifty wagons full of raw manganese was too much for these worn-out old rails whose fishplates barely held. The convoy would have to be divided in two and, since there was only one track, this meant that all traffic would be blocked for quite a while.

For two days, no trains moved. Travelers going from the Ocean to the river or from the river to the Ocean crowded the stations with their baggage and their merchandise, while those who had come from distant villages, unable to go back home, rolled out their mats and tried to sleep amid the crying children, bunches of bananas, and clucking chickens they were transporting. For two days they waited for trains that didn't show up, they vainly strained their ears to pick up the well-known sound of Massini's whistle. As the delay continued, the bananas began to rot, the odor of chicken droppings became more and more unendurable, the station became a vast expanse of garbage and putrefaction. The stationmasters tried in vain to evacuate the stations and appealed to the police for help. The travelers and their families responded by beseiging the ticket windows, demanding refunds, abusing the stationmasters and ticket-collectors, throwing rocks at the police.

Officials were sent out to explain things and try to calm people's tempers: the line was blocked by a convoy of manganese too heavy for the locomotive; they needed either a stronger locomotive or to divide the convoy in two, and either way, this would take time. But these explanations did not persuade the travelers or, for that matter, the population at large, because for them the "machine" was more than a machine and to accept that a locomotive was unable to pull freight cars would be like accepting that crocodiles no longer lived in the water or that water no longer put out fire.

As sanitation became more and more precarious and tempers became hotter and hotter, the administration decided to evacuate the stations by force. They sent armed guards who thrashed the malcontents, cut the throats of their chickens, destroyed the better part of their merchandise, and threw some of them into prison. Finally, the travelers resigned themselves to going back to their villages or neighborhoods, exhausted, bitter, and more skeptical than ever. There was certainly something fishy going on for them to be so brutally evicted from the stations; something strange must be happening to all these trains. Otherwise, how could this powerful locomotive be immobilized, without reason, between two stations? Or then again, could this be a sign of the foreigners' decline? Were things already beginning to slip out of their control?

The answer came on its own. The rumor began at the Ocean, it followed, like the train, the railroad to the river, then spread over the whole country: the trains had been stopped by the strongest man in the world, Moutsompa. Moutsompa was known in his own region for his extraordinary exploits; people had since learned that this was the man who fought elephants and buffaloes by himself, barehanded, for fun; this was the man who pulled out the baobab tree with the strength of his biceps, who could drive in a nail by smacking it with the palm of his hand, the man who never got into fights with people, preferring to swallow an insult than to react, knowing how fatal was his punch; the man who, one day, to amuse folks, let a heavy truck roll over his feet without feeling the least pain. There was only one thing he hadn't defied, which bothered him—the locomotive! Well, there it was, he wanted to prove his strength once again, so he stood on the track and stopped all the trains that passed. Moutsompa's name became a synonym for resistance to the foreigners, a name like a challenge, thrown in the face of the native guards and their masters.

At first the foreigners laughed, amused by the credulity of these folk with their irrational spirits, these big children who would believe anything. Then they began to be vexed by the cult which the name Moutsompa seemed to be inspiring, and they really got mad when Moutsompa's power began to be considered equal to their own. This had to be stopped. The authorities launched an educational campaign, mobilizing traditional chiefs, club presidents, venerable elders; they explained the value of thinking a little, reasoning, understanding that nobody could stop a locomotive with the strength of his bare hands; he would be snatched up, crushed, pulverized, leaving not a single piece of him intact. Besides, the trains had already started running again, travelers were once again making the journey from the river to the Ocean and from the Ocean to the river without any trouble, and Massini's train tooted its famous signal as it pulled in at the station every night. Nobody on these journeys had seen even the shadow of the notorious Moutsompa. Alas, this logical and reasonable argument had no effect whatsoever; people continued to swear by Moutsompa, "the man who inspires terror in the hearts of the foreigners." He became a hero of popular stories, a legendary figure.

At this point, the authorities remembered Massini Mupepe, whom they had forgotten ever since the end of the war, more than ten years earlier, Massini, the man who knew the railroad better than anybody, Massini, the man who had been the hero of an entire generation. Right away, they summoned him to the governor general's, assured him that he would soon travel over there, across the ocean, to the land of the masters, to the mainland, as they called it, to learn to build a train all by himself. They reminded him of his medals, of his record as a model employee: "You who have operated this powerful locomotive, explain to these folks that no human being could possibly stop one! Tell them about our unlimited power, you see, we've conquered the wind with the airplane that can fly faster than the eagle or the swallow even though it's heavier than the air, we've imprisoned sound with phonographs and radios, we've trapped images with photography and film, we dominate everything! Look at the cars in the streets, the ships on the sea, we invented all that, and it's a far cry from the tom-tom and the xylophone!

You're intelligent, explain to these people that compared with all this power, poor Moutsompa..." Every word the boss of the foreigners spoke only served to revive Massini's bitterness for, gradually, he understood that they were only asking him to play another role. He who had never been promoted above the rank of a simple mechanic after twenty-odd years of good and loyal service, he who had been forgotten after the war because he wasn't needed, now here they were, flattering him, telling him whatever it took to entice him. "...so, brave Massini, the first of the country's train conductors, intelligent man that you are, they'll understand if you explain all this..." The people are assembled, a big meeting, the entire capital is there; the governor and military chief of staff flank Massini, cooperatively wearing his decorations, standing in the middle of the platform.

The governor speaks first, his speech gets translated, the crowd applauds politely. Then he turns to Massini: "Massini, explain to them that no human being can stop one of our trains."

Massini gets up, they applaud him warmly, more warmly than they had the governor. He smiles and begins to speak, he needs no interpreter. "You all know me, I am Massini Mupepe, the man who mastered the locomotive; many of you have traveled in my train, and you all know that I'm the first and best mechanic in this land, our land, that belongs to all of us, whether we come from the South, the North, the East, or the West."

The crowd applauds. Some of them have never heard such language and suddenly discover that they have a lot more in common with each other than with the foreigners who have never stopped dividing them. The governor looks anxiously at the interpreter who translates in his ear: "He says he's the best train conductor in the country, whether from the North, the South, etc." The governor relaxes, reassured.

Massini Mupepe continues. Without realizing it, words spoken by the veterans De Kélondi and Mabiala come to his mind; the memory of young Poaty who, even though he was a member of another ethnic group, regarded him as his only relative, rises to his thoughts: "Please understand, we're all of the same land. And I can say this now, especially since I was the first to say publicly that it was idiotic to form clubs that only the members of one's own ethnic group can join, which means that every club event, sporting or otherwise, automatically becomes a little struggle between ethnicities. Don't we all have friends from outside our region or our clan? Look at the foreigners who live here, we should follow their example; they don't all come from the same village or the same region! So why do we always fight among ourselves?"

The crowd is surprised and moved; this is the first time they've seen one of their own speak publicly in this manner, in this brother tongue, they who were grouped in neighborhoods according to their ethnicities, to their place of origin, or in sporting teams built around their tribal clubs, encouraged by the foreigners. As for the governor, he turns to his interpreter for a translation: "He says we ought to follow the example of our foreign masters." The governor is very happy with Massini, he is proud of his own political acumen, of his ingenious idea of generously providing a platform for this native whom he has won over to the cause. They would name Massini a citizen of the mother country!

Massini keeps on unburdening his heart to the crowd, to the faces of men and women, sisters and brothers; he draws from his depths, from his experiences, he recalls the arrival of the foreigner in Lubituku, his village, he recalls the forced labor, the collaboration of notables such as his uncle, the death of his father, of his mother, the crippled veterans getting off the trains.

He cries out, as if smitten with a sharp pain: "Why can't we be masters in our own land? Why do we have to work for these people who've come here from God knows where? Let's be united, my brothers, and if you believe that I'm an honest man, then I beg you, listen to me and bear in mind what I've told you here today."

The interpreter: He says that they're all his brothers and so they ought to listen to what he's telling them.

The governor gives an approving nod of the head.

Massini: Do you all understand what I've told you?

The crowd: Yeeeesss!

Massini: You really understand, now?

The crowd: Yeeeesss!

Massini: We are all?...

The crowd:...brothers!

Massini: Good. And now, let's talk about the train, this famous train. I've always thought that the day we stop that train, that would be the beginning of the end of these lords and ladies standing here beside us. (Ironic winks, bravos from the crowd.) But since I've been asked to tell you what I've seen, what I know, let me tell you first of all that I've never seen Moutsompa.

The interpreter: He has never seen Moutsompa.

Massini: I've never seen him with my own eyes, but that doesn't mean that I know nothing, because here is what people have told me. In the spot where the train goes through the great mountain, just at the exit of the long tunnel at Mbamba, he stood up, his legs spread out on either side of the track so as to surprise the train. Then when he saw the manganese train come, he reached out his two arms, the comet just crashed into the palms of his hands, he stiffened his muscles, and the train came to a dead stop!

The crowd applauds and cheers: "Moutsompa, Moutsompa, Massini, Massini." The governor no longer knows what's going on. He asks the interpreter.

The interpreter: He's telling them the stories people tell about Moutsompa but says that he himself has never seen any of it.

The governor, furious: He should be talking about our power!

The interpreter: He forbids you to talk about Moutsompa.

Massini takes off again: "My brothers, I was going to tell you all the things Moutsompa has done, the strongest man in the world, the man who stands up to these foreigners. But here we are, the governor has given the order to not talk about him. (Loud protests from the crowd.) But from now on, if one of us says, "Let's stop the train," I hope you'll understand. (Cheers and conspiratorial smiles.) The governor says that it's not Moutsompa who's stopping the trains, but I ask you then, who is it?

The crowd: It's Moutsompa, it's Moutsompa!

The interpreter: He told them that you don't want him to talk about Moutsompa.

The governor: Tell him to talk about our power, if not I'll throw his ass in jail right now!

The interpreter's voice is drowned out by the insults of the crowd which is so excited it can't keep still; the guards increase their vigilance.

Massini: He doesn't want us to talk about Moutsompa, he's afraid of him!

The crowd: Yeeeesss! Moutsoumpa (they take up the chorus).

The governor shouted at the interpreter to make them shut up. He told Massini too. The crowd booed him and started throwing stones at him. The assembly turned into a riot. In a fright, the governor ordered the guards to disperse the crowd, and hastily left the platform, followed by jeers. The guards, who had inherited the functions of the old *mbulu-mbulu*, had also inherited their methods. There were no deaths but plenty of seriously wounded. This was the first popular riot in Massini's country.

In the following days, the country seemed to be hatching something indefinable and ineffable. The administration, the foreigners, the indigenous population, all were on the defensive; something had to be done about this oppressive atmosphere. The authorities decided to go into action and so, one day at dawn, the guards nabbed Moutsompa in a village, or at least somebody they said was named Moutsompa. They paraded him from village to village, they transported him from the Ocean to the river, they called another meeting, they presented him to the people of the capital: "Just look at this poor guy, he's nothing at all, he's just skin and bones, it's him, Moutsompa, yeah, take a good look, open your eyes wide, here's your notorious Moutsompa who, so we're told, stops locomotives!"

They give him fifty-kilo weights to lift, and the poor devil bends down, grabs them, and works hard to lift them. His skin stretches over his spinal column, his fragile vertebrae can be seen, people are afraid they'll snap; he gives up, exhausted. They call over a tall, burly, muscular guard, compared to whom Moutsompa looks like a feeble dwarf. Through the interpreter, the governor asks the guard if he can stop trains, no sir, I can't stop trains, I can't even stop a motorcycle, very good my brave fellow, now lift those weights; he lifts them without difficulty, first a shoulder press, then an overhead press, almost without trying, look, sermonizes the governor through the interpreter, look at this guard who just lifted these hundred-kilo weights, he can't stop a train, so how do you think that this poor sickly fellow you call Moutsompa can stop a train when he can't even lift twenty-five-kilo weights? Do you know how much a train weighs? Several dozen tons! Come on, stop acting like children, think about it a little, try to use a little logic, the few brain cells you have...

The governor is satisfied, the police and the guards are satisfied, they have demonstrated in flesh and blood that this Moutsompa is an imposter. The question has been settled, no need to talk about it any more.

Moutsompa—or the one they presented as such—was taken to prison and beaten so badly that he died during the night. Agitated, the guards who had worked him over buried him hastily and in secret, by the light of candles. Even today, nobody knows where to find the tomb of the great Moutsompa, the man who, for fun, fought barehanded with buffalo and elephants and who could stop trains with the strength of his arms...But in fact, is Moutsompa really dead? Then show us his tomb, liar! They only showed us a poor puny devil who couldn't even lift ten-pound weights and they wanted us to believe it was Moutsompa, the man who lifts a hundred kilos with a finger, the man who uproots baobabs, the man who pulverizes a gorilla's jaw with one punch, no sir, it's a con, a total con, Moutsompa has simply disappeared until the day he returns to set us free. Photos said to be of the real Moutsompa appeared all over the place on medallions pinned to clothes or cameos worn around the neck or wrist. Many, especially those who came from his region, would gather together at night in secret around a photo of their savior surrounded by flowers and illuminated with candles. A real Moutsompist organization was formed, part religious and part political, and the Moutsompists decided to no longer pay taxes, no longer carry identification cards, until Moutsompa came back to rid the country of all these foreigners. The governor, who until then had been just as sweet as honey from the hive, was transformed into a wasp's stinger. A terrible repression pounced on the land. All portraits of Moutsompa disappeared, and it was against the law to even say his name. All the well-known Moutsompists were thrown in jail. But that wasn't enough, a loud and strong assault was required: they announced that Massini Mupepe, first of the country's train conductors, had been laid off because of his subversive and Moutsompist activities. This measure caused a real shock. The people were now frightened, the Moutsompists became more and more discreet, and a year later it was as if hardly anybody remembered Moutsompa and his exploits. The governor general, head of all the foreigners in the country, was happy, he had finally won the battle. They called him back home, they gave him some more decorations merited by his policy of pacification overseas, promoted him, and replaced him with somebody else. Thus the first great popular movement against the masters ended in failure, but a seed had been sown.

Massini Mupepe had to give up that which, for twenty years, had been his sole passion, the locomotive. He was no longer the Massini Mupepe who came into town like the wind, with one long whistle, two short, one long; Massini Mupepe and his train that the children ran to see, amid the incessant click-clack, click-clack, click-clack of the metal wheels; Massini Mupepe, whose long and heavy train of cars loaded with manganese wrenched deafening moans from the fishplates on the rails. He found himself naked, without a thing. He was only Mandala Mankunku now. What was he supposed to do now that he had no job, how was he to survive in this new world where a person's worth was monetary, especially since he had never been to school and never learned to read or write? How could he learn a new profession at his age? He thought a moment about going back to his village, to his plants and his investigations. Meanwhile, in the evenings, he often sat in front of his house and watched the moon rise in the twilight hum of the city; and he thought of his past, of his youth, which was already so far away. He thought of his Uncle Bizenga and felt no remorse, he had done what he had to do. He also searched for his mother among the stars and, in the end, his thoughts always returned to his learning, the things he had discovered: the *mansunsu* leaves, the use of *kinkeliba* for malaria, the aphrodisiac *kimbiolongo*, and so many other things. Who knew what he might have discovered if he had stayed in his village? But all the same, it seemed to him that it all counted for little to the foreigners. What could he invent? Even if he invented water that wouldn't get things wet, it probably wouldn't change a thing. Nevertheless, he didn't quite feel ready to give up, he felt at ease in the society he lived in, for he was still capable of taking part in his country's struggles, as the Moutsompa affair had demonstrated. But he also felt that History was overtaking him with giant strides, he who had always been in the lead with a social custom or discovery. Why hadn't he learned to read? These days, that was probably the royal road to wisdom; could he still learn at his age?

Thus he lost himself each day in the meanderings of his thoughts, emerging only when Milete came to see him. Since their initial encounter, a little over ten years ago, when he had first said a word to that tearful young woman waiting to welcome a brother who never came home from a faraway war, an attachment had formed between them.

It was then that the daughter of the North suddenly appeared.

27.

At first they said she came from the North, then other people testified that she was originally from the South but had lost her way in the North. In any case, her reputation and her name set the country aflame like a brush fire in the dry season. Her story was simple, she told it to all her faithful: during one of those terrifying storms when the fury of God appears in the thunderous crack of lightning which tears the night apart and cracks open the shell of the sky with terrible rumblings, she'd had a vision; she had seen the son of God with Moutsompa on his right, telling her, "Woman, I've chosen you. Go, go and tell the people of this land that the hour of liberation is at hand. You have been chosen to continue the work that Moutsompa began but did not finish because, in the divine scheme of things, its completion has been reserved for you. Therefore travel through this country from North to South, from East to West, from center to center. Unite our people and guide them!" Then she had stood up with the wind and the sun and began to travel through the country, on foot, in canoes, and later in a litter carried by her faithful. She had abandoned her family, refused to marry the man her parents had chosen for her, and begun to spread the good news throughout the land. Her words traveled even faster than she did because they were carried on the wings of dragonflies, relayed by the rustling of leaves and grass which were mixed up with the sighs of the ancestors at nightfall and enriched by the secret meetings of the *mbongui* in the evening.

She had begun by preaching in the smallest villages, by traversing the narrowest streams; then she had spent days and nights trekking through the forests, she had braved the sun and the dust which reigned over the ferrous earth of the South, she had perspired in the burning sands of the Center, she had waded in the mud holes of the North. Several times she suffered acute attacks of malaria, but, at the moment she was given up for lost, she would suddenly get well without the help of any known medical treatment, she would be up again and would resume her preaching with renewed fervor. Finally her message and her faith traveled the length of the great river and reached the great city.

To prepare for the marvelous Second Coming that she foretold, she established a body of new doctrine, on the one hand inspired by the religion of the masters, on the other hand rejecting it. She said that there was only one omnipotent God, who had made himself known through the medium of Jesus Christ and Moutsompa, all other religions being idolatrous; she gathered up thousands of statuettes and sculptures and burned them publicly after a session of collective prayer for the destruction of the power of these icons. She forbade the consumption of alcohol but made an exception for palm and pineapple wines. She told the women to only marry husbands of their own choosing and to liberate themselves, like she had, from the protection of men; she authorized the men to marry as many women as they liked on the condition that they not make love to two wives in the same week, a week that had long since lasted seven days. She asked them all to forsake the foreigners' churches which housed nothing but lies and the perversion of God's word. In her hymns, inspired as much by tradition as by Catholic and Protestant choral music, she introduced the name of Moutsompa, and, along with a cross, she asked her faithful to wear the green palm leaf. As for sin, since it was an individual concern, there was no point in confessing so as to be cleansed, it was enough to be exposed to the rain, divine and benevolent water...

She had to be seen, this Saint of the North, Santu-a-Ntandu, among her thousands of faithful, while the churches, the temples, the mosques were deserted. She had to be seen, to be heard, this girl with the green cloth wrap and the white blouse, her head covered with a handkerchief, a palm frond in her hand, the light of her eyes changing with the emotion her words were charged with, like the shimmering and shifting colors of lantana flowers. "I've been sent to set you free, to free the land by continuing the work of Moutsompa; but as long as your hearts are not as clear as rainwater, as long as you haven't turned your hearts away from the false gospel of the foreigners and your soul hasn't attained to the dignity of a palm tree and the beauty of a royal poinciana flower, we'll remain in misery and sickness, we'll never recapture the happiness we enjoyed in the time of our ancestors and which Christ and Moutsompa have promised us..." She talked, talked, inspired, irresistible. Her voice was heated, warm, and generous, with the indefinable vibrations that must comprise the songs of angels. "Hallelujah," she would cry. "Hallelujah," the echoing crowd would throw back. She would clap her hands, launch into a hymn, the crowd would join in with the clapping of hands, the beating of tom-toms, the ringing of handbells. Then the spirit of God would descend upon the pure of heart, and the women who had been touched would cry out "Yesu, Yesu," and with a sudden gift of glossolalia, would launch into a Babelic chatter that only the Saint seemed to understand, then they would revert to their cries of "Yesu, Yesu," flutter, stamp, jump, fall down in cataleptic states, roll over each other, rattle their throats, let the white foam of the evil spirit flow from their mouths, leaving their finally purified bodies! And the Saint of the North, Santu-a-Ntandu, would cast her maternal regard over them, a regard full of a love that warmed them, calmed them, caressed them like balm, while the sanctifying hallelujahs, ceaselessly repeated, penetrated the very substance of their bodies and their souls.

And look, now there's another, even more inspired, suddenly standing up, her eyes translucent: "Hallelujah, hallelujah," the company responds; she speaks, begins to prophesy, looks over to the corner where the men are sitting: "Yes Lord. Brother Malonga, get up, reveal to us here what your sorcerer's heart is hiding." Brother Malonga tries to hide, to sink into the ground, they make him get up, he trembles, he has been unmasked like all the hypocrites, traitors, spies for the foreigners, sorcerers, thieves, magicians, whose only interest in the new religion is to allay their friends' suspicion. Well, when the Holy Spirit descended on the crowd, these rascals were also seized, they stamped, shouted, "Yesu, Yesu," but fell down thunderstruck, in a semi-tetanic state from which they would never recover... And this is what's going to happen to Brother Malonga... He senses that he's caught in a trap, he looks desperately around him and... takes to his heels in a desperate flight. People shout, run after him for a bit, then abandon him to his fate: the power of the Saint to detect evil spirits has been demonstrated once again.

Thus many people died, and this only added to the glory of the new faith, because there could be no religion without ordeal. They brought her women who were accused of adultery in order to determine if they were lying when they denied it, they brought her sorcerers who had been accused of "eating" someone, they brought her sterile women, paralytics, the incurably sick. She would walk among them, caressing the head of one, brushing another with her palm frond, blowing into the eyes of a blind man, calming a cry of pain with the touch of her hand, a true, beneficent queen in the middle of her domain. And the blind could see, the paralytics stood up, the cripples walked, the adulterous women confessed, the thieves returned their booty, and the sorcerers were unmasked; and those who could not be cured were those whose hearts were not as pure as the morning dew, those who were not sincere in their faith. These were then abandoned to the devil...

In truth, it seemed that there was only one person in the country any more: Santu-a-Ntandu. Long gone were the days of passionate enthusiasm for Massini Mupepe and his locomotive, for Wendo and his "Marie-Louise." The Christian churches badgered the administration with complaints about this false prophetess who was sowing trouble among their faithful; the police, for their part, complained to the governor about the disorder which would surely be caused by this adventuress who didn't conceal her reestablishment of a forbidden movement, Moutsompism. The administration hesitated between various courses of action, then finally decided to let things be, hoping that, as often happened with such millenarian movements, time would dull its impact, if not make it disappear altogether. But this is not what happened: on the contrary, the movement only gained momentum. Then the police, the army, and the church set out to combat this scourge together, this Saint of the North, Santu-a-Ntandu.

As it had ever since its arrival in Massini's land, the foreign administration only responded in one way to all problems: with force. So they sent out the army in search of the mysterious saint whose real name nobody knew. But the army always showed up too late, the saint was no longer in the place where her presence had been reported. Then the soldiers, like all the world's soldiers, became aggravated, pillaged villages, carried off chickens, goats, raped women, beat up men, just like in the good old days of the *mbulu-mbulu* before the war. Thus the soldiers spent six months tracking her, with armored trucks, by helicopter, on foot, in canoes, from village to village, from forest to forest, from river to river. One day, they thought they had trapped her in the swamps of the North; they had apparently surrounded her, the helicopters had located her, it was only a matter of minutes before they captured her, whatever you do, don't leave your receiver, it's me, the chief of state, the chief of the army, talking to you, news of the arrest of that criminal will be announced any moment now, maybe even before the end of this message.

But the minutes turned into hours, the hours into days, the days into weeks, and the saint was still not captured. Besides, was it possible to arrest a saint who could disappear when she wanted to, would go off to chat with God and come back whenever it pleased her? For example, one time her canoe was damaged by shots from the military and began taking in water on all sides; well, she rose and, like Jesus, she crossed the river by walking on water. Another time, she was among her faithful when some troops surrounded them; but hey, all of a sudden she wasn't there. Nobody ever knew what she became that day: the wind, a grain of sand, an ant, a palm frond? Finally, another time, getting really desperate, they sent out spies with cameras and tape recorders to catch her in flagrante delicto, preaching subversion; well, not only did the film refuse to register images, but the tape recorders also kept erasing what they recorded. In fact, as the reels unspooled, the words of the saint would fly away into the air, and the tape would be blank once more. And even that wasn't all. The great witch doctors were called in. They got together and decided to use a *kipoyi*. If you hung an object belonging to the missing person on a branch carried by two men, the branch would infallibly lead you to the person or the object you were looking for, after the usual adjurations. It was in this manner that sorcerers and other village miscreants could be detected. So they suspended on the branch of a *ntela* tree carried by a couple of burly fellows a green scarf lost by the saint; armored trucks and a military platoon followed behind the porters while a helicopter hovered overhead. And the witch doctors adjured, prophesied, spat tiny drops of palm wine onto the scarf, go *kipoyi*, as sure as the spirit of the ancestors is just and loves the truth, lead us to this Santu-a-Ntandu wherever she may be, wherever she's hiding, whether it's in the deepest part of the forest with the pygmies, or even if she's burrowing down like an ant-lion in its sandy tunnel, go *kipoyi*, go...The porters began to sway backwards and forwards and all of a sudden took off, like a motorcycle after racing its engine, and began to run to the place the hunted woman was hiding, followed by the helicopter, the armored truck, and the soldiers. The *kipoyi* was infallible, and its force continued to push the two porters, who stepped barefoot over shards of broken bottles without cutting their feet, they stepped over live coals, left smoldering under the turf by a forest fire, without being burned, they crossed through spiny brambles without being scratched by a single thorn, they stepped on vipers without getting bitten, they ran straight ahead, pushed forward by the power of the *kipoyi* just as iron filings are attracted by a magnet...right up to the great river which engulfed them all, porters, armored trucks, soldiers, and even the helicopter, the blades of which got caught in the trees. Thus they would never cross to the other bank, where the saint was! Even the great river protected her. And this was the person they thought they would capture! The Saint of the North, Santu-a-Ntandu: she was everywhere and nowhere.

28.

One night when Mankunku had gone to bed after spending many hours thinking about his life, as he did more and more these days, somebody knocked at his door. Surprised, he got up. Who could be visiting him? He lit his kerosene lamp and opened the door: it was Milete, alone, her face hidden behind a handkerchief. Mankunku was amazed; what would people say if they saw her here at this hour? She seemed preoccupied, she didn't even say hello. "I beg you, Mankunku, let us in quickly before somebody sees us."

He stood aside and was very surprised to see that she wasn't alone, that there was another woman with her.

"Look," said Milete in an imploring tone, "you've known me for years, Mankunku, you trust me, don't you?"

"Of course! What's going on?"

"You're the only one I can trust, and I've come to ask a big favor of you, a very important one. I beg you to welcome this woman and hide her for a few days."

"But Milete, I can't hide someone just like that! Who is this woman, what has she done? Is she running away from her husband?"

"No, rest assured, she isn't married, this isn't a question of man and woman; she hasn't killed anybody, she has committed no crime. She just needs help, protect her for two or three days, that's all. I beg you, help me, help us."

Mankunku looked at the woman standing in a corner. She was thin, seemed exhausted, at the end of her rope. With evident fatigue, she lifted the handkerchief that covered her head. In contrast, now a warm, evanescent flame, deep in her eyes, gave her emaciated face a quasi-surreal power and beauty.

Mankunku felt almost physically enveloped in the heat of this gaze. He seemed to perceive something familiar, to recognize something he couldn't quite grasp, a kind of energy that emanated from this person. "Woman, tell me the truth. Who are you? It seems that I know you, yet without knowing you."

"I am Santu-a-Ntandu, the Saint of the North."

Mankunku was flabbergasted. He was happy and he was frightened, he felt honored and he felt betrayed by Milete; so many contradictory feelings crossed his mind that he stood for a long time without uttering a word. The two women didn't budge, they looked at Mankunku's moving face. Finally he emerged from his internal struggle, his face apparently calm, his eyes radiant with pride and resolution. "Thank you, Milete, thank you Santu-a-Ntandu for thinking of me. For a long time I've been talking about liberating our country, about uniting us, but you see, between talk and action…You're a truly courageous woman! I'm not worthy to eat from your plate. Oh, am I honored! Yes, Mandala Mankunku is satisfied, happy. Stay here as long as you wish, stay a month, a year, your struggle is ours, and if they want to arrest you it'll be over my dead body."

"Thank you very much, Mankunku," said Milete. "I knew that you'd help us."

"Thank you," said the Saint. "God will bless you."

"Even without God's blessing, I'd have offered you this hospitality in the name of our common ancestors."

"Frankly, I couldn't go on, I can't go on, I'm tired of running from place to place, of going about at night in villages and forests, of not getting enough sleep. I need to lie down, to get my strength back before going on. I thank you too, Milete."

Milete turned to Mankunku. "I've known the Saint for a long time, but I didn't want to worry you, Mankunku, because of all the trouble you were having with the Moutsompa affair."

"In that case, I'm glad I had that trouble because, without them, the Saint would never have sought refuge here."

"That's true," said Milete, "it's because of all this that she asked me to bring her to you."

"You said that I was a truly courageous woman," said the Saint, "but you too, you're a courageous man. To give up prestige, fame, and money as you've done is also an act of courage."

"Alas, courage isn't everything. My demonstration of personal courage changed nothing in the predicament of our country, the foreigners are still here, and you're still being persecuted. They might as well have put me in jail or killed me, and I'd have sacrificed my life for nothing. No, we need something more, and that something more, which I don't have, you have."

"Without your defiance of the governor, I could never have done what I did."

"Maybe, but you managed to rouse the entire country, to throw the administration into a panic, you've managed to ridicule an army and a colonial police force against which no resistance had ever succeeded before; if only for that, Santu-a-Ntandu, you are an extraordinary woman. Stay here as long as you like. Rest up, recover your strength. I'm not afraid. Nobody can say what the future has in store for us, but, as I've always believed, History is like a great river, it makes its new turns and then returns. Well, good night, Milete, don't wait too long before going home, and be very careful."

"Good evening, Milete, and thank you," said the Saint.

"Good evening, Santu-a-Ntandu, good evening, Mankunku. See you tomorrow. You can count on me. The secret will be well kept."

She opened the door, inspected the darkness for a moment, took a few steps outside, and was snatched up by the night.

29.

While the exhausted army, the embarrassed police, and a governor humiliated in the eyes of the Minister of the Colonies and the religious authorities continued their laborious search, stepping up the repressive campaign, the Saint rested and recovered her strength for almost four months in the home of Mandala Mankunku. During this time, people still saw her everywhere and nowhere, in the North, in the South, in the central region, but nobody thought that she could be hiding in the capital, that new cosmopolitan metropolis.

Rumors began to circulate, however, according to which the army and the police were preparing to launch a house-to-house search through every neighborhood in the city. In this situation, the safety of the Saint was no longer assured, she would have to be hidden elsewhere. It was decided that she should go to Lubituku, Mankunku's village. He got busy preparing for her departure, buying things she would need for the village life, then found three people he could trust, two men and a woman, to accompany the Saint.

They set out shortly before dawn, taking narrow forest paths so as to avoid running into an army patrol; they crossed rivers, climbed up mountains only to immediately go down the other side, and, by the time the sun had reached its zenith, the Saint was worn out. So they stopped in a little village to rest. She was given water to drink and when she thanked them, some people recognized the Saint. At once the news spread, faster than her progress. When she arrived someplace, people were already waiting with fruits, eggs, chickens; women would run over to give her their babies to touch and to bless. The farther she went, the less possible it became to hide her. The faithful came to villages from a radius of ten leagues, the Saint was there, the Saint had come back! Thus the clandestine journey was transformed into a triumphal march. She had regained all of her ardor, her zeal, the passion of her faith. She held forth to her faithful: "I disappeared for some time to receive instructions from God and Moutsompa. Now here I am again among you. Does it seem that the army and the police are looking for me? Well, let them stop looking! Since they're incapable of finding me, I'll go looking for them, let them stop me if they have the nerve! Hallelujah!"

"Hallelujah!"

"The hour of liberation is at hand, my brothers and my sisters, this is what I've come back to tell you..."

The faithful applauded and made an about-face, the Saint in the lead, to take the road back to the capital, amid hymns and choruses. There were thousands of them behind the young saint, buoyed up by their faith and by their songs, which the echoes from the mountains and the depths of the forests amplified:

Telema-a-a...
Telema-a-a...

In their hands they held thousands of green palm fronds, and, after gravelly paths which tore up the bare feet of these new crusaders, after foggy valleys, sandy and dusty plains, they finally emerged onto the great asphalt avenue of the capital, much to the surprise of the urban population. All traffic was blocked. Columns of marchers advanced, singing all the while, then stopped in front of the train station, in Veteran's Square, the most famous square in the city. The Saint stood up at the foot of the monument erected in honor of the sons of the country, the "Senegalese riflemen" who went to defend the cause of liberty over there, and addressed the crowd of the faithful and the curious who had joined them: "Hallelujah!"

"Hallelujah," the crowd responded. People left their offices, their businesses, their work, to come and listen to her, as if the shadow of a general strike were hovering over the city.

Then, instinctively, as if she could communicate by osmosis with all these workers who were pressing around her, the meaning of her sermon changed, it became more immediate, more militant: "It is I, Santu-a-Ntandu, in the flesh and blood, I'm not hiding. It seems that soldiers have been looking for me for two years and couldn't find me; go tell them that I'm here and that I'm waiting for them. And now, listen to what I'm going to tell you. Hallelujah!"

"Hallelujah!"

"The hour of liberation is at hand, soon you'll no longer toil beneath the sun for a wretched salary while the masters stretch out in the shade of their verandas; all men will be equal, women will be equal to men, divine justice will descend on the earth. We cry 'no' to the injustices they impose on us, 'no' to exploitation!..." Enthusiastic bravos from the workers, hallelujahs from the faithful. "Go tell the soldiers I'm here; what are they waiting for? Now that I'm here, are they afraid? I've been sent by God to tell you that the hour of liberation is at hand..."

And suddenly they heard the sirens, the whirring of helicopters, the armored cars. The army and the police had sent no summons, they feared that once again the Saint would disappear by magic in her usual way. So they charged in brusquely, at first using their rifle butts, then tear-gas bombs, and finally both at the same time. The Saint was pulled from the monument at which she stood, she was thrown to the ground, stomped on, beaten; they dragged her by the hair over the rough macadam, they thrashed her with their rifle butts and boots all the way to the car they threw her in. Thus they avenged themselves for months of humiliation. The trouble spread, the entire city was seized with rioting fever; people threw stones at the police at all the intersections, and, in the Bembé district, the inhabitants charged armed guards with machetes. The riots lasted all day and all night. The Portuguese, Lebanese, and Greek shops were pillaged and burned, the white proprietors taken to task. So a curfew was proclaimed, and the soldiers were ordered to shoot pillagers on site. But, as is common when the military makes the law, the criminals were not the only ones to perish in the gunfire. On top of everything, a violent storm broke out in the city, pulling up trees and telephone poles which fell on buildings, thus causing serious fires, while waterspouts rushed through the streets, carrying off cars and houses.

The Saint was handed over to religious authorities who insisted that she publicly renounce all the heresies she had pronounced: she had told her faithful not to fast during Lent, not to take confession but to expose oneself to rainwater to be cleansed of one's sins, she had encouraged the men to be polygamous. She refused and launched into incomprehensible curses. All their threats—fire, hell, and damnation—couldn't make her bend. She kept on repeating that she had been sent by God and by Moutsompa, that her role was to put an end to the foreign occupation, to establish equality between men and women, as well as fair wages. She also said that she was going to help the workers and employees take possession of the factories and offices and kick the masters out. And all this, she said, must take place before the birth of the child she would one day carry in her womb, because her child could only be born free!

The religious leaders who feared the effect of such firmness on the attitudes of credulous natives thought they had found here an opportunity to degrade the Saint. They launched a campaign of disparagement against the heresiarch, repeating over and over, drumming it in in sermons, taking up the Cross as a witness: watch out for this sacrilegious woman, an offense to God, she calls herself holy while pregnant, have you ever seen an adulterous saint, a tainted saint...And the people learned the news, the Saint of the North, Santu-a-Ntandu, was pregnant, she was going to be a mother! Oh, bless her! She was a real saint, for how could one adore a sterile woman? And then a rumor got about that the Saint was not only pregnant but that she had already given birth and, moreover, not just to one but to two children: twins! She had done even better than the Virgin Mary! Respect for the Saint only increased. Besides, people no longer spoke of Santu-a-Ntandu, but of the Mother mother, Ma Ngudi, the Mother par excellence. The entire country performed ceremonies for Ma Ngudi's twins, despite the threats of the authorities.

One night Ma Ngudi was deported, nobody knew where. Some people said that she had been whisked away in a helicopter sent by Moutsompa and that he had taken her far away to wait for her triumphal return on the day of liberation. These became fervent Moutsompists; despite persecutions, they once again refused to pay their duties and taxes, to register their children with the government, to carry identification cards. As for the religious authorities, they maintained a discreet silence but had their flocks circulate various rumors to the effect that Ma Ngudi had renounced everything she had preached, converted to the true Christian faith after taking a vow of chastity, and retired to a convent.

The unrest continued for weeks, for months, throughout the country. The army couldn't restore order as easily as before. So the governor made it known, with a speech on the radio translated into all the major local languages, that the mission of the mother country was a civilizing and disinterested mission and that it was only concerned with the well-being of the indigenous people. In any case, thanks to a new "enabling act," porterage, forced labor, and obligatory recruitment were abolished. "A territorial assembly will be created with representatives elected by the people, that is to say, by yourselves, etc." Then they spoke of numerous indigenous officials, those who had gone to school and knew how to read and write; they spoke of the "political parties" that they would organize, the "deputies" that had to be elected; and they said that, thanks to all this progress, the country was going to become, for the whole world, a model of harmony and understanding between two civilizations.

Mandala Mankunku, like the vast majority of his compatriots who had never gone to school, understood few of these esoteric words which supposedly heralded the new institutions. He had the vague feeling that some people somewhere were in the process of winning an important struggle. In any case, he wasn't concerned with it at all, because of his great sorrow and his revived anger. He was still thinking about Ma Ngudi and her twins. In view of the little he knew about the customs of the foreigners in their own land, he was persuaded that Ma Ngudi had been burned alive with her two children and that their ashes had been scattered over the land or thrown into the river so as to avoid creating a pilgrimage site for her faithful. He could no longer stand still doing nothing. Had he become so indifferent, he, Mandala Mankunku, the man who had confronted and defeated his maternal uncle, who had also been one of the powerful? No, it was really time to wake up!

30.

Throughout the country, like air bubbles that rise, expand, and then burst on the surface of the water, dozens of women sporadically appeared, claiming to be Ma Ngudi returned, risen from the dead. Some said they were direct descendants; others declared themselves either independent saints, specializing in the cure of certain ills, or incarnations of the true religion of national liberation, a mixture of Christ, Moutsompa, Ma Ngudi, and the Virgin Mary. In this wave of anti-establishment religion there also appeared some sects from America, such as the Jehovah's Witnesses, who preached the apocalyptic end of the world and predicted a new order of things under the rule of the Son of God. While awaiting the new order of things, they refused, like the Moutsompists, to get involved in politics, vote in elections, or salute the flag. There were also many other local sects, the Kimbanguists, the Koma Cross, and the Zéphyrins, all more or less proclaiming the end of colonial domination. These sects had taken root among the common people in the cities and the peasants in the country. They did much more to sharpen the political, or at least the anti-establishment, feelings of the population than the campaigns conducted by the indigenous "counselors" and "deputies" who wanted to be elected to the new Territorial Assembly, recently created.

The foreigners, who for some time had been rather sure of themselves on account of the political liberalization they had effected in the rush of events caused by Ma Ngudi by nullifying the old discriminatory *code de l'indigénat* (code of the natives) and passing the new "enabling act," now began to get anxious, irritated, and unsure of their paternalistic stance. On the one hand they depended on the new deputies who had taken turns with the former tribal chiefs in broadcasting the blessings of the mother country, while on the other they took increasingly draconian measures to suppress the independence movement. The Christian churches also threw themselves into an enormous propaganda campaign aimed at eliminating once and for all the heretical, idolatrous, and sacrilegious cult of Ma Ngudi, which seemed to be taking root more and more in the hearts of the indigenous people. They launched a campaign to distribute thousands of holy medallions featuring beautiful profiles of the Virgin Mary and other foreign saints. The women to whom these medallions were given refused to accept them, and those who lacked the courage to refuse them ran and hid in the bush or the forest when the distributors showed up.

Then they changed tactics, and the civil, military, and religious authorities collaborated, each for its own personal interest. First the army would show up, surround a village at dawn, and catch everybody in its trap; they verified the papers of those who had paid their taxes; those who had not paid were led off to jail. Then they checked for voting cards, for those who had not voted were subversive Moutsompists. When the army and the police had finished their inspections, the distributors of holy medallions started their work: the destruction of all photographs of Moutsompa or Ma Ngudi, the sprinkling of holy water, the distribution of the cross of our Lord, of baptismal medallions. Finally, the operation was concluded with the gift of a sack of peanuts to each peasant, man or woman, and the agricultural agent made it perfectly clear that, for every sack, the administration would expect to collect three sacks full at the next harvest. Then they went off, leaving the subdued peasants murmuring their resentment.

In the cities, the agitation continued. The most spectacular gesture was that of the priest Zola, who broke with the Christian church. In protest against what he called "crimes" against his people, he publicly took a wife and shut himself in with her, while his flock surrounded the house singing glorias and hymns to the glory of Ma Ngudi. The priest continued his mortification for three days and three nights without eating or drinking, until one morning when a blood-curdling shriek was heard, followed by the woman's cries of terror: he had died hard at work, the first voluntary martyr in the struggle for independence.

As for Mandala Mankunku, he was also generally inconsolable. He was more solitary than ever, withdrawn into the depths of himself; the interrupted passion and the martyrdom of Ma Ngudi, the Saint of the North, had torn out a part of himself that not even Milete could put back. He seemed to be living outside this world, outside this life. And then, little by little, a deep resentment against the foreigners rose up in him. He who, in his youth, had known an almost boundless admiration for these foreigners who seemed to have invented everything, he who had been more honored in his youth by these foreigners than anyone, now he seemed to be obsessed by a single image, that of the man with a face red as *tukula* powder, hair straight as the beard on an ear of corn, protected by a white helmet, that man who had come into his village one day, a very long time ago. What would have happened if he had killed him instead of walking out on the meeting? Would the course of History have changed? Would it have made more or less of a detour?

31.

After the great adventure of living with Ma Ngudi, Mandala Mankunku felt that once again he had just lost a great battle.

How many such defeats would he and his people suffer at the hands of these foreigners? It seemed to him that all of his struggles up until now had been ridiculous, from the day he had objected to his Uncle Bizenga and abruptly walked out on the scene of bargaining between the latter and the first foreigner to set foot in his village, right up to this last battle over Ma Ngudi. At first he let himself sink into a deep pessimism about the outcome of the struggle for liberation; then he remembered his past, his ancestor Mankunku, old Lukeni, his own continual revolt against all that seemed to go against the idea he had of the world: defiance of the great river, defiance of nature, defiance of ancestor worship, defiance of Bizenga, defiance of the foreigner! No, he had to pull himself together, replenish his resources, and keep on fighting, if only to avenge the memory of Ma Ngudi.

For a moment, he thought of assassinating the leader of the foreigners or killing the chief of police; but when lucid, he realized that these were impractical acts, good for nothing but getting himself shot like a vulgar criminal. His action should have meaning, symbolic meaning. But how could he carry out a symbolic action in a world where everything was without roots, without tradition, therefore without symbolism? Then, suddenly, he remembered that he was a blacksmith and the son of a blacksmith.

In his backyard, on the edge of town, he built a traditional forge, just like his father's where he had learned the noble art of the blacksmith; and, instead of working with iron and lead, he had the idea of making jewelry out of the religious medallions that people did not want to wear. He asked men and women to sell him their holy medallions, and their response exceeded his expectations: they gave them to him for free. He melted them in accordance with ancestral techniques and made delicate ornaments out of them, necklaces, earrings, bracelets, U-shaped links for dancing. In his hands, the saints thus became mocking monkeys holding onto branches with their tails or hands, their fingers up their noses; they became delicate frightened does standing on fragile legs, massive elephants, ugly hippopotami with their enormous mouths, hideous warthogs. The blacksmith Mankunku could make anything, invent anything. He transformed the Virgin Mary into Ma Ngudi and Jesus Christ into Moutsompa. And the wives of the foreigners adorned themselves with these jewels made, without their knowledge, of medallions of saints while their husbands boasted about these marvelous products of the local craftsmen.

During this period, in a strange development that reassured both the administrative and religious authorities, the country was smitten, it seemed, with a renewal of religious fervor: the demand for holy medallions doubled, tripled, whereas less than a year previously, they'd had to use the army to distribute them. The bishops were satisfied, the ways of the Lord are mysterious, we should never give up hope: it was better this way, religion is an individual matter, it should not be imposed. The epidemic of piety only got worse, so much so that there was a shortage of all medallions, even the bronze cross of our Lord. Ever sensitive to the needs of their subjects, the foreign masters launched a desperate campaign in the newspapers of their country, brothers, help us, it's a matter of the souls of our natives, our dearly beloved little brothers in the faith... Then these generous people sent tons of crosses, of medallions, which wound up in Mankunku's forges. But the generosity of these people didn't stop there, they offered an exceptional Christmas for the pious people of Mankunku's land: reindeer were sent by special cargo plane; Santa Clauses dressed in red greatcoats and white beards were brought in, they rode around in wagons and waved to the people; on the roads there were holly and mistletoe. In short, only one thing was missing from this otherwise perfect white Christmas: snow; for nobody had been able to solve the problem of exporting it to a tropical land.

Mankunku made a lot of money thanks to the beauty of his jewelry, but his great satisfaction and his main motivation was to have in some small way avenged Ma Ngudi. Unfortunately, thousands of other little volcanos were rising up throughout the country, not vengeful like Mankunku's, but greedy. Mediocre craftsmen began to imitate Mankunku, only for the money, without his skill, and it was easy to recognize in a monkey's face a partly melted segment of the cross of Jesus, or on a hippopotamus the profile of the Virgin, badly transfigured. So the authorities began to suspect the actual destination of the holy medallions that were flooding into the country. The scandal was great and the sacrilege unpardonable. It wasn't hard to trace it all back to Mankunku.

They showed up early in the morning, surrounded Mankunku's house, opened his door with rifle butts and boots, pulled Mankunku out of bed, turned the house inside-out, and discovered a supply of sacred medallions waiting their turn to be transformed into sacrilegious objects by the maleficent fire of his athanor.

"You stupid dirty monkey nigger native of black tropical subequatorial Africa," fulminated the military leader, angrily repeating what he'd retained of the insults his masters had proffered when he'd crossed them, "so you're a fetishist and an idolater and don't respect the saints? You'll see what's what!"

He gave a sign with his head. Two soldiers pounced on Mankunku and began to beat him. He tried to defend himself by punching and kicking, but other soldiers joined in, he was subdued and dragged to the leader, his face all bloody. The man of the cloth who'd come along in order to authenticate the sacrilege kept shouting, "God won't forgive him because he knew what he was doing."

The soldiers tied him up and threw him in a truck to take him to the house of detention despite the lively protests of the neighbors who came running over.

News of Mankunku's arrest spread through the land like the shadow of a big cloud. The peasants were the first to protest, refusing to accept the sacks of peanuts and corn distributed by the administration for the state plantings. They fled from their villages as soon as they heard the sound of the big diesel-powered trucks laboring over barely passable tracks. The discouraged soldiers razed the villages and threw into special prisons every person they rounded up. The repression became so terrible that the peasants adopted a more passive strategy: they accepted the mandatory distributions but killed the seeds by boiling them in big kettles before sowing them. In time, the agitation also reached the urban population. It was no longer just these illiterate peasants who had come from the country to follow Moutsompa and Ma Ngudi, it was now the youth who had been to school. They contributed their support with the characteristic charm of youth, that lends new meaning even to things that are quite old. They had experienced neither the days of the machine nor those of the forced labor levees, they had never felt the sun burning their bent backs, nor the sting of the whip on their flesh, yet they spoke with conviction. To be sure, for them everything had become words, speech had been dissociated from all it referred to, but, as in all change, words became other things; they were less real, more independent from concrete things, but they had become more fascinating, more powerful by themselves. These youth had no need of interpreters, they conversed with the master like equals, they used the same dialectical subtleties. They had abandoned the old tribal clubs to form organizations they called "political parties." These parties organized demonstrations in front of the prison where Mankunku and others were incarcerated, signed petitions, distributed tracts, passed motions. The foreigners were caught in their own trap and no longer knew what course of action to take: they hammered and massaged, struck and caressed, shouted and sang. Finally, to disarm the mounting power of these parties, the governor general decided to call a meeting of the indigenous deputies of the new territorial assembly to discuss the situation. The demonstration that the political parties had been planning to hold that day was therefore postponed.

32.

The deputies and the foreigners had properly conducted their conversations, presided over by the governor general; they were flattered, these natives said to be *developed*, smartly dressed in their jackets and ties. It had been a discussion between civilized people; they did not at all approve of the peasants' protest against the planting program, quite the contrary, because the first priority was agricultural development in order to get the country out of the rut of underdevelopment; they approved neither of the irresponsible leftist agitation of the students nor those Marxist intellectual parties whose ideology was alien to Africa; they respected religion and freedom, the rights of man, they wanted to safeguard the friendship of the mother country whose civilizing and disinterested motives were really beyond question. On the other hand, they protested against the brutalities perpetrated upon the peasants because it was contrary to the humanistic tradition of the mother country. The governor and his delegation were quite happy to discuss matters with these developed people, these realists, who encouraged neither disobedience nor incivility. They deeply regretted certain minor excesses, but such excesses always occurred in the process of maintaining order; anyway, those responsible would be severely punished. Finally, when peace and order returned to this beautiful country, a plenary conference would be held to discuss the political and economic future of the territory. And the developed natives stumbled over their thanks, as was the custom among civilized people, and promised to reason with the public.

Everybody went out in the courtyard for one last handshake. "In the name of my colleagues and compatriots, we thank you for your gentleness and understanding."

"The important thing is to work together, to understand each other, to share a common language," responded the relaxed and smiling governor.

"Yes, that will enable us to avoid much weeping and gnashing of teeth; for our part, we promise to work toward a reconciliation of our two peoples, because a division of the world into good and evil, friends and enemies, is something of an oversimplification in which bad and good are no longer integral parts of the same instinctive situation and the same object relations," responded all in one breath and without hesitation the mouthpiece for the developed natives, the one with the eyeglasses and the attaché case.

The governor had understood nothing of the delegate's speech; he knit his eyebrows and felt afraid; these people were beginning to speak our language better than we do, and that's more dangerous than all the Mankunkus in the world. Suddenly he wondered if these people whom he treated with condescension, these people he thought he was manipulating, were not, in fact, putting him on; he wondered if, beneath their adopted clothing, their apparent docility, and their goody-goody smiles, they weren't hiding something sneakier, more dangerous; in brief, if, after all, they had him where they wanted him! For the first time in his life, he *saw* "his" natives. He adopted a cooler tone but didn't have time to answer...

At first it was the Os that reached them. They arrived quickly, rolled like hoops, then took flight, turning around on themselves like flying saucers. *O O O!* Then an immense cloud of dust, like those that precede large herds of animals running through the dried-up savanna. Finally, they saw them! Hundreds, thousands of men and women, students, peasants, the unemployed. In fact, while the governor and his deputies had been debating, the crowd, dragged along by the students and the party leaders whom the governor had refused to receive, had gone over to the camp in which Mankunku and the peasants were locked up, liberated them, and, on an impulse, had continued to march on the governor's palace despite the proscription against demonstrations. Some of them held green palm fronds or branches of other green trees in their hands. Those who knew how to read carried big posters with the names of Moutsompa and Ma Ngudi while others simply and directly called for the departure of the foreigners. They were all singing:

> *nsi ya beto* [our country]
> *ba mbuta zeto* [by our ancestors]
> *ba tu sisa yo* [was left to us]

and, when they stopped singing to catch their breath, you could hear the sound of their feet like an earthquake running after the Os, a profound and mysterious echo of the words of their song:

ba mbuta zeto
ba tu sisa yo-o-o-o...

Their mouths rounded out around the hoop of their lips, their chests expanded and contracted, their legs kept on marching: and there they were, surrounding the delegation of deputies and their great leader, the governor general. These latter stood there as if magnetized. It seemed to them that the Os were climbing, swelling, becoming a single O with an expanding circumference, becoming a sphere which imprisoned them. This O surrounds them, rolls them up, twirls around them like a hula-hoop. The governor and his delegation sweat, bleed, twist, crawl, groan; they feel themselves being crushed, stamped down, their flesh cut up in cannibal rites: the shots of a hundred cannon burst forth! The army, alerted, has come to the rescue. The charm is broken, the bubble that entrapped them is crushed, they can breathe. Panic breaks out in the crowd: men and women killed, hands caught in the spokes and the chains of bicycles, children crushed in the commotion...once again.

That, however, was the last of the bloody confrontations between the foreigners and the people of this country. The echo of the O spread out so rapidly over the country that it completely encircled the foreigners, who could no longer breathe, either in their daily lives nor in their dreams. There was nothing for them to do but leave. Thus two different people, two worlds, had lived side by side for nearly a century without really getting to know one another.

33.

The end of a reign is always sad. They left one morning in the dry season, gray as dry seasons in the tropics can be. In the presence of their last governor general, they slowly lowered, to the sound of a drumroll, their flag, which seemed old and tired, while they raised, to the cheering of the crowd and the sound of the bugle, the new flag of the new country. The old and new masters shook hands for a long time, each deeply moved, like two people who realize a little late that they have passed close to one another without seeing or understanding each other.

So they left one morning in the dry season.

Chapter Six

I accuse the night of having lost me.

—TCHIKAYA U'TAMSI

34.

Then came the surge toward the country of the old masters: those who wanted to become engineers, those who wanted to build a train all by themselves, those who wanted to become doctors, professors, lawyers, butchers, taxi drivers, those who wanted to become theologians in order to save souls, those who wanted to get rich quick. They went there by the hundreds and the thousands, they defied the snow and the frost, the Alpine wind and the north wind, rivers and cities polluted by industry. They put up with racist attacks and overcrowded apartments where they caught tuberculosis; they didn't shrink from chain-gang labor in which they lost their souls and their limbs. Nothing could break their will to go over there. Some stowed away in the holds of ships where they were eaten alive by rats, others thought they were taking off for Marseilles and wound up as slaves in a Gulf emirate, still others perished in the

Pyrenees or in the Alps, trying to retrace Hannibal's path without elephants. No, nothing could really discourage them, the main thing was to go there.

Once they got there they became students, ditch diggers, lawyers, street sweepers, skilled laborers, ambassadors, procurers, the important thing being to return home with a diploma, authentic or fake, for if they aspired to clamber to the top of the hierarchy in their country, they knew that power could no longer be acquired the way it was in Mankunku's youth, but that, from now on, it was linked with the knowledge that the strangers had introduced.

And those among them who couldn't leave continued to dream of those countries where people didn't die, where everything was clean, where science had made labor easy and fair, and where everything was for the best in the best of all possible worlds.

Chapter Seven

But since I do not wish to wander between shadow and

light, I prefer to remain engulfed in blackness.

— LU XUN, *Wild Grass*

35.

WHEN THE LONG FRATERNAL CELEBRATION OF INDEPENDENCE was finished, the country experienced a calm it had not known for a long time, as if it were catching its breath after so many years of tumult and trembling. Mankunku's life seemed to beat in the same rhythm as the country, a slow rhythm. He felt happy and free; he was proud to see all these educated young fellow-citizens sitting in the offices of the old rulers, bearing their titles, having themselves called Mr. Prime Minister, Mr. President, Your Excellency, and, among them was Bunseki Lukeni, great-grandson of old Nimi A Lukeni. To be sure, something had changed. What a road had been traveled, what detours and retreats it had taken to get here, since the day, he no longer knew how many decades ago, the stranger with red skin had come into his village!

He had taken part in the celebrations, in the best seats, so to speak, since, as a well-known and revered national hero, he who had never been to school and did not know how to read or write had been invited onto the official platform during the procession, standing beside these learned and intelligent people who now held power. He had admired the procession of tanks and trucks, he had laughed and applauded at the student skits which interpreted the great scenes of the struggle for independence, he had let himself be swept up by the rhythms of the folk dances, and, finally, he had drunk, drunk a lot. But there it was, the festival was over, the great struggles were finished, and there were no more enemies to fight, only everyday routines to put up with and the procession of successive civil or military leaders, each undertaking to bestow eternal happiness on the people. There were moments when even a hero might find himself alone and tired.

Mankunku reflected on his personal life as he had never done before. He felt old and weary, he wanted only to rest now, at least for a while. He needed one thing, a family life; he took stock of the fact that he had no children. Besides, not only was he reproached for this more and more, he was openly mocked. African society being one of the most conservative in the world, certain things must be done so that a man can be respected: for example, he must have a wife and children. Now, despite all his exploits, despite his celebrity, he still hadn't earned the title of *father*.

Maybe he didn't wish for it, but little by little his interaction with Milete changed and that which up to then had been simple friendship became love; at first, their handshakes lasted longer, their gazes became more intent...until the day they found themselves making love. Milete was happy, this was her first man; she moaned, wept in joy and pain. She cried out the name of Mandala, Massini Mupepe, she told him he was as strong as a buffalo, as powerful as a locomotive, but as light on a woman as the morning wind on her face. And he also talked, talked, he spread her before him in a ray of sunlight that pierced his thatched roof and ran his rough old mechanic's hand over her tender skin the color of a ripe papaya. And she, docile as a song, soft as kapok, embraced him...Finally, she got up, got dressed, and went out, hiding her face as if the neighbors had witnessed her amorous passion, Milete, tall and dark, noble as a solitary palm tree.

They went on like this for several months, finally living like husband and wife. Mankunku was astonished to experience such a child-like joy at his age. With Milete, he made once more the discoveries of his youth. They often walked, hand in hand, in the little forest on the edge of town, and there he taught her the names of flowers, of plants, he explained to her the origin of the morning dewdrops which rolled, luminous pearls, over the great green leaves of the taros and bananas. Sometimes he ran after butterflies and dragonflies, caught them, and placed them like delicate flowers on Milete's braided hair, and, while she tried to get away from him, he attempted to paint her face with micaceous scales scraped off the wings of multicolored butterflies. But their best times were the evenings when, sitting in the moonlight, he told her stories and heard her star-filled laughter rise up and lose itself among the Pleiades. He told her: "You'll come to my village, I'll show you the great river, my childhood companion who was both friend and adversary, you'll see the plantation where I was born, the bananas and the palm fronds, I'll show you old Lukeni's tomb..." He was happy, they were happy.

People from Mankunku's region looked with growing disapproval on their relationship, not so much because they were having extra-marital relations, but because she was a woman from another ethnic group, and, especially, as they said, a city woman. Nevertheless, they said nothing openly, thinking that this was one of those passing love affairs which flourish so often in the city, these cities with strange and dissolute customs. The scandal only broke when Mankunku let it be known that he was planning to marry her. The misery, the scandal! "You can't do that to us, you, the former president of our club, our Massini Mupepe, our hero, marry one of these city women of unknown origin? See here, aren't the women of our village beautiful?"

"Milete pleases me, I've known her for more than fifteen years. So many things, so many shared memories, tie us together!"

"No, you can't love her, you know these city girls, idle, indolent folk who prefer appearance to substance, women who are nothing but sound and fury. Isn't there a single one of our girls who's beautiful and who pleases you?"

Considering this situation, they called together a great family reunion over which the reigning elder of Mankunku's village presided. The old man talked, adjured, cited proverbs, called attention to his age and white hair, evident signs of wisdom; he flattered Mankunku, the celebrated man, role model for an entire generation, then finally asked him to pronounce the words of wisdom and thoughtfulness that everybody was waiting for: "You're right, I renounce Milete."

But Mandala Mankunku didn't listen, couldn't listen anymore. He thought of all the struggles he had undertaken for the country's independence, of the appeals to brotherhood that he had launched with the Saint of the North, of those two crippled veterans who said that it was absurd to fight each other in our country. *Our* country. All of a sudden, for him this land whose borders had been set at random by a foreign conquest, this land made of ethnic mixtures and fragments of disparate ethnic groups, took on an actual existence, a soul. He turned to the elder. "Why does it bother you if I marry a girl who's not from my village as long as she's young and beautiful and I love her?"

The elder interrupted him energetically: "I know you, Mandala, you've always had an evil spirit, you destroy everything you touch; well, we won't allow you to destroy our family, our clan. So try to understand: don't dilute our power with ancillary marriages and inappropriate progeny."

"No sir, I will marry Milete!"

A brouhaha among the audience. The old man's face is contorted, his eyes open wide, his lips, already thick, swell with rage. His face reminds Mankunku of his Uncle Bizenga's fiery temper. "Mandala Mankunku, man of destruction! Listen to this: a man loved his wife so much that in order to please her he was persuaded by the honey of her words and the beauty of her breasts to pick nuts from a sacred palm tree that grew in his village. In spite of the advice of the elders who counseled him against this extravagant project, he climbed the palm tree to look for the forbidden nuts. He climbed, climbed. Alas, the palm tree only grew taller, taller, so that the poor man disappeared in the clouds and was never seen again!"

The audience approves, murmurs, speaks, criticizes. The elder, still angry, throws like a demiurge his curse: "Well, go ahead, marry her! But let it be known that we won't bless this marriage; on the contrary, we'll curse it. If I'm really the elder, the oldest member of this great family, may the ancestors listen to me: you'll never have children, not one! I spit out this wine in their honor" (he rises, pretends to spit at the four corners of the horizon, takes up his cane). "From this day forth, we don't know you, you're no longer a member of our clan. The day when you understand, you'll be yourself again, contrite, ask our pardon; only then will we accept you again, will we reintegrate you into our great family, not before." He turns his back and begins to leave with the short paces of an old man trembling with rage and decrepitude.

Mankunku, in his turn, is also angry: "You have no rights over me! Go ahead, curse me, you forget that I am *nganga* Mankunku, who destroys even the powerful! You're mistaken if you think you can frighten me! I will marry Milete, do you hear, I will marry her!"

Everyone follows the elder out; they protest, they get angry, they leave, goodbye, Mankunku, goodbye, your marriage is cursed, you won't have any children until you've made honorable reparations.

Mandala Mankunku married Milete. He did not understand how anyone could resist the beauty, charm, and courage of a woman like Milete. It had been such a long time since he had met that forsaken young girl weeping for her brother who died over there, on the other side of the sea, "in defense of liberty." Since then, she'd always been at his side throughout the great struggle for liberation. And now a bunch of old idiots who had hardly been seen throughout that difficult time dared to come and preach morality to him in the name of the tribe. African society was already very—if not *too*—conformist; would this new Africa being born add intolerance to the conformity already suffocating everything? Let them allow me to live my life as I please, to make my own choices. For now, all that I want is to live happily with my wife Milete and my future children.

36.

Mankunku's wife is pregnant. They have gone to consult two different doctors, both are sure, she's six weeks pregnant: he's delighted, he rejoices, struts about. He misses no opportunity to challenge the family members he meets and shout at them, my wife is pregnant despite your curses, from now on I forbid you to ever set foot in or around my house; keep your evil spirits to yourselves, because if I catch one of you bunch of sorcerers hanging around my home, whether in the form of an owl, a bat, or a mere cockroach, I'll kill him, crush him as if he were a flea! Don't forget that I'm a *nganga*, a great *nganga*...

He coddles, protects, pampers his beautiful city woman. He has bought her Wendo's "Marie-Louise," the hit of his youth, and the songs retracing the struggles for independence; he brings presents from the coast, he spends a lot of money to buy her toiletries imported from Europe, and, in keeping with the latest fashion, he buys a layette for the baby during the sixth month of his wife's pregnancy.

He also wants to make sure that there are witnesses for the birth of his child, reliable witnesses, who will spare the little newborn his own misfortune, that of a man whose birth is in doubt; thus he has prepared a long list of people, as diverse as possible. Another innovation—his wife will give birth in a hospital. He has already chosen the midwife, given her gifts in advance so that she will take particular care of his wife, because with the sorcerers, men of his ethnic group, you can never be too careful, you never know what could happen, midwife, in any case, I'll be here, don't hesitate to call me if there's any problem, what, do you think that these pains are normal, yes, I believe you, no no, I don't want to be present at the delivery, I don't think I could bear it, yes yes, if a cesarian is necessary, I'll give blood, why no, why no, you see, I'm calm, I'm going to sit down, the sweat's running down my forehead because it's hot and I've forgotten my handkerchief...

Oyez Mandala Mankunku, there you go, the child is born, a boy! His eyes light up, he wipes his face, now a father's face, his hands stop trembling, he laughs, beams, I've got you now, sorcerers, I'm a daddy, he can hardly see the newborn through the window panes and the tears that cloud his vision. It's all over, he goes off with his hands his pockets, whistling gaily, dreaming about what he'll bring his wife tomorrow morning when the hospital doors open for visitors.

...They say that Mankunku's wife has brought forth a teratological being, a kid with a dog's head, an enormous head like a locomotive with owl's eyes that fear the light...They say that Mankunku's wife has brought forth a monster with the head of a goat, with owl's eyes like those of his father...They say that Mankunku's wife has brought forth a kid with white scaly skin like that of a fish...See, he was cursed, his marriage was cursed, you do not defy the clan with impunity...The hospital waiting room is full of family members, people of his tribe; there are toothless old women who have been waiting since the crack of dawn and who, already tired, have stretched out on their mats; there are old men chewing on their kola nuts to recapture a bit of youthfulness, from time to time spitting out saliva darkened by the bitter juice, proud in front of the many young boys and girls who have come to attend, to witness a concrete proof of the power of the ancestors and of the clan; they're all there gossiping or chattering, they're waiting for Mankunku, Mankunku the outcast, waiting to savor the revenge of the clan against the individual.

Mankunku arrives, the bleating and cackling stop. He's surprised to see all these people; he stops short, apprehensive. If they're here, it's certainly not to wish him well. With an intense inward effort, he pulls himself together and decides to ignore them, to treat them with contempt; in any case, he'll soon savor his victory over these backward conservatives, the victory of the solitary individual over the organized power of the group. He slaloms around the legs, the mats, the benches, the spit, climbs the stairs, goes down various corridors, and enters his wife's room. He gives her an affectionate smile, approaches the crib with little steps, noiselessly, so as not to wake up the dear little creature newly come into the world, tries to put on the funny clown face supposed to please children, leans over, and...Oh my ancestors, what have I done! The child is deformed, has an oblong head, assymetrical beacons for eyes, no, it's not that, the child has white skin, colorless white except for a barely perceptible light pink around the eyes, his hair is white like an old man's hair...an albino, Mankunku, father of an albino! He howls his sorrow, he shouts his anger. Making signs of incomprehension, he turns toward his wife for a moment, goes over to the window, casts a hate-filled look over the crowd gathered in the courtyard below, returns to the cradle, and begins to speak, what has happened, my child, what has happened, my child! The doctor in charge of maternity services comes in to calm him; he explains that it's nothing, an albino is a normal human being, he just lacks some pigment, a bit of melanin, it's a small, accidental genetic omission, a congenital, not a hereditary defect; he'll grow up normally, he'll marry, he'll have normal children. Mankunku allows himself to be calmed by the doctor's words, but his heart is heavy because, in spite of all the doctor's foreign science, his own explanation, which comes from centuries of tradition, remains with him. He caresses the child's head. This is, nevertheless, his son; paternal feelings get the better of him, he loves his child, he loves his wife.

37.

After mature reflection, Mankunku decided to reunite his extensive family for a frank discussion in order to, as his people put it, "open up the sin," just as one lances an abcess. Thus the infection would be publicly cleaned up, and, once the situation was aired out, his wife could bear him beautiful, normal children because, he thought, however far you wanted to distance yourself from your origins, they would always end up catching up with you; in other words, nobody could completely turn his back on his roots. And in turning to his roots, Mankunku remembered old Lukeni the just, who, in every dispute, tried to re-establish equilibrium, that unstable equilibrium which, paradoxically, was the guarantee of individual responsibility in a society otherwise perfectly arranged. Perhaps the others had not comprehended his position regarding Milete and that was the source of the misunderstanding. Did they think that he wanted to defy them for the destructive pleasure of defying them? All of this required a remedy.

So the day of the reunion arrived. He had bought palm wine, grilled peanuts, bananas, and boiled corn, red grape wine, a drink which was beginning to rival palm wine in popularity. Everyone was there, the elders of the clan, the youth, the former members of his club, and the elder of his village, the one who had pronounced the curse. The yard was full; it was a nice day, and the shade was pleasant under the palm, avocado, and *safou* trees which grew here and there on his plot. The guests drank the wine that Mankunku had served them, munched on the peanuts, gnawed the corn cobs. Only Milete stayed on the sidelines, flanked by a few members of her rather small family, seated on a mat next to her child who slept in his cradle in the shade of a traveler's palm.

Mankunku allowed them a moment to savor the wines and the food, then stood up. Silence. "I welcome you all with the respect that we've learned from the elders," he said, and he began to clap with lightly cupped hands.

The crowd made the same gesture in turn, and for a moment, everything was drowned out by the clapping sound, which was muffled by the concavity of its source.

When silence returned, he continued: "Dear relatives, dear friends, as the ancients have taught, it's good to open one's heart to one's family when something isn't working out. You all know what has been going on and the consequences for my child. If you don't rinse your mouth after you eat peanuts, something will always be stuck in your teeth; I asked you all to come here so that we can all rinse our mouths out and clear up the misunderstanding which has taken place between us. I've never wished to destroy the clan; I was born and I grew up before the arrival of the foreigners, and believe me, I know what misfortune can arrive if one isn't preoccupied with the greater interest of the group, the village, or the country. Many here are young and don't know our past: I'd just like to remind you that our village began to die the day that Chief Bizenga put his personal interests above those of all of us. You asked me not to marry a woman from the city, I told you that I couldn't accede to your request because I love this woman. She's a person I've known for years, who fed me when I was hungry, who took care of me when I was sick. It's a personal matter which has nothing to do with the clan or the tribe. I think that you haven't understood me; there-

fore, after what has just happened, we should all take a conciliatory attitude toward each other so that our great family may be
reunited again. That is all I have to say."

All eyes turn to the presiding elder. He empties his glass of
red wine; he smiles. "Mandala Mankunku, I'm glad to hear
what you just said. Only the heart of an animal is incapable of
changing. You've understood that the values established by the
elders cannot be defied with impunity. We're ready to take you
back into our great family. We're ready to offer you assurances
about the health of your future children. We only ask one thing
of you: renounce this foreign woman; it's the only condition we
impose."

Mandala jumps up as if he had been stung by a wasp. The
intense emotion which can't escape through his voice, which he
controls to some degree, finds an outlet in his eyes, now phosphorescent. "If I've invited you here, it's not to make honorable
reparations, nor to beg pardon for anything. I believed that
you'd understand my explanations, but alas, you are so sectar-
ian and limited. If you no longer wish to have me in your clan, I
couldn't care less! I repeat that I love my wife even more
than before and that, if I had to redo what I've done, I'd do it
again . . ."

Suspended glasses, jaws that stop chewing, open mouths:
everyone is surprised and the elder more than anyone. They
have come to see the famous Mankunku grovel on his knees
before them, begging their pardon; but no, they find a Mankunku
just as proud, just as arrogant and destructive as ever. The elder
moves the glass of red wine away from his lips and disdainfully
pushes away the plate of corn and peanuts he was savoring a
moment earlier.

But Mankunku goes on: "I tell you this: let the one who
bewitched my wife, who cast an evil spell on my son, confess it

Yesu," falls, rolls on the ground, foam comes out of her epilep-
tic mouth, it's evil coming out...*Vade retro Satana* cries a
Catholic priest who makes the sign of the cross, lifts the flap of
his cassock, and flees toward the welcome road without a backward glance, shouting, "It's the devil, it's the devil." Even old
De Kélondi, valiant soldier of the Second World War, was
frightened and took off, limping lightly on his left leg with the
help of a cane won from a German officer.

And there is nobody left. Mankunku's yard is like a field
after a battle; glasses knocked over and broken, shoes lost in the
rush, women's handkerchiefs...Nobody is left but Mankunku,
his wife, and the child who is still crying for food. Mankunku,
calmed, looks at the child with tenderness; after all, his head
isn't so big as all that, his eyes aren't really asymmetrical at all,
they're only a little green like his own. He's an ordinary albino,
nothing more, nothing less. And since his mother, in turn, is
leaning over the crib, Mankunku looks for some money in the
house and goes off to the pharmacy to buy what the doctor had
recommended for the baby.

Milete is left alone with her baby-monster. She caresses him
and begins to weep. She picks up the dear little child deformed
by the people from her husband's region, all sorcerers. She can't
live like this much longer, she'll go mad. She walks around in the
yard, the baby in her arms. She sings to soothe the child, her face
streaming with tears. The child continues to cry, demanding
food. Stop crying, my child, you're not a monster, I love you.
She sits down on a stool, opens her bodice, and offers the dear
creature her breast full of milk. The child sucks greedily, breathing noisily through his nostrils. Then he stops guzzling, burps,
and falls asleep. Milete's thoughts drift off for a moment with the
noisy breathing of the child, then come back to the yard. Now
her gaze rests on the ground littered with all kinds of rubble and

debris left by the panicky crowd. She can't go on, her decision is made. She quickly gathers together what she needs, puts everything into a suitcase, takes the child, and leaves...

When Mankunku came back from the pharmacy, his wife wasn't there. He looked for her everywhere, calling her, shouting; like a wild man, he ran from one place to another, pleading, Milete, my darling, my beloved wife, don't go away, I love you, you are the only woman in my life, I'll climb to the top of the tallest palm tree to get you fresh wine, I'll give you a brand new locomotive, Milete, my darling, where are you, come back, don't go away, you'll justify these idiotic tribalists, our marriage can be a happy one; the child is an albino, it's true, but what's an albino, we'll love him, we'll cherish him, he'll grow up and then we'll have another, a normal one, beautiful like you are with your skin the color of jujubes, Milete, don't go, I love you, you see, I can't drink I can't sleep I can't eat I can't live...He questioned the neighbors, but nobody could give him the right information; one told him that Milete had taken a taxi, another that she had taken the bus, still another that she had taken the train, and somebody even said that she'd gone off in the direction of the airport. He ran everywhere in vain. He never saw his wife and child again.

38.

After Milete's disappearance, Mankunku lived for several months in an unreal world, outside everything, dreaming of his wife, of a republic of teratological creatures and sirens, eating little, drinking little. Of all the battles he had fought in his life, it seemed to him that this was the first he had really lost and the last he would ever indulge in. Suddenly he had grown old, the least effort tired him, and he would remain prostrate for hours, alone in a house that was empty without Milete.

As time often takes care of things, he emerged little by little from his stupor and regained a taste for life. He would get up very early in the morning, first to watch for the birth of a new day, then to gather the morning dew from the leaves of the *ntundu* or the banana, and to quench his thirst by sipping it very slowly as if it were the elixir of life. Then, before the sun rose too high in the sky, he would go back home and stay there unless he had to go out in search of some food. But if his soul was beginning to recover, his body didn't follow. He was more and more tired, and he often returned from his morning walk panting like an asthmatic. Then it was no longer just his respiration, it was now a stiffness in his back or his knees, now stomach trouble. So he stopped going out in the morning, disappointed in the dawn; white light is bare and contains no truth. Henceforth he preferred the evening, seated on the porch of his house, waiting for the end of the day, the onset of night: the night was perhaps no more truthful than the day, but its light was deeper, more cunning, and consequently richer, both in truths and non-truths.

But when a person has lived a life of struggle, whether he wishes it or not, he can't totally escape from the life of his nation; so, that evening, tired, seated in front of his doorstep with a carafe of water and some kola nuts watching the Moon rise to the hum of the city sated with spectacle, he departed from his custom and turned on his little radio set to find out the reason for the feverish agitation which had taken hold of the city throughout the day. In fact, all morning, trucks had been driving around with giant portraits of the President and loudspeakers urging the people to go to the stadium for an important meeting.

And the radio was in the middle of broadcasting once again the speech of the day. At first he listened distractedly, then, recognizing the voice of the chief of state, more attentively: the latter was haranguing the crowd, ridiculing the cadaver of a political opponent who had been struck down the evening before and was spread out there in front of him in the dust, under the sun. Prior to this, some delirious supporters had circled the stadium with the corpse raised overhead, like football players running a lap with their trophy, abusing the corpse, threatening to bury it without its testicles, pulling out its hair and its beard, forcing a big cigar through its mouth, howling hysterically in an act of ritual cannibalism. Meanwhile, the supreme leader of the revolution continued to prophesy and speechify, strutting and preening beside the cadaver. Mankunku listened to the long speech without being provoked by a single passion or a single hope. The words of the leader of the revolution no longer contained anything dynamic, they lacked that reinvigorating, galvanizing power words can convey, especially in a civilization which had long regarded this power as the principal thread of historic continuity. Words such as liberty, liberation, imperialism, justice, struggle, these new leaders had so tainted them, used them so badly, that they were used up, like the soft and flabby breasts of an old prostitute; these words had become dirty, vile, sad, and heavy; they no longer rose to Mankunku's height; they no longer reached his heart and his soul except as insignificant babble and were as ridiculous as excessive things are.

He turned off the radio, terrified. He wondered if this was really still the same civilization that he had known since his youth or if he weren't living in a society *sui generis,* a sort of spontaneous society like the "spontaneous generation" of natural science. He wondered if this were not a world spinning through a vacuum, around itself, with neither values nor inherited roots;

if not, where was the continuity between a civilization of which one of the fundamental bases was respect for the dead and this new society in which a man was arrested for a yes or a no, tortured, mutilated, and thrown to the dogs? Mankunku, who believed in political morality, was completely lost.

He drank a mouthful of water from his carafe and began to chew on a kola nut. He thought about himself again. No, he had not deliberately kept apart from the course of events in his country, it was that these events had overtaken him with giant steps and pushed him into the rear guard of a new civilization in which he had no place. Just as the great river, once tired of him, had thrown him onto the bank in order to continue on its course, History had also thrown him far from its whirlpools. He no longer saw himself as anything but an old man destroyed by the love of a woman and a child, a ridiculous epilogue to a hero's life. And what if, after all, love wasn't ridiculous and was what was really hiding beneath the surface of things? And what if he had finally been defeated only by that for which he had searched and hunted in vain for more than half a century? This thought seemed to calm him for a moment, and he relaxed a bit. But little by little, as irresistible as the ascent of the evening star, an insistent and anguished question rose within him, invading his soul. His spiritual terror changed into a physical fear in the cunning black night that surrounded him: and what if beneath the surface of things there was ... *nothing*?

39.

Mankunku couldn't sleep that night; his soul was troubled, his body was troubled. He put a blanket over himself, took it off, put it over himself again, threw it off; sat down on the bed, went over to the window to look at the impassive moon and the cold stars, then went back to bed and tried to sleep. And what if beneath the surface of things there was nothing! This possibility, which had never crossed his mind his whole life, had become, in the course of an evening, a real obsession. He turned over in his bed, sometimes emitting a sigh, his brow covered with sweat. How could he know? Whom could he ask? And then he suddenly thought of Bunseki Lukeni and his wife, Muriel. He had not seen them for several months, although for a while they used to see each other practically every day. That had been right after their return from the United States, where Lukeni had completed his studies. Mankunku regarded this great-grandson of old Lukeni as his own grandchild, and the young couple returned his affection, especially the African American Muriel, who was trying to learn the rudiments of her husband's native tongue. Yes, he would go and see them, these intelligent people of the new generation, doctors of science or philosophy, the *ngangas* of the modern world. He would talk to them, humbly and without shame, because in the world today one had to admit it was no longer the old people with their white hair who possessed learning but people who had undergone long courses of academic study. Perhaps, finally, he would understand all these erratic events in the whirlwind into which he was tossed in this world without axis.

When old Mankunku was seated across from Bunseki Lukeni and his wife Muriel, he was suddenly aware of the weight of his burden of age. These children had been born long after man's conquest of the moon, and some of them, such as young Bunseki Lukeni, had reached the limit of the knowledge that it was possible to acquire in the schools of this world. He was a young man who had succeeded according to society's present criteria, and, in case that wasn't altogether clear, his beautiful car, his spacious villa, and his three children sufficed to attest to it. He played sports, particularly tennis, which made him seem younger than his thirty-five years.

For their part, Lukeni and Muriel were very happy to see him again. They introduced him to the children, then chatted, at first of unimportant things, of the color of the sky, of the chirping of the cicadas and the crickets, of the swarming of termites, of the taste of this season's palm wine. Then Bunseki Lukeni asked him to talk about the old days, about his great grandfather, Nimi A Lukeni, his namesake. So Mankunku told them about life in the village before the arrival of the foreigners, about the great love he bore for old Lukeni who had doubtless saved his life, his maternal Uncle Bizenga's coup d'etat, so to speak, his duel with him, the death of his parents, the *mbulu-mbulu*, his move to the city, his days of glory as Massini Mupepe. The young people listened attentively to this old man, a living museum and library of the past. Lukeni interrupted him several times to ask if colonization had been as hard as people said, while Mankunku tried his best to explain what was for this grandson nothing but stories about the past with no immediate reality, to persuade him that his tales were not exaggerations; he tried to bring to life the sting of the whip on the naked backs of workers laid beneath the sun...

The African American Muriel listened attentively, passionately. Her perception of events was different from her husband's, not so much because she was a historian, but because of the cumulative experience of her people's short history in America. Also, her husband's "detached" observations irritated her a little.

The old man stopped and took a gulp of refrigerated water. "I think I've told you everything. Besides, you who read so many books, you must know all of that. Ah, if only I could have learned to read and to write! Maybe I would be able to understand better what's happening now."

"Oh, you know very well, Old Mankunku, you can't learn everything from books. The knowledge that you have, your wisdom, is something that can only be acquired from a lifetime of experience. That's the kind of knowledge we don't have. Each life is an individual matter which always begins at zero, whereas science is cumulative, we take it up where our predecessors left off, we build on the sum of their achievement. So these two kinds of learning must nourish each other."

"Maybe. But I no longer know what is true or what is real, my girl. In people's speech, in their behavior, one no longer makes the distinction between a real act and the shadow of that act. In my youth, I believed that every force had a counterforce, just as every poison has its antidote: thus the world could control itself; but now, find me a counter-image, in a mirror, of an act which is nothing but the shadow of something that doesn't exist."

"I understand what you mean," interjected Lukeni. "You've explained your difficulty in comprehending the modern world well. Before colonization, you and everyone else of your generation lived in a closed world, a closed system in which exchanges with the outside were controllable, reversible. So it was easy to master the world. Since the onset of colonization, this system has become uncontrollably open, and everything in it tends naturally toward a greater disorder. It's no longer so easy to distinguish between cause and effect. In this sense you're right, things are more complicated than before, there's no longer any place for the ancestors and their balanced world."

Mankunku, who had more or less followed what Lukeni was saying to him, had only retained the last phrase. "No, don't say that," he said with a horrified cry hurled from the depths of his being, "don't say that the ancestors no longer have their place, or the world would be empty, atrociously empty."

"The world is empty, atrociously empty! Intergalactic space…"

"But in that case, there'd be nothing behind the surface of things, nothing would make sense anymore!"

"Why look for meaning in things? The *why* is without interest, it's the *how* that matters."

"I don't want to believe you, I can't believe that there's nothing behind the appearance of things, that there is no meaning…I would have been chasing an illusion all my life…I'm afraid…"

His look had changed in the blink of an eye, as if he had plunged deep inside himself, and his pupils had recaptured the sea-green phosphorescence of his youth. Muriel and Lukeni suddenly felt themselves snatched up by this interior fire burning in the old man's gaze.

After a moment, he exclaimed in a voice pierced as much by anguish as by resignation: "Oh, it was a world made to our own measure!"

"But the world today is also ours," Bunseki Lukeni said forcefully. "There has never been a golden age."

"I never believed in a golden age," Mankunku replied immediately, as if stung to the quick, "even before colonialization! If I had, would I have spent my life overturning the powerful?"

A long silence fell on the three of them, then Mankunku became calm, his eyes lost their strange gleam. In a tired voice, he said, "Excuse me, I'm old, and I've let myself become a bit nostalgic. I no longer have a place here, I'd better leave. But of course I agree with you, the world keeps turning, we have to go on living. We must have hope. And then, we belong to the race which was present at the creation of the world, we have a duty to be there when it ceases to exist."

"You bet," said Lukeni, quite moved by his words. "Old Mankunku, why don't you write your memoirs?"

"I don't know how to write."

"You could dictate them to Muriel, and it would be an extraordinary document for our children."

"Oh, I don't think that the memoirs of an old illiterate would interest many people. I'm so tired and my mind is too; I've lived long enough, and my only concern is to find out if I'll be able to die one of these days."

"See here," said Lukeni, laughing, he who knew nothing of the doubts about the reality of Mankunku's birth, his rational mind amused by the old man's senseless fears, "see here," he resumed, "everybody has to die someday, you can't just fade into the cosmos."

"Come on, let's go," said Muriel. "It's time to eat."

40.

When they had finished eating, and while the houseboy was clearing the table, they went into the living room. Lukeni gave a big cigar to Mankunku, who, lounging in a cushioned armchair, amused himself by blowing smoke rings.

"Allow me to surprise you. My wife and I collect old records, records from your younger days, and we're going to play them for you."

"That would make me very happy, it's been an eternity since my phonograph worked."

"You have a phonograph?"

"Yes, a very old one."

"What's the matter with it?"

"The spring is broken."

"That's right, those things used to be powered by a mechanical spring."

"Yes, the spring is broken and the needles are all rusty."

"I've been looking to buy one. Would you sell me yours?"

"Sell it to you? That old contraption that doesn't even work, when you have this magnificent stereo system?"

"Absolutely. I'll even give you what I paid for my laser disc system."

"I'll give it to you for nothing, my children. I don't need it anymore; I'll send it over to you as soon as I can."

"No, Old Mankunku, we want to buy it from you."

"I wouldn't hear of it, my children. That device has been a very important part of my life, I couldn't sell it. I'll give it to you because I love you and think of you as the children I never had."

"Thank you very much, that old phonograph will be as important to us as it has been to you."

Mankunku suddenly burst into laughter. "When I think of the first time De Kélondi brought that device over to my house and started it up, what a panic there was! People were afraid. They thought that there was a little demon hidden inside who imitated the human voice."

They laughed together. He told them about his radio, about his home which had become the meeting place for all the youth and all the veterans, the former to listen to the latest songs, the latter to follow the news about the war in Indochina. Now when you can see that a peasant from the deepest depths of his native bush country finds nothing extraordinary about little transistor sets that you can hold in the palm of your hand, about mini-cassette players, about VCRs, you fully realize how times have changed.

Lukeni turned his stereo on. Mankunku sank down a little deeper into his armchair in the afternoon torpor. And he listened to the scratchy old records from the good old days, from his best years. He felt his eyes swell with emotion. He listened to Wendo singing "Marie-Louise," Wendo weeping over the death of his friend Paul Kamba, he listened to the San Salvadors, Jimmy the Hawaiian, the old tangos of Carlos Gardel...He listened...My God, why are memories so sweet and yet so sad? Milete, oh, Milete! He couldn't go on, he wept, once again overcome by love. Silent tears rolled down the wrinkled cheeks of an old man plunged into the depths of time lost and found again. Muriel, moved, came and took his hand.

"I haven't always been alone," he said, "in my long life I've loved one woman, only one. Her name was Milete, she was beautiful and intelligent, like you, my girl."

Muriel hugged him; that was all.

Mankunku finally emerged from his memories. "It's time for me to be going, thank you so much."

"Can't you stay a while longer?" protested Muriel. "We'll drive you home this evening."

"No, really, I don't want to put you out anymore."

"You're not putting us out, besides, we've planned an outing for this afternoon."

"Tomorrow we have to work, so let's make the most of the weekend."

"Exactly what kind of work do you do, my boy?"

"I'm doing research in the field of molecular reactions, how can I explain it? I'm trying to see how elements can be combined to manufacture new products."

"Are you trying to find out, I mean, discover the hiding places of products and things that have never been seen?"

"Not exactly; I manufacture, I create, I invent molecules, products which don't exist in nature, which have never existed before."

"Create...products which don't exist in nature? How's that possible? I don't understand."

Lukeni didn't know how to answer. Muriel intervened: "Why don't you take him to visit your laboratory?"

"That's a very good idea, it'll replace this afternoon's outing. Phone Sita to see if we can also visit the observatory."

The old man assented with joy. Muriel made a call to the astronomer, then they took the car to the laboratory.

Mankunku arrived at the laboratory excited but intimidated by the white coat that Professor Lukeni had just put on. The latter started by showing him the strange products of his laboratory; he prepared solutions with changing, fluctuating colors, he mixed two colorless liquids which reacted to yield a solid with bright colors; he showed him liquid gases, solid gases...Mankunku's ears buzzed with such words as atoms, molecules, molecular orbits, electrons, quarks...He was in a veritable state of mental inebriation, everything was turning around in his head. Was it possible that all things could be found in this chemical laboratory and in the brain of this grandchild whose birth he had seen not so long ago? His mounting excitement peaked when Lukeni took a little flask and poured a fat silvery drop onto the worktable. The fat drop burst into finer droplets which formed spherical balls and kept rolling. Mankunku had his breath taken away; his gaze, for a moment phosphorescent green once again, rolled along with the droplets. "Water which doesn't make things wet! I knew that it existed!" he cried out.

Intrigued, Lukeni asked him what he was talking about, but the old man was down on all fours, chasing after the balls, as fascinated as ever.

"What's happening?"

"I knew that it existed!"

"Oh, you mean the mercury?"

"You see, my son, I knew that there was a connection between the water you can hold in your hands and the solid iron we blacksmiths can deform and reform."

Also intrigued, Lukeni started telling him about the properties of mercury in words which he hoped were accessible: "You see, it's a liquid metal, the only metal which is liquid at room temperature. Its expansion coefficient...I mean its ability to expand is remarkable, that's why it's used in thermometers."

Mankunku interrupted him, as if Lukeni's words were of little importance, for they seemed only to brush the surface of things. "After seeing this water that doesn't wet things, I'm sure that there must be a transition, a way, a state between the world of the forgotten ancestors and us the living, between life and non-life; that's the transition I've been looking for..." And his hand darted down, trying to crush the drops of mercury between his fingers, to hold them, feel them, but they were infinitely fragmented, fleeing, evasive, just like a shattered mirror infinitely multiplies the same image.

"Watch out, this metal can make you go crazy!" Lukeni grabbed his hand roughly, pulled it away from the droplets of mercury, and forcefully wiped it off for him.

Mankunku did not seem all that surprised by what Lukeni had just told him. He replied quite casually, as if it went without saying, "It's in the very nature of things that it should make one crazy. It couldn't be any other way."

Lukeni was really fascinated. Where had this old man heard about mercury, the quicksilver of the alchemists, the prince of essences, and most of all, by what unanticipated coincidence did he accord it exactly the same importance as alchemists all over the world since the beginning of time? Only then did the old man's intelligence strike him. He had been talking to this man for hours and, until this moment, his mind, closed in prejudice, confusing intelligence with academic instruction, had not registered the fact that he was talking to a scholar, even though the man had never been to school. When questioned about the connection between life and non-life, Lukeni was about to respond that certainly this link existed: viruses, which were situated on the threshold separating living matter from inert molecules; but he held his tongue, for he was beginning to understand the profound separation between them, the fundamental difference between their two approaches to the world. He, Bunseki Lukeni, had a scientific approach to the world through knowledge, the old man a holistic sapience. Their roots were nourished by different sources: the old man, profoundly rooted in the thousand-year-old culture or civilization of which he regarded himself as inheritor and repository; the young man, new representative of a science whose essentials had been almost totally elaborated elsewhere, even if it plunged its original roots in the earth of Egypt and Nubia, a science that had proven its universal utility and which no civilization could do without. The ideal would be to combine these two approaches; he felt this in the deepest part of his being, that there was something essential here that Africa was bringing forth, and that this was intuited by the old man, something which could without doubt give new vigor to his own learning, to the Western science which he had acquired. But how? Wouldn't this entail too long a quest, whereas what he had to do, for fear of falling behind in his discipline, was to be au courant with the knowledge being added to it? How would it be possible to appropriate, or, rather, reappropriate this African gnosis, especially since Mankunku's world and all it implied were receding further and further toward the horizon, just as a landscape recedes faster and faster as the train picks up speed?

Night had fallen in a few minutes, as it does at this latitude. Muriel reminded them that it was time to set out for the observatory. Lukeni poured out a little liquid nitrogen on the droplets of mercury which, in turn, became hard and brittle, and he easily put them back into the flask. He washed his hands, made Mankunku do the same, then took off his lab coat, closed the door, and the three of them went back out to the car.

The astronomer Sita welcomed them in front of the gate of the great domed building. He knew the old man well and greeted him warmly. They went up the steep stairway leading to the telescope. He adjusted the instrument with infinite care, and, when everything was ready, he asked Mankunku to take a look.

As soon as Mankunku placed his eye on the eyepiece of the apparatus, the sight surpassed his wildest dreams. The Moon shot toward him, or, rather, he bounded toward it. He explored the craters, the contours, the seas. Then the astronomer focused the big telescope on Mars, explaining all the while: "That's where the astronauts who'll be sent up next month are going. We know a lot more about Mars than we knew about the Moon when men first went there. You see those geological faults? The ancients thought that those were irrigation canals traced by intelligent creatures! And here's Saturn, with its innumerable rings...Jupiter, the largest planet in the solar system...the Pleiades which you know so well..." He spoke to him of nebulas, of galaxies, of supernovas, of black holes, of stars which grow cold and die, of quasars...

"Could men ever reach those distant galaxies pulsating in this infinite universe?" Mankunku dared to stammer.

"It's not certain that the universe is infinite...or, rather, it's quite possible that it's infinite but closed, and to that extent finite...how can I explain it...let's say that if you could look straight ahead and your vision could extend to infinity, you'd see the back of your neck. Do you understand?"

"Yes, yes," said the old man, full of wonder. "It's...it's like an inflated balloon, right? An orange, for example. An ant could walk around it indefinitely, but we know that it's a finite object."

"Bravo," said young Sita, astonished by the rapidity with which Mankunku's mind grasped what he was trying to make him understand. "To answer your question, the big problem with such an expedition, at least for now, is that the speed of light seems an impassable barrier; no material object can travel faster than that. But," he concluded, "that's no reason to despair. We have reason to hope that one day we'll really understand this universe of ours."

Old Mankunku dropped into his seat, exhausted. And the planets, the stars, the quasars, all the little molecules were whirling around in his head. All that he had just seen made what he knew seem ridiculously miniscule, he who boasted of being a *nganga*! Oh, he told himself, now I know that I know nothing. Then, turning to the three young people, he stammered: "But...but what's behind all that?"

Always this same obsessive question! "Nothing, old Mankunku, *nothing*," Lukeni exclaimed to him.

"But yes," said Sita, "there's the law of gravity that keeps the planets together and guides them..."

"What's a law?"

"It's something people invent in order to explain how things function or how they ought to function."

"*How* they function and not *why*," Lukeni observed.

"Then there's nothing!" exclaimed Mankunku desperately.

Muriel came up to the old man, put her hands on his shoulders while the two boys kept quiet. Mankunku could not get used to the idea that the ancestors were buried, and well buried, and they were no longer the supreme authorities in this new technocratic world. He saw his soul naked, with nothing to lean on. These young people could live with nothing, with nothingness, but he could not. In a weary voice, he said: "I'm really glad to have seen what I've seen. There's no place for me here, please take me home."

They left Sita, got into the car; Lukeni, who was at the wheel, headed for Mankunku's home. But after a moment, Mankunku stopped them, preferring to go on alone, by foot, as if their paths separated here, as if they could no longer go along the same path together. The two young people got out of the car to say goodbye to him. Muriel took him affectionately in her arms, and then, when she let him go, he took Lukeni's hand and shook it slowly before withdrawing his own hand, just as a relay runner withdraws his hand after passing the baton. Afterward, he looked at the couple still waving him goodbye, two children, their arms around each other's waists, happy, the world wide open before them. Nothing was impossible for them: Lukeni had married a woman from the other side of the world without any problem whereas Mankunku couldn't marry the woman he loved on the pretext that she was a foreigner and that her city, a day's walk from his village, was too far from his village for him. He turned his back; the couple got into their car and drove off.

He took the long way home, walking with steps as steady as his age would allow, so as to feel the solid earth beneath his feet, a solitary soul under stars scattered across the celestial vault like grains of corn thrown to chickens with the sower's broad gesture. Once again, he dragged the Moon behind him in the dust of the Milky Way, while his soul floated with the currents of a wave of cosmic plasma. He searched among all the constellations that he knew for his mother's star; he didn't see it. He felt even more alone, lost among the galaxies, the supernovas, and creation's initial big bang.

It was at this point that the patrol of militants defending the revolution, which was threatened by the forces of evil and imperialism, fell upon him.

41.

After the scenes of ritual cannibalism in the stadium, whipped up to a white heat by the chief of state's speech, militant bands had swept over the streets to defend the beleaguered revolution, although it was winning greater and greater victories every day, as the opposition leader whose body had been exposed at the stadium had discovered at his own expense. They ran through the streets, crying, "to the firing squad," stopping people to verify their identity so as to rout out spies and the vanquished enemy's accomplices. One of these patrols came across old Mankunku, walking alone beneath the starry vault and the palm trees swaying in the warm evening breeze. Two militiamen leveled their guns at him while a third, probably their chief, shouted at him: "Hey old man, show us your papers."

Mankunku did not hear them because his mind was still floating among the stars; he continued along his way until the sharp pain from a rifle butt in his back made him double up, bringing him abruptly down to earth.

"Quick, your papers, or else it's the slammer!"

Painfully, Mankunku pulled his old body up and looked in bewilderment at his interrogators. "My papers, I don't have them with me, I forgot them at home...in any case, I'm in my neighborhood...you can come to my house and check them..."

"Come on, you dirty reactionary spy, we're taking you in!"

Mankunku protested, swore, pleaded; they dragged him along for about ten yards then threw him in the back of a van chock full of other spies who, like himself, lacked identification papers. The van continued its rounds until very late at night; finally in the first hours of dawn, he was thrown out with all the others into a stinking little room which was shut again with heavy locks.

They were pulled out of the nauseating room in the afternoon, clothes lice-infested and muddy, bodies exhausted, to be presented to the Party member in charge of security. They were seated on hard benches made of wooden boards, on the wall across from which there hung an immense portrait of the President. They waited for nearly an hour, then a voice cried out: "The Party comrade in charge of public security has arrived, Comrade Anastase Kaduma."

The militiamen stood at attention with their rifles, and everyone got up. The comrade responsible for security entered the court to general applause, while applauding himself, and took his place at the rostrum. Everybody sat down. Then he began to talk, showering obloquy on the enemies of the revolution and their spies, some of whom, arrested during the night, were in this room. He opened the great register containing the names of the detainees. Mankunku was the fifth. He was clearly the oldest person in the group. Tired and hungry, the curve of his back somewhat accentuated, he tried, with visible effort, to support himself on the back of the bench in front of him. The Party functionary, a man of experience, realized right away that this poor old man had nothing to do with spying, he'd simply let himself get caught in the net cast by these slightly over-zealous young militants. No, really, there was no point in being ridiculous. In a conciliatory tone, he said: "Old man, why were you out walking at such an unseasonable hour without your papers?"

"I forgot them at home."

"Forgetfulness is no excuse."

"I was in my own neighborhood, two steps from my house; I asked them to come over and check out my papers but since these young louts are so badly brought up..."

"Listen here, old man, I was well enough disposed in your favor, but if you insist on publicly insulting these devoted young people who are benevolently defending the revolution, I'll throw your ass right into the clink."

"You should teach these young fellows to respect people; you don't know who I am."

This was too much for the president. His forbearance vanished, and it was in a severe and pitiless tone that he thundered: "I don't give a fuck who you are, you illiterate old man; from the moment you threaten the State Revolution, you're expendable, and the Party must crush you like a roach..."

At this moment, a member of the presidium seated to the right of President Anastase Kaduma whispered something in his ear. The latter scowled, astonished, then continued: "I've just been told that on Independence Day you were acclaimed a national hero. Well, that only aggravates your case, because your behavior is unworthy of a national hero. Instead of contributing to the well-being of the country…"

Mankunku was no longer listening to him. The sound of the president's voice was now only a distant, inconsequential murmur that had lost the power to vibrate his eardrums. He plunged back into himself. What was he doing here, he who had also been a great man? He who had tied the seasons to the Pleiades? He who had discovered the aphrodisiac properties of *kimbiolongo*, he…His thought forced itself out in a loud voice, interrupting the Party member who was still lecturing him: "Why, *I* discovered that *kinkeliba* cures malaria!"

Astonished by these words which didn't fit into the range of his own habitually wooden language, the one in charge of security became angrier than ever: "Why should *I* give a fuck about your kinkeliba, anyway? When I have a touch of malaria, I take a couple of chloroquinine tablets and I'm back on my feet! You're delirious, you're too old. Well, I'm not going to put you in prison, the revolution knows how to be magnanimous. I'm going to send you back to your village, first thing tomorrow morning, and that's where you'll spend your last days, a fallen national hero. Don't you ever set foot in this city again. Guards, take him away!"

Now it was Mankunku's turn to get angry. Suddenly he pulled himself up, the curve of his back brusquely disappearing as if he were supported by an intense internal power. He was panting slightly while his eyes regained the phosphorescent ardor of the days of his youth when he'd braved moments pregnant with consequence. The guards who approached to seize him came to a dead halt, as if hypnotized. "I am Mankunku the destroyer, the one who defies the powerful and the drums which render them homage. I've struggled all my life, I've killed my maternal uncle, I knew Moutsompa and Ma Ngudi…"

And then, all of a sudden, he realized that these words were, for these young people, for the one in charge of Party security, empty, hollow words, sonorous echoes of an epoch which meant absolutely nothing to them: for them, he was raving, saying whatever came into his head. Confronted by a modern State, with its arms, its laws, and the apparatus of its Party, he had nothing but the strength of his faith, which was a derisive thing. A man alone could not hold out against the power of a State. He felt that time had completely passed him by, the ancestors were dead and buried. He became silent as suddenly as he had begun, walked out of the courtroom without anyone making the least gesture to stop him: for them, he had already ceased to exist, he was no longer a threat to their revolution.

The energy which sustained Mankunku did not give out until he got back home and sat down on his chaise longue. He was worn out, physically and morally. He seemed to be turning around in a world in which History had rejected him just like the great river once had, a world made for the Lukenis and the Party members who had interrogated him that afternoon. Where could he go? Whom could he visit? All of his old companions had passed away. There was nothing left for him but his village, which he had not seen for ages, since the day he had left it to become Massini Mupepe, the man of the machine and of the wind. Yes, his decision was made. He would go back to his village to live out his last days, to converse one last time with the birds, to listen to the great river, to listen to the wind, and maybe, who knows, to rediscover the purity of things and the pristine brilliance of the fire of his origins.

Chapter Eight

The whole universe, all things

animate or inanimate,

are gathered here—look!—enfolded

inside my infinite body.

—THE BHAGAVAD-GITA, XI: 7
(TRANSLATED BY STEPHEN MITCHELL)

42.

WELL BEFORE DAWN, HE GOT UP, RAPIDLY WASHED HIS FACE, picked up the little bundle he had prepared, went out, took one last look at his now useless house, then set it on fire. For a moment he contemplated the flames as they totally enveloped the thatched roof, then walked quickly away without looking back, as half-asleep spectators rushed over, too late, to the site of the fire. Thus nothing remained of his life in this city. And for those who would never see him again, Mandala Mankunku would be nothing more than some ashes mixed in with those of his burned house.

Ordinarily, after walking for half a day, he could already pick out familiar scenery indicating that he was approaching his native region. But today, after about ten hours of walking, he still recognized nothing. He stopped for a moment, standing under the overwhelming sun, wiping the sweat off his brow, and his gaze encountered a crystal of sand-glass strangely gleaming in the radiant sunshine. Mankunku forgot everything around him and remained fascinated by this strange reflection. Then, all of a sudden, the crystal was bombarded by a particle of light from the sun, and, incapable of containing it, discharged it onto a blade of grass, which caught fire; the grass caught fire, everything caught fire, everything began to burn. Mankunku panicked, threw away his bundle, and began to flee, to run straight ahead. Behind him was nothing but fire, as if all fires had become Fire, an image of a burning and collapsing world. He ran, ran, thorns shredding his clothes, tearing his skin, plowing his flesh; he tore off the scraps of clothing which hampered his flight and threw them away; the fire instantly swallowed them. He ran like a winged gazelle but breathed as noisily as a locomotive. His body began to tire, but his soul impelled him forward.

He had overestimated his strength, for, now that the sun had plunged to the other side of the earth, he still had not reached his village. His aged limbs ached, he was obliged to stop after such a mad race. Far behind him, the world continued to burn. He took off the worn-out shoes that hurt him and walked barefoot in the grass which was beginning to be heavy with evening dew. He was cold. There was no moon, but all the stars were out in an exceptionally limpid sky. He walked painfully, his heart beating quickly, quickly as if it were racing, and he had a suffocating feeling each time a heartbeat sent a wave of pain shooting into the left side of his chest. Finally, he emerged in a clearing: he recognized the plantation where, according to the statements of his mother, he had first seen the light of day, he recognized the *nsanda* tree that his mother had planted in order to perpetuate the memory of his birth. This meant he wasn't far from his village, so what was the point of hurrying? He had to rest, he had run too much, he was too weary.

He sat leaning against the tree of his birth a long, long time. Then he wanted to stretch out. With a great effort he cut off a large banana leaf, as tall as a man, set it on the ground, and lay down on it; the hard central spine penetrated his ribs at the same time as the cold of the dew-moistened leaf; he curled himself up a little more, like the hammer of a gun. He was all alone in this vast abandoned plantation, in this cool night of the dry season.

He was acutely aware of his solitude. The rustling of the palm and banana leaves shaking in the wind was transformed in his mind into the crackling of flames, as if the fire were beginning to catch up with him. He wondered if he did not carry within himself his own negation, if the one who had borne all those names, Mandala Mambou Mankunku Maximilian Massini Mupepe, shouldn't also be consumed, just as he had set fire to his dwelling, just as the world was ablaze behind him. Thus might he be finished once and for all with this world which had grown old for him, so old that some things had two, three names, and sometimes more, thus dissimulating the very essence of things most beautiful and pure in their nakedness. How could such a world regenerate itself without first destroying itself?

He had promised himself, at the time of his investigations, to reinvent the creation of the world—or at least the myth of creation—so as to finally understand it; now he wondered if that wasn't what he was living through, or else the myth of the end, he who had always destroyed everything. But was there any difference? Every end contains within itself a hope, that of a beginning. It was perhaps this hope that he was in the process of living through now, that he was perhaps in the process of regerminating along with kernels of corn and grains of millet. And suddenly, in a brief moment of lucidity, he finally discovered what he had been searching for all of his life: *to rediscover, as on the first morning of the world, the primitive brilliance of the fire of origins.*

Then his body and his soul relaxed. There he was, suspended, a being without beginning or end, outside the time measured by man-made clocks. He watched the great river dive into the immense ocean, mirror of a new sky and a new world. All around was only the noisy silence of the universe, the whirling of the galaxies, the wind, sovereign spirit reigning over all things conscious and sentient. But, of course, these stars were not stars, this wind was no longer the wind, the planets, the suns were no longer planets and suns, since nothing had yet been named. And he, born without birth, without origin therefore without end, listened, contemplated; bedazzled, he did not know if it was he who was breathing, kissing the earth, climbing up to caress the tops of the trees, if it was he who was shining over there, up there. He did not even dare to gaze upon these things moving and burning like a wave surging from John Coltrane's saxophone, these things pure as a cry on the first morning of the world, beautiful and gravid as a dawn, for fear of deforming them, transforming them. And least of all did he dare, for fear of soiling them with words, to bestow a name on these naked things.

Montpellier–Boko–Brazzaville–Tokyo,
1975–1978, 1983–1986